AUTHOR
AVIS, P.

CLASS
F GEN

TITLE
Playing the harlot or, mostly coffee

VIRAGO
MODERN CLASSICS
418

Patricia Avis

Patricia Avis was born in 1928 in Johannesburg to a Dutch father and an Irish mother. She travelled to England in 1946 to read medicine at Oxford, where she met and married a fellow student, Colin Strang, moving with him in 1951 to Belfast. There she met Philip Larkin and they embarked on a year-long affair. Through Larkin, Avis met many brilliant writers associated with 'the Movement' and often known as the Angry Young Men – Kingsley Amis, John Wain and Bruce Montgomery who wrote under the name Edmund Crispin. Increasingly estranged from her husband, Patricia Avis moved to Paris where she met the Anglo-Irish poet, Richard Murphy, whom she married in 1955. They lived in Ireland, where their daughter Emily was born. Patricia Avis had several of her poems published and in 1957 started writing *Playing the Harlot*. After her second marriage ended in divorce she settled in Dublin, editing a poetry magazine. Her emotional life had always been complex and often unhappy and she became increasingly reliant on barbiturates and alcohol. In 1977, after a second novel was rejected, Patricia Avis died of a fatal combination of drugs and alcohol.

CPP ✓	CLN
CBA	CLO
CFU	CMI
CIN	CPE
CKI	CRI
CLE 6/01	CSA
CLH	CSH
CLHH	

PLAYING THE HARLOT
or
Mostly ~~C~~offee

Patricia Avis

Introduction by George H. Gilpin
and Hermione de Almeida

I am a railing alongside the stream; whoever is
able to seize me, may seize me. Your crutch,
however, I am not.

Nietzsche, *Thus Spake Zarathustra*

A *Virago* Book

First published by Virago Press 1996

Copyright © The Estate of Patricia Avis 1996
Introduction copyright © George H. Gilpin and
Hermione de Almeida 1996

The McFarlin Library of the University of Tulsa, Oklahoma is
acknowledged as owner of the manuscripts of this novel and other
literary documents of Patricia Avis.

A CIP catalogue record for this book is available
from the British Library

ISBN 1 86049 004 2

Typeset in Goudy by M Rules
Printed and bound in Great Britain by
Clays Ltd, St Ives plc

Virago
A Division of
Little, Brown and Company (UK)
Brettenham House
Lancaster Place
London WC2E 7EN

Introduction

'The thought of your great work makes me shudder.'
postcard from Philip Larkin to Patricia Avis,
11 January 1959

Amid the circle of English writers in the 1950s who became
known as the Angry Young Men was one very angry young
woman who remained unknown: her name was Patricia Avis,
and she was known to her friends as Patsy. She was born in
Johannesburg, South Africa, in 1928. Her Dutch father, reared
in Holland, had fought with the Boers against England and
founded a shipping business; her Irish mother raised her two
children as Catholics. Her family's wealth allowed Patricia to be
unusually well educated for a woman of her time; she attended
the Roedean School in Johannesburg then went to England in
1946 to attend Somerville College, Oxford. There she read
medicine and developed her interest in French literature,
encouraged by Enid Starkie, the well-known French scholar
and one of the few women on the faculty. Patricia completed
her Oxford degree and qualified to be a doctor in 1951, though
she never went into practice.

At Oxford, Patricia met Colin Strang, a student of philosophy at St John's College and son of the diplomat Sir William
Strang (later Lord Strang), and they married in July 1948. The
couple moved to Belfast in 1951 when Colin took up his

appointment as lecturer in philosophy at Queen's University. There she met the poet and novelist Philip Larkin, a St John's graduate like Colin. Philip was sub-librarian at Queen's, and he and Patricia began an affair in 1952 which is documented in their letters to one another. Their correspondence reveals a tender and complex friendship between two highly intelligent people at an exciting time in their lives when they were caught up in the post-war revival in English letters. When Philip first met Patricia, he had already published two novels, *Jill* (1946) and *A Girl in Winter* (1947), a collection of poems, *The North Ship* (1945), and a privately printed collection, *XX Poems* (1951). During their affair, Philip was composing the important poems that would appear under the title, *The Less Deceived* (1955), and in October 1953 he was identified in *The Spectator* as one of the poets who was 'In the Movement'. Patricia's literary interests were stirred by contact with Philip; following his example she began to keep a journal. She became acquainted with a circle of lively literary friends from Oxford, especially those who were Philip's – and Colin's – contemporaries at St John's. Kingsley Amis and John Wain, both named as members of The Movement in poetry, were finishing first novels – *Lucky Jim* (1954) and *Hurry on Down* (1953) – that would establish their reputations among the Angry Young Men; in addition, Bruce Montgomery, who was a close friend of Philip, was already well known for detective fiction that he published under the pseudonym 'Edmund Crispin' and for musical scores for film. Patricia's affair with Philip continued into 1953, during which time she became pregnant by him and suffered an early miscarriage, as Philip's letters show: on 11 August 1952, Philip wrote to Patricia, 'I'm sorry about the little creature, but it's not for me to say, really. I dare say my pride in it would have been over balanced by a distressful knowledge of double dealing.'

When Colin was appointed Lecturer at Newcastle University, the affair ended, though Patricia and Philip remained friends and correspondents for the rest of her life.

When Colin took up his new position, Patricia gradually detached herself from him by living on Boar's Hill on the edge of Oxford, where she began to write short stories and poems. During this time she became involved with historian Lionel Butler, then a Fellow at All Souls College, later Vice-Principal of St Andrew's University, and finally Principal of Royal Holloway College, University of London. In the summer of 1954 Patricia moved to Paris with the idea of continuing her writing while researching the letters of the nineteenth-century Breton poet Tristan Corbière; she renewed her journal and considered beginning a novel on the model of *Under the Net*, the just-published first novel of Iris Murdoch, a contemporary of Philip at Oxford who was sometimes identified with The Movement. However, Patricia, as her journal reveals, was too preoccupied emotionally in considering divorce from Colin, the end of her intimacy with Philip, and her relationship with Lionel to write or to pursue her work on Corbière. In late October, she met the Anglo-Irish poet Richard Murphy. Richard, a graduate of Magdalen College, Oxford, was living in Paris while he prepared his first collection of poems, *The Archaeology of Love*, which would be published in 1955. In spite of admonishments to herself in her journal – 'it's Philip all over again' and 'I've had enough poets in my life', she admitted, 'I've met what I've been looking for.' Consequently, during a trip together to Brittany, Patricia and Richard became engaged. However, Richard's poetic portrait of Patricia on this occasion, 'Girl at the Seaside', reflects his sense of her emotional – nearly suicidal – instability; the poem, told from the girl's point of view, concludes:

> *I've argued myself here*
> *To the blue cliff-tops:*
> *I'll drop through the sea-air*
> *Till everything stops.*

The couple spent the winter travelling in Greece, and after Colin divorced Patricia, she and Richard married in London on 3 May 1955, and moved to Ireland. During this period, Patricia's literary efforts intensified, and, as well as keeping a journal, she wrote poetry. In January 1956 Patricia and Richard began to renovate a Regency period lodge called Lake Park, purchased from the writers Ernest Gébler and Edna O'Brien. A daughter, Emily, was born that year.

Lake Park was located in the Wicklow Mountains, twenty-five miles from Dublin, and at first its beauty appealed greatly to Patricia; in time, according to Richard, she found its remoteness uncongenial, and she remained restless in her longing for a literary life. Richard tried to encourage her writing and provide an intellectual milieu. Philip Larkin, Donald Davie, Sean O'Faolain, Julia O'Faolain, Conor Cruise O'Brien, Thomas Kinsella, the historian Hugh Thomas, Honor Tracy, Charles Monteith and J.R. Ackerley were among the visitors to Lake Park. With Ackerley Patricia and Richard visited Elizabeth Bowen at Bowenscourt.

Patricia's poems began to be published: in Ackerley's *Listener* (1955), in G.S. Fraser's anthology *Poetry Now* (1956), and in Larkin, Bonamy Dobrée and Louis MacNeice's *New Poems 1958*. In September 1957, soon after a traumatic miscarriage, she began a novel, *Playing the Harlot*. Richard had asked Ackerley to encourage Patricia to start the novel, for at the time she was, as Richard recalls, 'reading French novels and writing poetry, hour upon hour in her study upstairs, filling the air with cigarette smoke: and I felt that work on a continuous fiction would satisfy her more than writing occasional lyrics'. In the autumn the family moved to Kensington Church Street, London, in an effort to satisfy Patricia's need for a greater intellectual life while she continued to write her novel. In June 1958 Patricia went home to visit her parents in Johannesburg and from there wrote to Richard asking for a divorce. The divorce was granted in the spring of 1959 with Richard granted custody of Emily. Richard moved to the west of Ireland where he continued to write poetry, publishing *Sailing to an Island* (1963), *The Battle of Aughrim* (1968), *High Island* (1974), *Selected Poems* (1979), *The Price of Stone* (1985) and *The Mirror Wall* (1989). Patricia took up residence in Wilton Place, Dublin, where she lived for the rest of her life. There she edited four issues of her own literary magazine, *Nonplus*, from fall 1959 to winter 1960. In 1963 Patricia submitted the completed manuscript of *Playing the Harlot* to Charles Monteith, then a director (and later chairman) of the publisher Faber and Faber.

For character and plot, *Playing the Harlot; or, Mostly Coffee* draws heavily from Patricia's own experiences among her generation of young English and Irish literary intellectuals; the novel portrays a group of university students and the story of their passage through to adulthood. It opens in a university town and then moves to locations in London, Paris, and the English countryside. The characters include Mary Gallen, the daughter of an Argentinian industrialist, who marries a medical student named Pete Mason; Theodora Folding, her room-mate, a medical student who marries another student lecturer, Bernard Whitworth; Abigail Rubel, an artistic student who settles for marriage to an ageing European count named Prince Oberall and ownership of an occult-arts boutique in London; Raphael de Groot, the homosexual and unlovable son of

Oberall; Anderson Cully, also homosexual, a music lecturer and writer of demi-opera; Daniel Frost, also homosexual but for his liaison with Mary, a medievalist instructor with prospects at the university; Martin Freemantle, a sculptor whom Mary meets in Paris and divorces Pete to marry, though she is aware of his penchant for young men; Dermot McNeill, poet, historian and diplomat, with whom Mary has her longest and most destructive affair; Rollo Jute, a 'bachelor of regular habits and inadequate private means', whom Mary meets in a café while she is lodging in St Saviour's, a hostel run by Catholic nuns. Rollo, like Byron, keeps a diary of his friends' sexual exploits; Mary has her first flirtation with him and her last affair.

As *roman à clef*, the novel ascribes to the room-mates, Mary and Theodora, colonial and medical backgrounds comparable to Patricia's. Her father in Johannesburg is the painful model for Mary's rich father in Buenos Aires. The ill-fated marriage of Mary and Pete Mason arises from Patricia's imagination playing on memories of her first marriage; as her Paris courtship, marriage, house renovation and divorce are transformed into Mary's experiences with Martin Freemantle. Her emotionally bruising entanglement with Lionel Butler, who, she told Richard, 'used to send her brief notes of his desperation, written in violet ink under the heading *All Souls – 2 a.m.*', underlies her creation of Daniel. A slight resemblance to Bruce Montgomery may be detected in the grand inebriation of the writer and composer Anderson Cully. Patricia's liaison with Larkin, more of wit and eroticism than sex, as their letters reveal, clearly inspired her presentation of Rollo Jute.

The most significant and attractive attribute of Patricia Avis's novel – as its very title, *Playing the Harlot; or, Mostly Coffee*, would suggest – is that it is a woman's novel. The focal stories of the novel are of the women – Abigail, Theo and, most of all, Mary, who as the foreign-born, intellectual, rich girl both mirrors the author's situation and provides a female version of the perspective identified with the Angry Young Men of her generation. While Jean Rhys, Djuna Barnes, Katherine Mansfield and Laura Riding (whose work Patricia particularly admired and whose *roman à clef* called 14A had been withdrawn immediately after its publication in 1934 because of libel) had written women's narratives in the period between the wars, Patricia Avis's novel clearly works from within her postwar generation – its preoccupations, its social and political aimlessness, its situation-driven personal tragedies. Her special perspective is of the women of the generation, a point of view that is *new* and so far undocumented in fictional or dramatic form. To the 1950s literary 'outsiders'' cynical and disillusioned attitude, that expressed in the fiction of the Angry Young Men and the poetry of The Movement, is added the alienation of a female – and feminist – point of view. Patricia's original inspiration in Paris for a novel, Iris Murdoch's *Under the Net*, had been told from a man's point of view, and the only novelist with a similar perspective to emerge in England at the time was the then little noticed Doris Lessing (another woman with a colonial upbringing) who published the first three volumes of her *Bildungsroman, Children of Violence*, in the 1950s. While the men in Patricia's circle like Larkin, Amis, Wain and Murphy were published and celebrated, a highly educated woman like Patricia Avis who shared their experiences remained virtually unknown. As she had complained in her journal in 1953 in a phrase that was subsumed into the title of her novel, her life seemed to be 'mostly cups of coffee'.

Accurate and moving is Patricia's portrayal of her women characters' situation; they are educated, well born and moneyed (usually), yet serve as ornaments in marriage or objects in

multiple unfulfilled relationships. Written two decades before
the feminist movement of the 1970s, the novel anticipates
most of that movement's concerns for the female individual
and her situation within relationships in contemporary society.
This is true in terms of obvious and direct references in the
novel: Mary Gallen is at once schoolgirl and 'defrocked goddess' prone to multiple miscarriages; the women's situation in
their society is summed up as 'Fine feathers make fine birds at a
distance, don't they? But plucked . . . plucked, gutted and
trussed. There's no concealing it'; and the novel ends with the
image of an increasingly suicidal Mary seeing a deer caught in
barbed wire. More subtle and feminist is the treatment of the
heroine's search for love and self-worth in sexual relationships
with homosexual men – 'a certain lack of precedent is always
attractive, a challenge to womanhood' – and the portrayal of
the unexpected dependencies within these real, albeit equally
abusive (as is Mary's most traditional heterosexual relationship
with the politician, McNeill) liaisons. Particularly compelling
is the scene in the Arab quarter in Paris where Mary accidentally meets her current lover, Daniel Frost, and her future
husband, Martin Freemantle, while they are both cruising for
Arab boys. Equally compelling and truly original for its time is
the letter Mary writes to Freemantle after they have both confessed infidelities with other men suggesting that they reconcile
and work jointly on rebuilding *his* dream house with *her* father's
money as the place to foster best into reality *his* sculpture and
her fantasies of personal connection.

   This thoroughly engaging novel can well hold its place
among published works in the canon of Patricia Avis's angry
generation: the dialogue is real and abundant, the characters
sympathetic, and the personal encounters between them
absorbing and very often moving. Readers of this fully

contemporary British novel will find in it a fascinating mix of the conventional and the new in narrative forms. They will recognise aspects of the traditional Dickensian family saga, the nineteenth-century French novel of adultery, the naturalist novel of Moore and Gissing, the sparsely detailed and epiphanic modernist novel of personality and impression, the myths of sexual awakening and rootlessness of post-war fiction and drama, the post-colonial novel narrated by a partial outsider to British society and culture, and, finally, the patterns, arguments and ideologies of the new and emerging form of the feminist, or gender-driven, novel.

But *Playing the Harlot; or, Mostly Coffee* was much ahead of its time – and as *roman à clef* too much of its time. Patricia Avis's manuscript was turned down at Faber and Faber because Charles Monteith, according to Richard Murphy, thought that 'sentence by sentence, it was well written but the structure was weak . . . He thought it a borderline case, publishable, yes: but he did not want to publish it because it slandered his friends.' Disappointed in her literary life, Patricia lived on in Dublin amid a circle of intellectual friends; after about 1963 T. Desmond Williams, Professor of Modern European History at University College, lived with her. In 1977, Patricia completed a second novel in the tradition of the British anarchist-spy travel thriller popularised by Graham Greene. Called *A Second Adam*, it, too, was rejected by Faber and Faber. This disappointment may have contributed to Patricia's death, according to her daughter Emily. Like Sylvia Plath, Patricia Avis felt her situation as a rejected woman artist acutely; her sense of rejection was real, and was compounded by her lifelong tendency to suffer depression. Avis's premature and tragic end mirrors Plath's. Over the years she became increasingly addicted to alcohol and barbiturates. On 2 September 1977 she died as a result of an overdose of Nembutal tablets while drinking nearly two half-bottles of Benedictine and Cointreau.

George H. Gilpin and Hermione de Almeida
The University of Tulsa, Oklahoma, 1995

CHAPTER ONE

Rollo Jute felt for his nail scissors. There was a photograph on the back page of *The Times* that particularly interested him. After some patting, groping and quiet cursing he remembered that he had lent the scissors to his landlady, on the understanding that she would not use them on her chow. Not even the finishing touches he'd said firmly, knowing very well that the short, curved cut was just what she fancied for the ears. It was May. He made a few tick-tack signs to attract the attention of his favourite waitress, the one with the chignon and the most elaborate belt.

'And how are the buns this morning?' he said ogreishly.

'Toasted or plain.' She knew him well enough not to wink too soon.

'As a matter of fact,' he cleared his throat, 'all I need is a knife, a really sharp knife.' He had her there, at least he hoped he had.

'No young ladies today?' she cooed, lingering over him.

Rollo, grinning like a toy panda, shyly averted his gaze from the damp, splitting seams under her nearest most motherly arm.

In this ancient, provincial university town, certain people could be presumed to be present in certain places at certain

times. Among these Rollo Jute, aged thirty-five, bachelor of
regular habits and inadequate private means (supplemented by
afternoon classes in Musical Appreciation under the auspices of
the Girls' Public Day School Trust), bore himself with dubious
distinction. Of fluctuating fact and figure, the least variation in
either being detected instantly, if not long prophesied, by the
owner. Of chaste reserved demeanour. Of pastel weaves, with
such subtle additions as his uncle's watch and chain and a set of
fisherman hats, Rollo was to be found every morning, except
Saturday, drinking coffee in the Kardomah. There his acquaintances would seek him out, and there too he would find enough
time, enough, on the whole, to comment on such extracts of
their private lives as they saw fit to offer him. Several young
ladies, glad of so sympathetic and understanding an audience,
provided weekly, at crucial periods even daily, instalments on
how the world was treating them. It must be assumed that these
instalments diverted him. On Saturdays he attended a Swedish
drill class and on Sundays he wrote to his mother, whom he
supported on the Isle of Man. His evenings were largely devoted
to embellishing his diary. This notable scrapbook was now on
its twentieth leather-backed ledger. For some time now the
problem of safe storage had been troubling a good many people,
particularly those few more intimate male acquaintances to
whom late-night extracts had occasionally been read, along
with the appropriate gestures of one sadly but steadily possessed
by the predictability of people and events. A few months back
a large sealed parcel had been consigned to a local bank. This,
Rollo swore, had disposed of the fire-watching years at any rate,
though no one closely concerned with these years quite
believed him.

The Times photograph, a rural pony show scene, had just
gone into the wallet, between a laundry list and the latest

report on decapitation of seals, when one of Rollo's young ladies arrived.

'Hallo, dear.' He made as if to get up. 'And how are the nuns?'

Mary Gallen slumped into the nearest basket chair.

'I'm leaving them,' she announced, easing a squashed packet of cigarettes out of a music case stuffed with notebooks and dictionaries.

Mary was eighteen, tall, fair, well-built, to be called beautiful as often as most later on, only now her features were amiable, unformed, her skin unreliable, her hair like a furze-bush. Any odd pounds above the slot-machine average were minimised, or so she hoped, by a variety of thick-knit sweaters, pleated skirts, knee stockings and brogues. She had no party dress, long or short, as she'd never been to a party.

Rollo got out his Dr Barnardo matches and signalled for another cup of coffee.

'Well,' he said, 'what happened? Did they catch you in bed with a lover?'

'Not quite,' she laughed shyly. 'They caught me taking a light off one of the Sacred Heart lamps. You see, I think the Sacred Heart is an unpardonable aberration. And then there was more fuss about the electric fire. Mother Paul said that even if I did come from South America there was no need whatsoever to leave two bars burning in the bedroom all the time I was having a bath. And no need to lie about it. No need either to have the bath so full. No need to help myself to the National Cocoa Powder both before and after Benediction. Didn't I know it was only intended for girls who were working late?'

'Do the nuns bath you?' Rollo said.

'Don't be silly. One of the lay sisters must have been snooping about. Or Mother Paul herself. I shouldn't put it past her. You'd think they'd have better things to do there, wouldn't you? After all St Saviour's is meant to be a hostel for serious-minded young ladies. Not an open prison. It's not all that open either,' she went on. 'You can't get in after 10 p.m. without a special indulgence. One of the girls slipped off the chapel roof last week – did I tell you? – climbing in after a lantern-slide lecture, on the Gobi Desert I think. Somewhere glamorous like that. Anyhow, she managed to crawl up the steps, get a bit of sleep on one of the back pews. Then at first mass she had to explain she'd been praying all night and the limp was only pins and needles. They spotted the flowerbed of course. It's really very depressing, a lot of women living together, the way they fuss about. Still, I suppose men only manage better by being a bit more brutal about it. Well, well.' She blew at her cup, gathering skin. 'I'm leaving, going to live with a cousin.'

'Cousin?' What sort of cousin?'

'No special sort. Her mother just happened to be at school with mine. Of course they didn't believe me, said they'd have to write to South America, and could my cousin provide a good Catholic home.'

'And can she?'

Mary smiled. 'She's a bit busy at the moment, but I could always try converting her. Anyhow,' she went on, as if to convince herself, 'I'm pretty sure my mother won't mind. She's been sending the Foldings a Christmas card for years. And my father never trusted nuns. Theo – that's their daughter – has the handiest digs I know. You just put the lid on the bath and it makes a kitchen table.' This clearly impressed her. 'The landlady is deaf too, never leaves the basement, so she won't bother us much. In fact,' she concluded firmly, 'it's an ideal arrangement.'

Rollo nodded several times running, which was most unusual for him.

'Not Theodora Folding the medical student, by any chance?'

he said casually, staring hard over her shoulder at one of the ornamental pillars.

'That's right.' Mary looked pleased. 'So you know her?'

'Well, I've *heard* of her.' Rollo paused cautiously. 'Rather – er advanced ideas, hasn't she?'

'You're worse than the nuns.' Mary laughed. 'She *was* at a co-ed school, if that's what you mean. *And* she wears slacks. Very nice too.' She fingered the safety-pin holding her skirt together, then breathed in deeply to feel thinner. 'After all, I'm sure your protégées wear slacks on Sundays.'

'I'm afraid I shall never know.' He smiled sadly.

'And how did they get on with the castanets?'

'On the whole the type of girl most suitable for the castanets prefers to stick to the triangle.'

'Oh.' Mary sighed, toying with a fresh cigarette. 'I suppose I'd better be getting back to work. All these libraries, and not one little fire-proof annexe. You'd think they didn't want anyone to learn anything.' She lit up. 'My father is of the opinion that only prostitutes smoke.' She waved out the match round and round like an indoor firework. 'You know . . . life without exams must be a sort of perpetual convalescence. As it is, if I don't get one of these scholarships, I'll probably be summoned home.'

'But surely your old man's not all that hard up, is he?'

'No,' she smiled, 'he is not. It's a matter of honour. I've always had to be first. In a warm climate it's easy enough. You just don't play games. But here . . . '

'Never mind, dear.' He grinned encouragingly. 'Perhaps you could bribe the authorities with betel nuts or slender cheroots.'

'Bananas might be more wholesome.' She shook out a handful of saccharine tablets, setting four aside for further cups of coffee. 'Look,' she said, pouring the rest back, 'I really ought to write a letter. Would you mind?'

'Not in the least.' Rollo smoothed out the crossword. 'Give my love to the *pampa*,' he said.

Mary pulled out her writing pad, wishing, as she did every week, that an air-letter would do. She had left home for the first time six months ago, to acquire, by way of St Saviour's, such information as might, produced at the right time and place, provide written and spoken proof of a sound capable enquiring mind. In fact, like several thousand eighteen-year-olds up and down the country, she was hoping that one of the four local residential colleges bent on higher education for women would gladly find room for her. If she hoped more drastically than most, it was because, as her father's daughter, she had very little alternative. Her father, in case this does not become clear, made no allowances, none whatsoever. Occasionally, the world being what it is, he let things pass, but on the whole he got what he wanted, the way he wanted it. At seventy-two he was, if not the biggest, certainly one of the least vulnerable industrialists now based on the Argentine Republic, living within ten minutes' driving distance of his not luxurious, not 'Mediterranean modern' office in Buenos Aires. His wife, thirty years younger, mediated as best as she could between her husband and such sections of society as would trade with him. Being of Swiss puritanical pastoral origin, he had little else in common with them, and had indeed never been known to invite anyone, apart from his own executives, to his house. Nor were his family permitted to do so. Nor could they leave this house, except in his absence. And his absences, with the telephone always at hand in and out of office hours, were very rare, short business trips, during which his daily letters had to be answered in detail by return post. On longer trips he took his family with him, along with the current nanny, governess or tutor. And 'home life' was soon re-established in the first-floor

suite of the Grand Hotel of whatever large town he happened
to have business in. No nanny, governess or tutor had ever
stayed very long. His wife had been brought up as a Catholic,
middle member of a large expatriate family with a father in the
Irish Guards, missing since Ypres. And Mary, who had started
off life with a twin brother, was by this time their only child.

Dearest Daddy and Mamma,

Thank you very much for the food parcel. Unfortunately
the nuns expect everything to be shared round, but I must
say it was a great relief to see some fruit again, after weeks
of pilchard pie and tapioca fritters. Oranges are still
rationed, dished up like grapefruit once a month. Actually
I think the austere life can be carried a bit too far for
'growing girls'. It's also bitterly cold. This is the Spring
Term, you see, which means all the heating is off. Even
that little radiator I brought with your Christmas cheque
has been confiscated, which makes it very hard to study at
night, once the libraries are shut. You know what these
old damp old places are, Daddy. Not a penny spent on
them for years. St Saviour's is hardly more than a glorified
string of barges, really. Even the mouse-holes leak. Of
course, not everyone is as uncomfortable as this; that clipping you sent about accommodation here was meant as a
joke mostly, I'm sure. It's only that St Saviour's does rather
seem to take advantage of the situation, though Reverend
Mother herself, I'm told, has recently acquired an electric
blanket.

I was thinking it might be easier to get on with my
work somewhere warmer and drier, where I could cook my
own food, have a bath every day, change the sheets once
a week.

You remember the Foldings, Mamma? I believe Sir Basil is back from Portugal now, doing something very private and confidential in Whitehall. Anyhow their daughter Theodora is here studying medicine. She's attached to one of the colleges, but not living *in*, as medical students stay here so long that they can't live *in* all the time. She has a lovely flat overlooking the park. It's one of those university flats with an authorised landlady, who keeps an eye on everything – just like the colleges, only much more comfortable. The flat has two nice bedrooms, a large sitting room, kitchen and bathroom, and Theodora would very much like me to share it with her. The rent would work out much the same as St Saviour's, what with all those Chinese missions. I could go to the University Chaplaincy for Mass, Mamma, and there's also a Newman Society, where all sorts of interesting people give talks. Anyhow, you think it over and let me know. Theodora has promised not to make any other arrangements till I hear from you. The landlady seems very sweet and motherly – a great baker apparently.

I told Reverend Mother I might be leaving, going to a cousin (so as not to hurt her feelings). She seemed rather angry, but that's probably because St Saviour's is half empty anyway. My tutoring would, of course go on just the same. There's an awful lot of General Knowledge that seems peculiarly English to judge from the specimen papers – *Brass-rubbing* for instance . . .

She turned to Rollo. 'I'll never go back,' she said fiercely. 'Never.'

'Where to?' He almost looked up. 'St Saviour's?'

'No.' She clapped up the written pad. 'Home.'

Rollo returned to his pencillings.

'Any quotations from the Lady of Shalott?' she said a little later.

He shook his head. 'Any sort of a banner carried in lacrosse?'

CHAPTER TWO

'Ma – a – ry!'

'Yes?'

'Do turn that machine down a bit, would you dear? We'll never hear the telephone.'

Mary slid aside the music score she'd been trying to follow by skipping the fast bits. As she leant towards the volume control of the third-hand portable gramophone, something exploded in the kitchen. There was no smoke, just a swinging sort of knock getting weaker and weaker. Eventually it stopped.

'My God.' The deep sweet voice from down the corridor could be tragic too. 'That's not the iron again, is it? Do have a look. I'm covered with grease.'

Mary switched off the gramophone first. Last time everything had fused, but this evening it was just that the mock copper kettle, designed to disconnect itself, had actually done so.

Mary managed – by fiddling about, getting angry and interested – to uncouple the plug along with its cord from the back of the gas cooker.

'I say, Theo,' she called out, 'do you think it matters if one or two of the wires don't quite meet?'

The said Theo came out barefoot from the bedroom to have a look. She was wearing a champagne-coloured crêpe de Chine petticoat, trimmed here and there with black lace. If the makers of the champagne-coloured crêpe de Chine petticoats, trimmed here and there with black lace, could have seen her, they would have hired her on the spot. Laying aside her nail-varnish brush – across the spout of one of the bath taps – she took up the plug and shook it. Two more screws dropped out.

'Perhaps we'd better leave it,' she said. 'They do say a hot damp towel, but I'm sure surgical spirit would do just as well. Those herbal masks are a nonsense anyway.'

She sat down on the lidded bath, brushing out her hair. This she kept dark, shiny and straight, as in Tahiti, concealing a somewhat knobby forehead to varying degrees, depending on how dreamy or abandoned she could afford to be looking. On formal occasions, such as presenting herself to the dean after breakfast, or passing anatomy vivas, it was caught back in a scrolled silver clasp, very severe, leaving her face all taut and eager. Like a mare held back at the starting gate, a young prize mare.

Mary was wondering how she was going to make coffee without a kettle. 'Is it *Lucifer and the Lord* again tonight?' she said.

'I very much hope not. We should be trying out some revue numbers soon, *if* they're written that is.' Theo speeded up the hairbrush to get the sort of crackling you should get, when you start experimenting with electricity. She was engaged quite a lot at present in amateur theatricals.

'Will Anderson be there?' Mary said, not engaged in anything very much.

'Anderson Cully? Oh yes, I suppose I will. Everyone got awfully angry with him last time. He would keep fooling about with the accompaniment. As if you could have *any* of those camp scenes starting off with "There'll be a Hot Time in Ole Town Tonight!"' Theo put down the hairbrush, remembering her half-varnished toes. It was too late now to do anything but clean the whole lot off.

'Are those Anderson's records you've been going through?' she said, reaching for the bottle labelled Rennet, containing acetone.

'No, of course they're not.'

At this point the telephone rang.

Theo grabbed a raincoat off the banisters and rushed downstairs, missing all the splits in the linoleum, which had been known to trip people up.

Coming back was much more sedate. She had a young man with her, a tall, thin, stooping young man in spectacles. And he was wearing a pink check wool shirt half tucked into a pair of shrunken chocolate-coloured corduroys held up by an old school tie. One half of his face was concealed by a tongue of uncombed hair. The other half, sketchily shaven, looked kind and content.

'You two haven't met yet, have you?'

Theo, very gracious in her raincoat, led the way into the sitting room.

'Dear Pete!' She squeezed his forearm under the flapping pink check sleeve. 'I don't know how I'd manage without him. He's brought all those embryology slide drawings I missed, learning squash last term. And a way to work out the last stages of the Head and Neck too. I told you, didn't I that our body's already going bad, and my dissecting partner still has something wrong with his nose, which he can't help, but which makes it impossible to breathe anywhere near him.'

'I thought you were going to get another partner,' Mary said.

'I know, but this one has to have some partner, and he is doing his best to get cured. Anyhow it's all right now. I need hardly appear, thanks to Pete.' She smiled at him, most thankful, most pleased.

Pete Mason was a fifth-year medical student, who happened to have kept all his notes. They were very neat notes with helpful diagrams in coloured inks, and he was quite happy to lend them to Theo any time she wanted them.

'Would you look after him dear?' she said to Mary, going towards the mantelpiece from which her stockings were suspended by a vase and an ashtray. 'I simply must get dressed now or they'll give my part to that girl from Guatemala.'

'I suppose Abigail will be there,' Pete said. He had a pipe with a storm-lid, but the storm-lid had stuck.

'I really don't know.' Theo hung on the door, leaning back, swinging a bit, trying not to seem rude. 'The scenery's not quite her line this time, but she may be there, providing ideas or something. She often is.'

'I might look in later,' Pete said, having another go at the storm-lid. 'To keep an eye on Anderson.'

'Yes! Do!' Theo gushed herself out at that.

And Mary lent Pete her safety-pin for the storm-lid. 'Is Anderson Cully a friend of yours?' she said.

'Good Lord yes. Same school, same college, same staircase.'

'Are you both still there?'

'Sorry,' he said, handing back the rest of the safety-pin. 'It needs pliers.' He smiled obligingly, like someone just arrived on the scene anxious to know if there is anything they can do to help.

'Do you have nice digs?' she said.

'Oh yes. Quite nice. Anderson's, actually. I moved in there when he got his piano.'

'So you share?'

'Good Lord no. He had to find somewhere with french windows to get his piano through.'

'And did he?'

'Oh yes.' Pete chuckled happily. 'He did.'

They sat for a while, and then Pete saw the score.

'So you like Wagner too?' he said, reaching out for it.

'Well yes, I do. At least I'm beginning to.' Mary wriggled a bit. 'Would you like a drink or anything?' she said quickly. 'I'm afraid there's only cider, or sherry with cork in it. Or perhaps you'd like something to eat? There's lots to eat . . . Ham? Corned beef? Tinned salmon?'

'I don't know, really.' He looked up from the score a little bewildered, but patient, still prepared to help. 'You haven't any eggs, have you? Or a cup of milk?'

'Of course.' Mary got up. 'Would you like an omelette?'

'Oh no. Just boiled eggs. Two. Four and a half minutes. And bread and butter, if you have it.' He smiled encouragingly. 'And – er *cold* milk.'

Mary found Theo in the kitchen ironing a flared red taffeta skirt. What wasn't being ironed was mostly caught up in the legs of the ironing board, or lying on the floor.

'He looks awfully hungry,' Mary said, ripping open the latest food parcel from South America.

'Pete? He always does. I expect it's because he's in love with Abigail Rubel.'

'Who's she?'

'A rather exotic art student. Auburn tresses and grey grey eyes. Very mysterious. I'm afraid Pete isn't quite the diabolic enchanter she's looking for, though he's *echt* enough I should have thought.'

Mary started opening tins.

'By the way, dear,' Theo held up the skirt all dimpled where water had been shaken on it. 'Will you be in on Thursday night?'

'No, I don't think so.' What Mary meant was that she would not too much mind taking herself and books to the library or to the cinema café for a few hours, instead of staying in the sitting room. On the whole she preferred the café to the library, though the tables were sticky and wobbled, and the lights kept flickering. One of these days she hoped that Theo would do the same thing for her. But one of these days, nights rather, was a long time coming.

On getting back with the tray to where Pete was, she found him very busy annotating the *Meistersinger* with a fountain pen.

'It isn't mine, you know, that score,' she said, putting down poached eggs on sweetcorn, sliced peaches, peanut butter on toast and a tumbler of milk. 'I got it with the records from the Gramophone Society.'

'That's fine then,' he said. 'I was just marking the record sides for you. I say,' he swivelled round, rubbing his hands. 'How nice.' Then his face dropped, and he went on making room for the tray.

'I thought you might have got hungrier.'

'Oh . . . I see. You wouldn't by any chance have a cup for the milk?'

'Well yes, I suppose so. I mean there *are* cups, but I thought . . .' She didn't know what she thought really.

'It doesn't matter.' He was looking pretty glum by now. 'No, no. Please don't bother.' He reached for the glass first, made a bit of a toast and then started drinking, as if it were spa water and he on a cure.

By the time Theo had got herself ready, Pete had almost finished with the score. He had also eaten most of the yolk of the two eggs, drunk most of the milk, and was clearly not going to eat or drink any more.

'Going now,' Theo said from the door, 'just to make sure they can all manage perfectly well from now on without me.' Though she looked of course by this time well worth waiting for. 'Are you two going to have a little concert?'

But Pete was already standing up. 'Another time perhaps,' he said. 'You see,' he was kind, gentle, very polite to Mary, 'I'd more or less promised Anderson I'd look in.'

'See you later then, dear,' said Theo to Mary, kind gentle, very polite too, the way people often are going out, leaving others staying in.

After they'd gone Mary went back to the gramophone.

CHAPTER THREE

Rollo Jute and Anderson Cully were having coffee in the Kardomah. Anderson, aged thirty, could still describe himself, where such descriptions are called for, as a student, a postgraduate student in Middle French. He was more than plump and could be heard most evenings in his favourite pub attributing this to too much beer and too little exercise. Apart from chain-smoking, which he interrupted for an hour or two after breakfast every other month for the sake of his heart, he treated his body with benevolent indulgence, clothing it in monogrammatic slumberwear, silk shirts, bow-ties, wide-lapelled suits and copper-bright pointed shoes. His fair curls were boyishly cut, regularly dented and creamed, and one or other well-manicured hand usually carried a signet ring of no known significance. Because of a long childhood illness, he had for some time now been very advanced for his age, too bright too soon to be eager any more. At the present time an academic career in the offing still provided the handiest cover and contact for broader enterprises, mostly musical. His concertinos, intimate operas, part settings of English verse, both lyrical and biblical, had not as yet been very rewarding. Nor had his serious short stories. This morning he had come to elucidate certain knotty problems in a film so far entitled 'Murder in the Ballet'.

'What about the cast?' Rollo said. 'I suppose they'll be only too glad to let you wander up and down the practising bars, taking your pick.'

'Of course, my dear fellow. That's the whole idea.' Anderson had what must be called a rich, fruity voice, which his more admiring associates did their best to imitate, saying of course they'd had it first, which of course they had not. 'It's not going to be easy, mind you,' he went on, very bishoplike, 'to find a male dancer who would dream of handling a gun these days.'

'Couldn't make it a poisoned joss-stick or a Bushman's little blow dart, could you?'

'Oh dear no.' Anderson shook his king of the beasts head reprovingly. 'This is an all-British job. Just plain, honest, decent folk like you and me out for a good cry.'

'No ballet mistresses then?' Rollo seemed a little despondent. 'No pince-nez?'

'Well, we'll see. There'll be a few backstage palpitations, of course, but if you're thinking of corridors of crushed slippers, keyhole orgies, no. Certainly not. Covent Garden must be kept up somehow, you know.'

'No jazz I suppose.' Rollo's morose abstracted expression eased slightly as he saw Mary making her way through the tables. Mary hadn't noticed Anderson on account of the ornamental pillar. When she did, she said 'I'm sorry, I didn't realise . . . No, please don't get up. I can't stay.'

And Rollo said 'Nonsense dear,' drawing out a chair, with Anderson miming faint offers of assistance.

'We did meet once I think,' Mary said, glancing at Anderson, who did not disagree. 'At a party of Theo's,' she added more firmly. 'Did you get that book in the end?'

'Book?' Anderson did not seem to remember any book, wanting as he was to go on thinking about 'Murder in the Ballet'.

'Wagner's life, wasn't it?' she prompted delicately. 'You were trying to get someone to swap it for Pascal.'

'Oh yes, that's right.' He remembered now. 'What an ass he was, that young man. Fourteen stately volumes if you please, for a scrap of ancestral junk. And he was so sure I was trying to do him, which indeed I was. I wonder what else he's salvaged from that little *Schloss auf dem Gipfel* of his.'

'Who's this?' Rollo said.

'Oh, just some morganatic princeling, who quarrelled with his dad over the tailor's bill or something. Now goes by the name of Raphael de Groot.'

'Oh. Must he?'

'Yeth, I'm afwaid so . . . Well now.' Anderson flapped his six-inch silver cigarette case at Mary. 'Perhaps you can help. Ballet. All nice girls are fond of the ballet, aren't they?'

Mary smiled. 'Are they?' she said, feeling this was not quite the moment to start explaining how very far from fond she was of the ballet.

'Now the thing is,' he had his rolled gold pencil out, 'how can this budding ballerina get it across to the second horn that there's a gun in the oak tree, aimed at her, going to go off at the first cymbal clash? Oak tree to the right, flowers busy dancing to the left. Not all the flowers are friends, remember.'

'I see,' she said, though she didn't at all. 'I suppose, if the girl were a good thrower, the horn might catch the message done up as some sort of a petal . . .'

Anderson smiled fairly politely. 'The horn,' he said, 'would be playing at the time. No, no. It must all turn quite naturally on the movement of the dance.'

'I see,' Mary looked towards Rollo in case he might have something to say about the movement of the dance.

'And how is flat life suiting you?' he said.

'Oh fine, though it's hard to get down to anything there. Theo's been pretty jumpy lately. I can't think why.'

'You didn't check up on that Founders' Song of hers, did you? . . . "Nigh forty years",' he started, quite wistful.

She laughed, embarrassed. 'I'm sure Anderson wouldn't want to hear all that.'

'Don't mind me, ducky.' The rolled gold pencil was draughting away, oak tree to the right, flower dance to the left.

' "Nigh forty years laboured they to create us",' Mary murmured uncomfortably, ' "dreamed for us, schemed for us, gave us our . . ." Look Rollo, I really don't see why you're so interested. It's not even funny.'

Rollo said he really didn't see why either and he wasn't all that interested anyway. He drew her attention to the mild purposeful approach of a familiar ragged figure, nursing a flat rectangular parcel done up in mauve tissue paper and gilt thread.

'Hallo Pete,' Anderson said. 'No twins on the way, I take it?'

'Not that I know of. And anyhow the student midwives would get them. It's always their turn, as far as I can see.' He settled the parcel finally between the pillar and an abandoned trolley.

'What on earth is that?' Rollo said. 'The rugger fifteen?'

Pete grinned awkwardly. 'As a matter of fact it's Abigail's. She's – er just given it to me . . . another self-portrait, I think.'

'Well, let's have a look at it.' Anderson shifted a bit, so that the trolley could be wheeled elsewhere and Pete and the picture sat down. 'There's bound to be something phosphorescent somewhere,' he said. 'Abigail's evil genius, bless her dear little head. Last time it had tusks.'

This time it had horns, camouflaged by wisps of mauve tissue sticking to the varnish, but horns nevertheless. A bottle-green gargoyle with nut-brown horns leered over one creamy shoulder of Abigail. For this King Cophetua's beggar maid with a touch of the grave inscrutable East was Abigail – Abigail lost, found, lost again, Abigail entranced. Apart from the gargoyle, which had a slight look of Pete, the background was dark and stormy with blurred traces of a fiery multiparous planet in the top left-hand corner.

'Dear Abigail,' Anderson said. 'Tempted again. And what's the arrangement with this one, Pete? A commission basis?'

'I'm afraid not.' Pete was studying the terrazzo floor. 'You see, it was a kind of parting gift.'

'Oh, it was.' Anderson studied the floor too for a moment. 'Well, my dear fellow,' he burbled on with a jovial nudge, 'never mind. You're not the adoring type, you know.' He looked again at that auburn hair, those grey grey eyes, so very far away. 'It would make a lovely firescreen. Don't you think so, Rollo?'

Rollo muttered evasively, being very particular about the useful or beautiful or both, especially when it looked like coming into his own bed-sittingroom.

Pete made one more attempt to replace the wrapping, being clearly in no mood to abandon a parting gift. 'I think I'd better be off,' he said, once he'd got some of the gilt thread to meet.

'What about your coffee?' Mary moved it a bit nearer.

'Not for me, thanks. Never do.'

He was half-way out when she thought of the notes. Getting herself and music case unravelled eventually from the wicker-work, she hurried after him, catching up at the swing doors.

'Theo asked me to leave these for you at the maternity clinic,' she said, pulling out a crumpled pink file. 'You couldn't take them now, could you? It's rather a walk. And there was something else she wanted, something about heated cats I think. Would that be right?'

'Oh yes.' He hollowed an arm to take the file. 'The decerebrate reflexes. Did she miss those too?'

'I suppose so.'

They stood aside to let more shopping baskets through, Pete still holding the pull door with his foot.

'If you wouldn't mind just coming round to my digs,' he said, 'we could pick them up there.'

Mary looked back down the tables, mostly set now for lunch. She could see just enough of Anderson to be quite sure he was conducting with a fork.

CHAPTER FOUR

Pete's bed-sittingroom was large and dark and never dusted. Apart from a desk and a cracked cane chair at the window, both stacked criss-cross with books and papers, and a family-size legless divan in one corner, the furniture consisted entirely of open bookshelves assembled in various handyman styles by student lodgers over the years. The most stable section held medical books, very neat, decisive and opulent. The rest was a gay, sagging jumble of twentieth-century literature, the product largely of Pete's long-standing association with Anderson. Mary, who had never seen anything like it before, was most impressed.

After a few friendly exchanges on the more obvious aspects of this scene, she and Pete settled down to listen to the gramophone; that is Pete changed the records from the edge of the divan, while Mary sat cross-legged some yards away on the only mat. An hour later they were both sitting on the mat, holding hands, following extracts from *Tristan*. At the start of each side – short-playing sides – their hands renewed contact with increasing goodwill. Just before Kurwenal's death, Anderson arrived. Pete and Mary promptly disengaged hands and all three sat silent till the side ended.

'Ah!' Anderson rubbed his hands happily. 'The master at

work.' He seemed as pleased as if he'd done it all himself.

'Next one?' Pete put up his hand to the lid.

'Oh no, I don't think so.' Anderson waved him gently back. 'I must say I don't much like listening to music any more, except my own of course.' Here he chuckled like a Father Christmas in one of the better stores. 'I was wondering . . .' He looked at his watch. 'Damn. They're shut. You haven't anything left in there, have you?' He looked hopefully at the old school playbox wedged into the grate.

This, on being opened, had the sort of smell which is at its most unforgettable in the upholstery of the second-class bar of the Irish mailboat. After some desultory rattling, squinting and tipping, Pete remembered a nearly full bottle of gin deposited some days ago with a teetotal divinity student up the road. As only a toothmug of this had been stipulated at the time – for urgent unspecified purposes – he went off to reclaim the rest.

'Dear me,' Anderson said at the gay slam of the front door. 'Here I am – come to console, guide, and generally fortify.' He glanced at Abigail's portrait abandoned in its gilt thread by the door. 'It looks as if I need hardly have bothered.' He grinned at Mary and she grinned back.

'Have you known her long, Abigail?' she said, moving round behind the desk, starting to look out of the window.

'Long enough, bless her nymphish little heart. Not that her heart's exactly the first thing you'd notice.' He lumbered idly up along the bookshelves towards the desk.

'I'd always wondered,' she said, still gazing out on the network of back entrances, 'just what went into those pig-litter bins.'

Anderson squeezed himself up at last, past the desk. Stretching one arm across the window, just above her head, he leant out cautiously.

'My God.' He peered at the scaly hens staggering about in a

maze of ashpits directly below them. 'So that's where the Sunday breakfast comes from.' His arm was now resting across Mary's shoulders. For some seconds they stood quite still, watching the hens, except that his arm was now at her waist.

'Well, ducky?' he said with a slight squeeze. 'Shall we sit down?' Without loosening his hold he turned her slowly towards him. Several books fell off the desk.

'Just a minute.' She disengaged herself as deftly as she could, 'I think the gramophone's still on. Are you sure you wouldn't like to hear something?'

'Quite sure,' he said. After a few increasingly undignified attempts to recover lost ground, he set himself gingerly down on the divan, which creaked all the same.

'Now really,' he said, mopping his neck, stretching his legs, 'a big girl like you should know better than that.' He patted the space beside him invitingly, very rueful and boyish, also cross.

'Oh well,' he sighed, 'some people will never know what's good for them.' And he unclicked the six-inch cigarette case. 'Have one?'

Mary, a little put out by all this, went on sorting records noisily. And then Pete got back with the gin and three cracked cups.

'So the girlfriend didn't need it after all,' Anderson said, cradling his cup, happy again.

Pete cleared his throat disapprovingly. His gestures were very clear-cut on the whole, designed to be readily understood a long way off. 'Nothing to go with it, I'm afraid,' he said, starting to pour it out cup by cup. 'The plumbing's off again.'

Mary decided she could not stay. She borrowed a book though, and nearly forgot the notes for Theo.

'By the way,' Anderson said, soon after she'd gone, 'I got those seats in the post this morning for the *Rosenkavalier*.' He was referring to the first post-war performance at Covent Garden. 'Of course it's not for months yet, but I was wondering about that third ticket. I don't suppose you'll want it now, will you?'

'What about you?'

'I doubt it. You see, none of my women would last out the first act, except perhaps at the back of one of the higher boxes. Oh dear no. Abigail was the only one who could ever have carried it off. Mind you, I'm not at all sure just how far her trance would have taken us either. If women get ignored too long, they start losing their gloves, getting pains, begging you to drive them home. Once in the car of course, they feel much much better. Bless them. But we can't have any of that on the first night of the *Rosenkavalier*.'

Pete agreed, as he usually did, being long indebted to Anderson for much worldly advice. 'Still,' he said, 'I might manage to find someone . . . Mary, for instance.'

Anderson seemed doubtful. 'It's the Grand Circle, you know. Do you think she might possibly smarten up a bit?'

Pete was sure that could be arranged. On the subject of dress he could be very cool, aloof, almost formidable. 'How much do I owe you?' he said.

'My dear Pete, don't be absurd.' Anderson, liking, as he did, to move in a world of jovial approbation, having, as he often had, more money than most of his friends, could be remarkably generous. 'This is on me,' he said.

By the time Mary got back, she was doubled up with the sort of pain that comes from swallowing air instead of food, and can only be dealt with by lying face down on a hot-water bottle. This she did, equipped with the two most promising of Theo's textbooks. Both had colour plates, but what she most wanted to know was once again not made clear. Absorbed in the index: cross section of . . . events in . . . mechanism of (in spinal tract) . . . see hypothalamic level . . . the clicking to of the front door roused her immediately. And when Theo came in, she was poring over the Eye as an Optical Instrument. But Theo had her own worries. In fact it looked very much as if she'd been crying.

'No post, was there?'

'No,' Mary said, 'but I got those notes for you.'

'Oh, did you?' Theo had certainly been crying.

'Look here, I'll make some tea, shall I?' Mary led the way into the kitchen, Theo following, twisting and swinging the front door key on its label and string.

'I say, Mary,' she said at last, 'you don't really believe in a principle of evil or anything like that, do you? I mean people are just people, aren't they?'

Mary switched off the toast. ' "Lest Satan should get an advantage of us",' she said, smiling a bit. ' "For we are not ignorant of his devices." What's happened to you?'

'Nothing really.' Theo was still at the key on its label and string.

Mary watched her, wondering. 'I'm afraid I'm pretty well bound to settle for hell sooner or later,' she said. 'Either that or some metal monster spattered with primitive rites. Only you need a hot climate for primitive rites. There's always Jehovah of course – cruel, capricious enough to sustain the fear and trembling. Still, I shouldn't have thought you needed anything like that.'

'What about the East?' Theo said, smiling a bit too by now.

'I, for one, would be terribly bored in the Bound Lotus position.'

And then the telephone rang. When Theo got back, she ran straight to the mirror. 'Oh God,' she said, 'just look at my face. Come on, Mary. Leave all that mess. We've been asked to a party.'

CHAPTER FIVE

'You haven't any tomato juice, have you?' Mary said. She was sitting on one of the windowseats, feeling slightly giddy and hoping, by staying where she was, not to attract attention. By now most of the guests had paired off for the evening, some dancing to the gramophone, others sitting out. Expert, enraptured, abandoned or just plain drunk, they all seemed to her to be getting on pretty well, the way people do at parties when you're sitting by yourself. Mary's prospective partner, on hearing in their first five minutes together that she neither knew nor cared to know anything about Latin American music, had excused himself early on. It would, in this case, have been no use at all even trying to explain why she so much disliked everything to do with Latin America. The prospective partner was now practising Andalusian stamps in one of the stone passages outside.

One whole side of the large, bow-fronted room had been turned into a cocktail bar, attended by two well-seasoned college servants, very spruce and knowing in their white jackets, and clearly determined to get everyone drunk as quickly as possible. Seeing that their services had not been required after 10 p.m. it was natural enough they should be doing their best to hurry things on, for Daniel Frost, the present occupant of these much-coveted apartments, was well known for his parties. Not too well known, though. As a client of Clio's – or, as he generally preferred to hear it put, as a promising medievalist all set for a fellowship, who knows a Chair – anyhow, as Daniel Frost, he had, on the grounds of chronic ill health, severe mental stress, scholarly gifts, great charm, youth and beauty, managed so far to keep not only these much-coveted apartments, but also, oh yes also the nods and winks, goodwill and respect of almost all the most influential members of his senior common room.

Just now he was reclining in a deep, not-too-shabby armchair, reciting Swinburne – 'Atalanta', beginning at the beginning. Frail and flushed, with long glossy hair (jet black) tumbling down his forehead, and a pair of eyes, which must have been wondered at from the cradle upwards (translucent royal blue), he looked the picture of tragic youth.

Theo, who had not left his side all evening, was now sitting on the floor with her head in his lap. Those gathered about made sporadic attempts to join in the choruses. But only one, a hairlessly fair pink sleek young man in belted jacket and velvet pants, appeared to know the words.

The tomato juice was anything but a success. Mary managed to find her way to a small, damp bedroom, where she lay in the dark, the bed a raft, herself surviving just as long as she kept her eyes open. Now and then heads would look in, mutter surprise or annoyance at finding themselves forestalled. One hand felt the bed. Nobody stayed, until Theo came in and kindly explained the best thing to do.

When Mary got back to the party, a lot of goodbyes were going on; for most of the guests were obliged to report back by twelve. Even those without porters or landladies waiting up for

them were coming round to such topics as transport, 9 a.m. lectures, what a wonderful evening and must see you soon. The
young man in the belted jacket was ushering them out. So was
Theo. With Daniel ensconced by the fire bucket at the head of
the stone stairs, leaning gracefully on a silver-knobbed hickory
stick, shaking, or very subtly *not* shaking, hands, very pleased
with his party.

'I think,' he said, back from all this in the armchair again,
with a large glass of liqueur brandy, 'we might have a little
music now. What do you say, Theo? A bit of the old Seventh
perhaps.'

'Just as you like,' she said.

The young man in the belted jacket had retired to a corner
couch with a big thin book entitled Hans Memling, *The Shrine
of St Ursula*.

'Right again, Daniel,' he said soon after Beethoven's seventh symphony (third movement continued) had begun. 'It
was Pope Cyriacus, erased from the list of pontifical sovereigns
for joining the pious cohort of virgins. Here imbued,' he giggled
a bit, 'with touching solemnity.'

Daniel smiled over his brandy. The music spun on. 'And
how's the beautiful Argentine?' he said. 'All better now?' He
studied her tenderly.

And Mary, once more not even trying to explain how very
little connection she really had with all things Latin American,
looked flustered, pale, but happy.

'Come on,' he said. 'You have this chair.' And he made as
if to get out of it, leaning hard on the arms, frowning a bit. 'Do
stop fussing, Theo, please. I'm quite all right.' He shook off
her helping hand, rose a bit further, then fell back, panting
and coughing. Nobody spoke. The record ran down but did
not switch off. Theo turned it over, got it going again, several

bars late, and went off towards the bedroom.

'Do take that filthy stuff away,' Daniel said, on seeing her back with bottle, spoon and measuring mug. 'The mere look of it's more than enough to give anyone palpitations.'

She banged the lot down on the sideboard, unsettling corks and ash, rinsed out a glass with the last of the soda water and went over to the filing cabinet, where the liqueur brandy was kept. The music churned on, abandoned, aggressive, on and on the relentless merry-go-round.

'Ah!' Daniel was crouching forward now, head between fists, heels tapping spasmodically. 'What energy! So many worlds, so much to do, so little done. Dear God!' His head was on his knees.

The ultimate tug and jerk, take it or leave it but you damn well better take it, gave way to a persistent, no longer patient tapping at the door.

'Oh, Raphael, do be a dear.' Daniel looked up, between his fists, to the young man in the belted jacket still studying Flemish art on the couch. 'You'd better tell them the orgy is over, though it's probably only poor old Finch with his war memoirs again.' Poor old Finch was an elderly ailing college don with somewhat less influence in college affairs than Daniel had once supposed.

Raphael groaned, stretched, groaned again, but before he could get his suede slippers on properly, the door was already open, introducing another young man, tall, bony, very bleak in his monkish spectacles, outgrown schoolboy pyjamas and dressing-gown.

'Look here,' the prim, fastidious lips were tight with rage. 'It is now ten minutes to one. If you don't want to sleep . . .' He stopped short, seeing there were women present, gathering in his dressing gown, much embarrassed.

'All right, old man. Very sorry.' Daniel grinned placatingly. 'Come on in. Have a drink.'

'No thank you.' The lips stayed tight, one hand still clutching the dressing gown, the other back on the doorknob.

'Well, good-night then. Sleep tight. We'll be closing down shortly.'

'I hope so.'

The door clicked to most precisely, slippered steps retreating up the stone stairs.

'Who on earth's that?' Raphael said.

'That, my dear friend, is Martin. A new arrival. Sleeps, as you see, upstairs and divides his waking hours between the chapel and the river walk.'

'Good Lord!'

'Come, come now. He'll be all right. A sweet boy, really. Just a little retarded by sixth-form scruples and the old home gone.'

Raphael, yes Raphael de Groot, shrugged his well-padded shoulders, pouting, sulking, as only he could pout and sulk, so he thought.

'And now,' Daniel said, 'I suppose I'd better see you girls out, or we'll be getting ourselves a bad name.' This seemed to amuse him. Most things amused him this time of night.

'What about all this?' Theo said, scooping a handful of matches and stubs into the nearest ashtray.

'Oh yes, oh yes,' Daniel sighed. 'Of course.' He started towards the sideboard. 'You don't mind waiting a bit, do you?' he said to Mary. 'Can't leave it all to the staff, you know. It wouldn't be fair on them, really.' He was up now, shaking dates, pickled onions and cocktail sticks out of a favourite vase, polishing it very carefully with a silk handkerchief. Raphael tidied the bookshelves. Theo and Mary did the rest.

'On such a night,' Daniel said later, seeing the girls out, with the clearing up all done by them, apart from the washing of certain glasses which he always attended to himself. He waved his stick at the moonlit wisps of cloud speeding high across the quadrangle. 'On such a night as this, I'd love to walk back with you, but . . .' He touched his chest apologetically.

They moved on over the lawn, passing one by one under the arches, through the spiked and studded door, a side entrance to which keys could be come by on certain scholarly pretexts.

'Now, you must have a taxi.' Daniel straightened up, breathing in deeply. 'This way, I think.' He started out up the pavement leaning hard on his stick.

'No, don't you come.' Theo held him back. 'You've done quite enough already for one night. I'll just run round to the call-box . . . And there's no need to hang about, no need at all,' she added quite sharply, as if much the same had happened before.

'That's very sweet of you, dear.' Daniel took her hand, kissing it as if this too had happened before. 'Here now, you take this,' he closed the same hand, under his, round the silver knob of the hickory stick. 'Just in case there's any bother. All the same, if you don't mind, I think I'd better wait here with Mary.' He turned to Mary. 'Still a bit shaky, aren't you?'

Mary moved her head doubtfully.

'Of course she is. What do you say, dear?' he appealed to Theo.

But Theo was off, pretending not to hear. As soon as she'd turned the corner, Daniel drew Mary back through the doorway into the unlit cloisters.

'We should have met long ago,' was all he said, tilting her head back against the crumbling stone. Such occasions flesh records with indelible precision.

'Soon, very soon,' he whispered roughly, as they went out again to the street light, meeting the taxi before it drew up. Mary nodded, getting straight in, while Daniel went round the other side to say good-night to Theo.

'What exactly is wrong with Daniel?' Mary said, quite casually, as they drove along.

'Well, he's said to have mitral stenosis.'

'Oh. Is that serious?'

'Now look here Mary, don't you start worrying about Daniel's health, do you hear?' Theo sounded pretty fed up. 'He's got plenty of nurses already. Damn him.' She started fussing about in her handbag, looking for her purse. 'Were you sick, by the way?'

'Not quite.'

'Enjoy yourself?'

'Off and on.' Mary wound down the window, facing the night breeze. 'It's been quite a long day one way and another,' she said dreamily.

CHAPTER SIX

Abigail Rubel's bed-sittingroom was an elegant little boutique, fashioned largely by her own slender artistic fingers out of the choicest remnants she could afford. Her father, by now the principal shareholder in a worldwide travel organisation, preferred to distribute his excess profits among those more demonstratively appreciative, or, as he often put it, more deserving than his own large family, who were regularly admonished to stand on their own feet, as their father had done before them.

Abigail's more serious attempts in this direction, fostered since the age of two by a wide variety of advanced educational methods centring on self-expression, were at present confined to her landlady's box-room, studio rather, since it had a leaky skylight and Abigail had introduced the customary black stove. Occasionally canvases, boards, muslin-wrapped clay figures appeared in the sittingroom on special demand, but in general these goings on in the box-room were accepted as a deep secret, an inner temple to which delicate allusions would not be unwelcome.

This morning these slender artistic fingers were hemming a

small pair of curtains to screen the contents of what had once been half a large bird's nesting box and would soon be a cosmetic cabinet.

'I like your hair like that,' Theo said, kneeling off her tapestry footstool to reach for another petit-four.

'Do you, dear?' Abigail glanced down fondly at the thick foxy plait now nestling in a ribbed fold of her bottle-green polo-neck sweater. 'I was up terribly early this morning,' she said, picking at a fleck of paint on her slim, trousered thigh. 'One or two little problems to work out.' Her tone suggested some highly exclusive dawn rite. 'By the way, were you ever in Greyfriars Abbey?'

'Well, I did look round with Mary once. Rather austere, isn't it?'

Abigail nodded gravely. 'The monks there lead a very simple life,' she said. 'I was thinking we might perhaps look in for Benediction this evening.'

Theo was not too enthusiastic. 'All that chanting can get a bit monotonous,' she said. 'Anyhow, I'm afraid I more or less promised to do a bit more rehearsing.'

'But I thought you'd given up all that.'

'Did you?' Theo looked a bit wary.

'What about that paper you had to prepare for the Medical History Society? Monks and Mandrakes, or something. I know it all sounded quite fascinating.'

'Oh that.' Theo was busy brushing crumbs off her shirt. 'I didn't *have* to prepare it, and anyhow, I don't suppose anyone would have turned up, seeing it's not on the syllabus. One gets these odd enthusiasms now and then. Silly, really. All for the sake of . . .' she looked up. Abigail was well away with scissors and books and expanding wire. 'You might ask Mary to go with you this evening,' she went on rather more loudly. 'Though I must say she doesn't seem to be quite so interested in the Church as she used to be. I gather the new man down at the chaplaincy spends most of his time on the rugger field, when he isn't repairing his motorbike. Hardly setting the best example for growing girls.'

'They've a big old bell at Greyfriars,' Abigail said. 'You just pull the rope and someone will come to you any hour of the day or night.'

'Dear me. You aren't thinking of being received, by any chance?'

Abigail shook her shapely, dreaming head. 'Just ripples, beautiful ripples of truth,' she said.

'I see.' Theo smiled at her, the way she often did. 'Did I tell you our dean came back from Tibet last term, equipped with two photographs of God the Father? You could see his beard quite clearly brushing the mountain tops.'

'How extraordinary.'

'She passed them round at the last meeting of the Theosophical Society. Bernard Whitworth was there taking notes for some article of his. Plato again, Plato and the Vortex of Visual Fallacies, I think it was this time. Probably all about helpings of marmalade, ending up with no spoon, no jar, no such thing as marmalade at all. You know how homely these philosophers like to be. You ask for a key to the front door and they set about making it quite clear how there's no front door, never was, and if you happen to find yourself locked in or out it's only because you haven't learnt to talk properly.'

'Really?' This time Abigail was not the least impressed. She was not going to have her sacred well polluted by any such frivolous talk. Philosophy, art, religion dwelt there, along with the latest developments in psychical research. 'And how is Bernard getting on these days?' she said.

'Oh fine. You know he's not nearly as conceited as we thought. It was mostly stage fright, if you ask me, all that patronising world-weary stuff. And I don't suppose anyone could produce a play without losing their temper at least once a night. He's given up those Apache scarves, than goodness. On to stiff collars and college ties now, the allegorical ones.' Theo paused, not sure how she felt about college ties, even the allegorical ones. 'Your scenery is very much missed,' she added, seeing this was true, in a way.

'Well, dear, you know how I feel about abstract art. And Bernard would insist on cones.'

'It's all black now.' Theo stretched out her arms to prove the all-blackness, the nothingness of it. 'Some sections just a bit dustier than others. By the way,' she got her arms back somehow, wishing they'd never gone out at all. 'if you'd like to do any illustrating next term – not the squiggly bridge and gas-pump sort, but something more in keeping say with the *Contes drolatiques* – Bernard is thinking of starting a new magazine. I'm to deal with the readers' queries, from a purely medical standpoint of course. It should be fun while it lasts.'

Abigail was not so sure, but pleased all the same to be asked. She went on adjusting small folds of striped silk. With its curtains up the cosmetic cabinet looked like a puppet theatre, all set for some minor Restoration comedy.

'And Daniel?' she said, with that gentle persistence that commonly passes for unerring instinct.

'Daniel?' Theo did not look up. 'I really don't know. I dare say he's surviving. Managed to wangle a nice long holiday for himself in Rome, looking up archives.' She almost laughed, nothing like outright. 'We had our farewell scene in the park, just behind the anatomy labs – he with one eye on the cricket nets, she reeking of formalin. Well, well.' Grasping her ankles, she started rocking slowly to and fro on the tapestry stool. 'There it is. If we are cut out for sacrifice, as they say, one does like to be the only victim on one's particular little pyre. Don't you agree?'

Abigail looked a bit puzzled. 'I must confess he always struck me as a most ordinary young man,' she said. 'Those ears for instance.'

'Yes. They did stick out rather, didn't they?' But further analysis on these soothing lines was forestalled by the rhythmical flutter of fingernails on the other side of the panelled door.

Abigail jumped up, slender artistic fingers at the thick foxy plait. A few sweeping strokes with the silver-backed hairbrush, a rapid meticulous replacement of fuchsia lipstick and she was over the threshold embracing someone in a tweed cape with the largest nose Theo had ever seen.

'Nillie darling.' One last hug and she ushered him in. 'This is Theodora.'

Prince Stanislas von und zu Oberall offered a topaz-crested hand and a martial trace of a bow from the hips. 'How do you do,' he said.

'So you didn't go after all.' Abigail started helping him off with the cape.

'No. Fortunately not. *La tante*' – this with slight Teutonic emphasis – 'finds herself a trifle indisposed this weekend. *Pas grave*,' he added with mild amusement, as if the idea of expecting anything other than querulous Sunday luncheons from this tenacious recluse, his last untapped source of highly problematical riches, was mere childish optimism. 'The RSPCA were back there last week.'

'Oh dear,' Abigail said, curling up at his feet. 'Not again.'

'Bedroom after bedroom made over to diarrhoetic cockatoos.' He shuddered a bit, and Abigail shuddered too.

At fifty-three, Prince Stanislas von und zu Oberall bore his threadbare elegance with wistful good humour. When exposed to the rough intractable world, he gave the impression not so much of a moulting eagle, chained to its perch in some fenland zoo, as of a borzoi, trapped in the dog-pound, gently repulsing the more importunate mongrels snuffling round the same cage. Over many long years of exile, spent largely in boarding-houses on and off the Gloucester Road, he had come to blood-brotherhood terms with a few fellow sufferers, who gathered most nights in some continental cafeteria on or off the Gloucester Road to discuss minor exploitations of the gullible, along with the latest monarchical alliances, the latest herbal cures, the price of fillet steak. When all these failed, there were always childhood reminiscences to fall back on.

'Ah,' he said, helping himself to the rest of the petit-fours. 'Delicious! What about a little *café*, my dear, *mit Zahne*. Yes? And you might take off those prostitute's pants.' He gave them a passing smack.

Theo withdrew soon after this, on the pretext of a luncheon engagement.

'There now, Nillie,' Abigail was back at his feet, stretching up to stroke what remained of his hair. 'What you want is a real *gemütliche Hausfrau*.' She pronounced this like a small child repeating a nursery rhyme.

'Well, not a hermaphrodite hoyden anyway. In fact, if it weren't for these . . .' He bent a bit closer, outlining her breasts appreciatively.

This same Sunday it looked very much as if Mary would not be going out. For some weeks now she had hardly been out at all, waiting for the telephone to ring. But twenty-four hours ago she had received a postcard from Daniel in Rome. This was the first time she had heard from him since that night soon after the party, when he had arranged to meet her for supper. She had sat for two hours in the appointed corner of the appointed cocktail lounge, tipping the waiters more and more heavily each time they came too close to ignore. He was terribly sorry, he'd got caught up. He hoped she'd eaten. She was sure, quite sure she hadn't minded waiting, not in the least, and yes she had eaten, thinking of the cocktail cherries. It being high summer and a fine night, they had gone for a walk by the river, singly at first down the towpath, then arm in arm through the meadows, above the plopping of water rats, the islands of swans asleep.

'No mortal sins,' she had whispered.

'No, no mortal sins.'

Since that night she had not heard from him till this post-card featuring four river gods arrived in a typewritten envelope from Rome. The message, written apparently in the Papal library, read as follows:

Working, alas. Not even the fountains play all the time. I fear you'll be caught up with the Celts before I can get back. The river here has little but history to recommend it.

Molte belle cose   D.

None of this, needless to say, was being included in this week's letter to South America.

Dearest Daddy and Mamma,

I hope the dogs are over their ringworm by now. I suppose the dye will take some time to wear off. Thank you for explaining about those state monopolies, Daddy. As

you say, most military men have severe limitations. Are
letters being censored, by the way? I shouldn't think
women getting the vote would make much difference one
way or the other, unless of course they were all intimately
acquainted with the federal police. As to these women's
higher education, I hope very much there will be room
enough for all, though I imagine that until things settle
down a bit not even the Córdoba could be regarded as a
very healthy spot. No bombs about here unfortunately.
But I don't think you quite realise, Daddy, what a long
queue there is for higher education, especially with so
many ex-service-women still trying to get back. They get
preference, naturally enough, and are mostly pretty good
at modern languages. Still, if you do want me to try for
that other set of scholarships, it might perhaps be wiser if
I stayed on here during the long vacation, rather than
going to Ireland. After all, if you'll forgive me, Mamma,
they're a very horsy lot, especially Aunt Iris. And after a
certain age riding isn't too good for one's inside – tightens
the wrong ligaments – at least so Theo says. Anyhow it
wouldn't be very easy to study there. It never is in someone else's house, especially with horse-boxes rattling all
round . . .

'Oh, hallo Theo. You're back early.'
'As it turned out I was a little *de trop*.' Theo helped herself
from the keg of cider. 'Not very nice, is it?'
'No.'
'Guess what. Abigail's gone and got herself a prince.'
'A real one?'
'Real enough, though I wasn't actually shown the hand-
tinted family tree.'

Before the bulletin could be concluded someone whistled out in the street, an imperative two-tone whistle suggesting a dog-owner more than anything else. At the third repeat Mary looked out of the window.

'Your bell must be broken,' Pete called up. And she went down to let him in.

Pete looked tired and even thinner. He'd been acting as junior house surgeon for the past three weeks in a vague attempt to placate his father, whose fourth advance in prostatic surgery was all too famous, and also less vaguely to placate the hospital authorities, who laid great stress on practical experience. Twenty-one days and nights of such experience had convinced him, more than ever, that if he was going to placate anyone from now on, it would have to be the Medical Research Council.

'There now,' he said, having fixed the bell and explained to Theo which Bs in the notes stood for Bacillus, and which did not. 'Who's coming to the Marx Bros?'

'I'd love to,' Mary said.

CHAPTER SEVEN

Rollo and Anderson were having coffee and mince pies in the Kardomah.

'Are you going anywhere for Christmas?' Anderson said.

'Isle of Man,' Rollo said.

'Oh. One can get there then, in the winter?'

'I'm afraid so. What about you?'

'Home too, I think. I quite like it there. Have to come up again though, for the wedding.'

'Wedding? Don't tell me . . .'

'Heavens no. I suppose the invitations will be along shortly. Peter Mason, only son of Sir Rupert Mason – here fully commended for unspecified advances in the war which knows no armistice – to Mary Gallen, only daughter and so on. This being a mixed marriage the Very Reverend Father d'Egbert St Bone, SJ cannot permit a choir. But I'm to write the wedding march.'

Rollo spluttered a bit over his coffee.

'No really, my dear fellow, I should know. I'm to be best man, after all.'

'But she's under age.'

'I did hear that the paternal blessing had been somewhat delayed. In fact if the old boy hadn't been up in the Andes recovering from a bad attack of *Peronismo*, I dare say things would have been a bit different. He's quite a character, apparently.'

'That,' said Rollo, smiling slightly, 'is what's known as a slight underestimation.'

'Anyhow I don't see what the Gallens should have to complain about. Poor old Pete, he's not even qualified yet. And it's not as if he'd ever want a soufflé, or a pair of pants pressed. I can't believe he's missing his mother either, doesn't even remember her, and he won't go near his sister, in case she'd insist on a change of clothes and a haircut. You know how he feels about smartening up. So there he is, surrounded by sex-starved nurses, and he has go to and get himself a wife. Wonderful, isn't it, what a kindly disposition will do for a man. Lord knows what they'll live on.'

'But Mary hasn't been cut off, has she?'

'Cut off? You mean no more pocket money from home? I expect, apart from the wedding feast, a few postal orders may be counted on. Christmas and birthdays, that sort of thing. Just about cover the instalments on the washing machine. My God!' Anderson hissed out more smoke through his teeth. 'Poor chap, if he only knew what he was letting himself in for.'

'There again, I don't think you quite realise . . .' Rollo paused mildly. It was not on the whole in his nature to enlighten others.

'I suppose the engagement was announced in *The Times*,' he said, as if this were the finishing touch.

'Oh dear yes. Mother-in-law saw to that. It was going on all the long vac, you know, this affair. Started with Mary bringing him bottles of milk for breakfast, leaving them on the window-ledge with little notes. That's the trouble with *nice* women, always giving you things you don't want. And the one thing you do want they make such a damn fuss about.'

'Do you think Mary did?'

'Well, maybe. I don't really know. Pete was rather cagey about all that. As far as I can see they spent the whole time mooning over the gramophone and going for country walks. Think of it, Rollo,' he shuddered, 'country walks, midges, mud, carting round pocket books on birds and wild flowers. Still,' he picked out a cigarette somewhat flatter than the others, sniffed at it doubtfully, 'I don't think Mary is quite the Dublin type – *noli me tangere* where it really works. As a matter of fact . . .'

'As a matter of fact what?'

'You won't let this go any further, will you?'

Rollo did his best to look reassuring.

'It was after the *Rosenkavalier*. Not bad really, for Covent Garden, though the horns could have done with a good rinse.'

'Yes?'

'Well, Mary had been holding my hand at the high spots. My hand, mind you.'

'I don't suppose you were keeping it in your pocket,' Rollo said a little sourly. 'How do you know she wasn't holding Pete's hand too?'

'All right, all right. Pete was busy following the score with a throat torch. Anyhow, afterwards, when we got on the train, the midnight special, you know the one, picks up milk churns all along the line. Well, we were all fixed up very early; empty compartment, coats, wallets still with us, but no drink. So Pete slipped off to the nearest hotel to try and get something on medical grounds. And while we were waiting, no lights yet, no corridor, Mary made it perfectly clear just who it was she wanted to spend the night with.'

'What do you mean made it perfectly clear?'

'Now, now, my dear Rollo.' Anderson patted his shoulder benevolently. 'Surely you don't want the details? I'm afraid I was not quite on form after all that over-the-counter champagne. And no Rennies. Slept most of the way back. And when I came to the next morning, there they both were, skipping about on the doorstep, all brimming over with the good news. Can you imagine how I felt?'

'Not really.' Rollo sounded a little more distant than usual.

'Of course I couldn't say anything with Mary there. What is there to say, come to that, but thank God it's not me. Not that I've anything against Mary, though I must say that sort of naive intensity depresses me rather. And as for marrying her . . . Naturally, I felt pretty sure the whole thing would blow over, but when I got back from the summer school – must tell you about that some time, quite a place Derbyshire – anywhere there they were as before, cooing away, all pussy-my-love and sweetie-pie. Pete had even stumped up with a ring, if you please.'

'It seems he's not the only one. Have you seen Abigail's ring?'

'What?' It was Anderson's turn to splutter this time. In fact he nearly choked, though this was quite accidental.

'She was in here displaying it last week,' Rollo went on, as the coughing wore off. 'Some bit of feudal rock, probably used for branding serfs, from the look of it. I suppose that's about all most northern princes can produce nowadays.'

'You don't mean to tell me she's seriously thinking of getting herself hitched up to old Oberall?'

'I gather so. At least she was doing her best to give that impression, in strict confidence of course.'

'But he's married already.' Anderson was mopping himself, breathing fairly steadily again. 'At least he *was* married, to a

Dutch swimming champion. She must be a bit on the flabby side these days, but I shouldn't have thought he could just dump her back on the dykes for that. He's not in his archduchy now, after all.'

'No,' said Rollo, fixed and fierce, very much the jury-man, 'he certainly is not. Just hasn't found the right moment, would you say, to get it all straightened out? Or perhaps he's still waiting on some special dispensation. Come to think of it, Abigail was pretty hazy about the nuptial arrangements. Any one church would be rather too narrow for them, and had I heard Chaliapin singing the Credo, yes all in Russian, massed choir, quite fascinating, but wasn't the whole thing just a tiny bit too theatrical. And why not be married like Romeo and Juliet. I must say I thought then there must be something tricky going on.'

'What about the son? Was he mentioned at all?'

'What son?'

'Oberall's, of course. He's not exactly the olive branch his father might have had in mind. In fact they're only on speaking terms when the funds run really low. You must have heard of him, surely? Goes by the name of Raphael, Raphael de Groot.'

Rollo looked as if he'd heard more than enough for one day. 'We can only presume he'll be introduced later,' he said.

CHAPTER EIGHT

I t was Sunday morning up on the hill. The bells, six miles away, were not audible. In this once fashionable retreat for senior members of the university, with long-legged brainy bicycling children, nothing was audible between the milk round and the midday bus. The resident population at present was largely confined to rich old ladies, wheeled out on fine days from their silent, spotless mansions by trained nurses, daughters-in-law or other potential poisoners accompanied by shrill packs of constipated corgis. On weekdays the scene was slightly enlivened by distant clippings and mowings, demonstrating the survival – in presumably good health – of the only gardener, who governed the district with shrewd inexorable obstinacy. Now and then a salesman or grocer's van would call.

Mary was writing to South America.

Dearest Daddy and Mamma,

Thank you for your letters. I'm sorry not to have written before, but I've just got back from the nursing home, not pregnant any more. It must have been all that rushing about getting the house ready. Some insides apparently need more resting than others. The nursing home wasn't too gay, but very efficient and Pete taught me how to play piquet, which helped a lot. Pete, by the way, has got himself a Nuffield Research Scholarship in biochemistry, which lasts for two years. The grant itself should nearly cover the running of the car, but it's quite an achievement all the same, just the start-off he needs at the moment. The car is going very well, Daddy, thank you. We shall of course keep it in the garage at night (yes, there is a padlock), see that the tyres are properly checked at least once a week, and complain to Dunlops if the new set wears out too quickly. I admit one could walk, or take the bus, but there are only two buses a day from here, and Pete is often kept late at the laboratories. This scholarship will provide a lot of advanced technical experience, which will be all to the good when applying later for jobs. There aren't any further qualifications he needs at the moment, Daddy. When you're doing research you just go on doing it till you discover something. Then you write a paper about it. There aren't any exams.

As far as my work is concerned, I shall have to wait now till the beginning of the next academic year. Meanwhile, when I'm feeling a bit stronger, I shall arrange to attend some of the lectures. Please don't think I'm wasting my time. There is always a great deal of reading to be done, and normally I study most of the day.

Thank you very much, Daddy, for helping with the rent. We were not exactly 'living like navvies', but it is nice to have a bit more space, and of course you're right about growing one's own vegetables. The way ginger is brought on in China I shall not forget. The gardener's wages, by the way, were included in last month's 'personal accounts'. It is not at all easy to get any servants to come here, let alone stay, but we may try to get someone from Ireland, as this house is really too large for me to manage on my own, especially the floors. I'm sorry we weren't able to do more house-hunting for the sort of property you had in mind. As it is, I should apparently have had my feet up every afternoon. I must repeat, it just doesn't seem possible to find a soundly built house without a little dry rot somewhere. The last one we got surveyed was not by any means the 'criminal proposition' you had in mind. Nor a 'derelict folly', for that matter. That corrugated iron was only on one of the outhouse roofs, and I'm afraid *all* the local building stone is somewhat porous. I hope you managed to get those granite steps finished all right. No granite here, as I said, no one who'd dream of handling it either. Forgive me if that surveyor's report upset you. He was not, I assure you, in league with anyone, and the owners' asking price was not by any means the product of a diseased mind. Anyhow we're all right here for a while. The lease can always be renewed. I was unfortunately obliged to sign that repair clause, but it doesn't look as if anything serious will need doing for a long time.

I'll do my best, Mamma, to get those slippers you mentioned for Rupert's birthday, either those or the special shoe-horn. We don't see very much of him, as there are so many surgical conferences he has to attend. Jake is quite over his distemper now, just a little short of breath when chasing cars.

As to the new Constitution, it sounds high-minded enough, hard to know how it will work out though; 'private property has a social function' is not so far removed after all from storming the Bastille. Still, I shouldn't think . . .

'Oh, hallo dear.' She looked up. 'Any mail?'

'Only this.' Pete, half in and out of the french windows, felt through his dungaree pockets, producing among other things a large grease-thumbed envelope. 'Looks like the bill for the furniture,' he said.

Mary opened it, easing out the long stiff card. 'It's Theo.' She looked pleased. 'She's getting married to Bernard after all. Reception at . . . Oh, we must go.'

'As you like,' Pete said.

'It's on a Saturday. We could miss out the church,' she smiled encouragingly. 'And we might go on somewhere afterwards. Rollo should be there. And Abigail . . .'

Pete nodded, no keener than before. 'Who is this Bernard anyway?'

'Bernard Whitworth. Don't you remember all that fuss about the magazine?'

Pete did not. 'There was a Bernard Whitworth in college, ages ago. Classics scholar. Came from the Midlands, I think.'

'What did he look like?'

'Oh, nothing in particular.' Pete frowned hard as he always did pursuing rare tracks of thought. 'Steel-rimmed spectacles . . . Or were they? Let me see, now. Didn't he carry his books about in a rucksack? Yes, that's it.' His brow cleared again. 'I tried to borrow the rucksack once for beer. Nothing doing though.'

'This Bernard is very elegant.'

'Can't be the same one, then,' he said, obviously relieved.

'Still . . .' She turned back to the invitation. 'His parents do seem to live in Nottingham. Look, here.' She held out the card, silver side up, but by this time Pete was busy laying out box spanners on the carpet. 'Car all right now?' she said.

'Well, I've got the decarbonising done. Just putting back the cylinder head now. It's a bit more cracked than I thought.' He mused a while. 'Needs welding, really.'

Mary was twisting the card about, clipping at it with her thumbs. 'I suppose Daddy was right,' she said grudgingly. 'We should have got it properly looked at first. Perhaps the green one would have been better.'

'Nonsense,' Pete said. 'It's done very well for its twelve years. You must always allow for maintenance, you know. Fair wear and tear.'

'You haven't forgotten, have you, that Anderson is arriving this evening? Six-fifteen.'

'Good Lord. Is he?' Pete rubbed an oily hand right through his hair. 'Oh well, he'll have to come up on the bus, that's all.'

'But darling, you know very well he'd never do that.' The card was now in four roughly equal sections.

'No, I suppose not.' One foot half-laced in a stained split tennis shoe started beating time slowly. 'There are such things as taxis, aren't there?'

'But I said we'd meet him at the station.' Mary's voice trembled a bit. The tennis shoe beat on.

'You've got five hours,' she said.

He started collecting up the spanners, very precise. 'Might try cold soldering, I suppose, though it never makes a satisfactory job.'

'What about lunch?'

'Oh, you could bring me out a couple of boiled eggs and a cup of milk some time, if you like.'

'Nothing else?'

'Perhaps a bit of bread and butter, if you have it.'

*

'Right-oh, dear, I'm coming.' Anderson could be very reassuring. Rapidly downing the last large gin and tonic he followed Mary out through the littered tables of the station refreshment room.

'Mind your coat,' she said, as they got into the car. 'Pete's been doing a few running repairs.'

'How nice this is.' Anderson sighed happily, patting her knee. They drove on. 'And how have you been getting along?'

'All right.'

'You're looking thinner.'

'Am I?' Mary smiled. 'It must be moving house.'

'How is the house? It sounds very grand.'

'Oh no, it's not grand, just large. A not too successful stock-broker's residence, acres of stained floor. It was all we could get really, apart from digs, and anyhow the family more or less approves, which is something.'

'And Pete?'

'He likes it well enough, plenty of room for tools.'

'He wasn't serious about the Gold Coast job, was he?'

'Serious enough. He'd live anywhere. I mean it's all the same to him, hot or cold, black or white, as long as *The Times* and the test tubes are there. Do you know,' she paused, changing a few gears, 'I'm not sure Pete needs a wife at all.'

'Now, now.' Anderson beamed benignly. 'Don't tell me you're having troubles already.'

'No, it's just that . . . well, take the books, for instance. Pete's books. They don't seem to have any connection.'

'You mean he's not quite the highbrow you bargained for?'

'Nothing but cars,' she said shortly. 'Cars, co-enzymes and cricket.'

'Dear me. I'm afraid, you'll find most masculine pursuits amount to something like that. I must say, mind you, I've always been a little in awe of Pete's mind. There's something almost fourth-dimensional about it at times. Have you noticed?'

'I'm mostly asleep by then,' she said, flashing headlights on and off.

'What about you? Signed on anywhere yet? Or are you a lady of leisure still?'

'Not really. Things got a bit interrupted, that's all. And somehow marriage seemed less of a risk.'

'Less of a what?'

'I mean a better excuse, if you like, for never going back to South America.'

'My dear girl,' Anderson chortled incredulously. 'Don't tell me it's all that backward there. You haven't cut loose altogether, have you, by any chance?' He looked at her, quite curious now, not chortling at all.

'Can't afford to at present.' Mary swerved, cursing a bit. 'Pete hasn't the least idea of what things cost.'

'Doesn't his father help?'

She shook her head. 'Prefers to think we're doing quite nicely thank you, for a young couple.'

'And so you are, dear, so you are. House and car already. Furs next. What more could you expect?'

They crossed the bridge in silence.

'How about you?' she said next. 'Any luck with the festival?'

'Gracious no.' Anderson waved an ample airy hand. 'I didn't even bother to enter this time. Far too busy with the impact of science on the Outer Hebrides. It means a lot of tartan tom-foolery, of course, but I must admit I'm rather pleased with the Leucocytes Lullaby. You see –' they just made the last set of traf-fic lights – 'there's a plane crash, as usual, to get in the coastline, fishermen's nets, candlelit spinning-wheels, natural way of life and so forth. And then outer space takes over.' He rubbed his hands happily. 'The switch always works better with a primitive

society. No moral problems to fuss about. Just sex and sea –
toiling and blind acceptance of fate. That's where the fun
starts. The whole thing is based on blood-cell mutations this
time.'

'I see,' she said. At the top of the hill she slowed down a bit.
'Rather nice, isn't it?' She half-glanced back at the town lit up
below them.

'You might stop for a moment,' he said, easing himself round.

Mary drew up by the ditch. 'It looks as if the floodlighting's
come to stay.' She went on looking, liking it.

Anderson laid his free arm over her shoulder.

'Do you see our bridge?' she said softly. 'The one with the
green lights?'

'I'd rather not,' he said.

'You should get those gears shifted,' he murmured some
minutes later.

'Come on now,' Mary smiled, stroking his hair. 'We'd better be
getting back,' she said. 'Pete will be wondering what's happened.'

'You know perfectly well he won't.'

'Come on,' she said once again. 'We really must go.'

Anderson straightened one knee tentatively. 'It is a bit
cramped here,' he admitted.

'Does anyone want more beer?' Mary said some hours later. 'If
not, I think I'll be going to bed now, if that's all right.'

Pete looked up from the chart of haemoglobin absorption
spectra, which he had been plotting for the last hour and a
half, ostensibly for Anderson's enlightenment.

'That's it, dear,' he said. 'You run along.'

'Sure you don't want anything?'

'No, no. I'm doing fine. What about you, Anderson?'

'Not for me, thanks.' Anderson laid aside *The Oxford Book of*

Mystical Verse, which he had been rendering, for Mary's hesitant amusement, into nightclub lyrics. 'Come to think of it, I must have had six double gins on that train.' He sounded a little overawed. 'I say, Pete, you will check over that murmur of mine again some time tomorrow?'

Pete raised one hand like a car-park attendant, plotting on with the other.

'Well, good-night then. You won't be long, will you dear?' Mary said to the back of Pete's head.

'Umm?' He turned slightly.

'Don't be too late, will you?'

'Oh no. Just finishing this. You go to sleep,' he said soothingly, back at his board and chalks. Whenever possible Pete spent most of the night in the armchair over this board, solving problems by various methods. Any problem would do, including those featured on the back of the box of a certain breakfast cereal. Most mornings Mary came down to find crumpled calculations all over the floor, and a few neat sheets of figures pinned to the board. Very few problems remained unsolved. Several letters had been written, but not posted, to the purveyors of the cereal, pointing out fundamental fallacies, which they would be well advised to avoid in future.

When Mary came out of the bathroom, there was a light in the spare bedroom.

'Are you all right?' she said at the half-open door.

'You haven't another towel, have you? Just a small one.'

On going in she found Anderson in a paisley silk dressing gown, laying out his toilet accessories. 'There you are.' She put the towel down on the bed. 'I'm sorry the room's rather bare but . . .' Anderson caught her arm.

'Aren't you even going to kiss me good-night?' he said, quite hurt.

'Good-night then.' She kissed him quickly.

'There now.' He drew her closer. 'You know you're just the right size for me.'

She stood passive for a moment, then made abruptly for the door. 'You might have done something about it before,' she said from there, very tense and tall.

'Sorry ducky.' His small eyes glistened with mock apology. 'You might have told me your father was a millionaire.'

CHAPTER NINE

Rollo helped himself to more fruit cup. Champagne did not agree with him. 'Isn't it amazing,' he said, 'the miles people will cover for a free drink or two.'

'I must say I hardly expected to see you here.' Anderson nestled back in his red leather chair. 'We're quite well placed, don't you think?'

They were sitting at a corner table in the hotel ballroom, as far from the wedding cake and as near the bar as they could be, without dressing up as staff. Well before the wedding speeches, Anderson had come to a firm understanding with one of the more experienced attendants about the quality and quantity of refreshment required in this particular corner.

'Don't let anyone ever flatter you into being their best man,' he said.

Rollo did not seem to think this likely.

'I spent the whole of Pete and Mary's reception dealing with car-hire firms. It was raining, of course, thunder and lightning, the lot. And then there was that row with Moss Bros over Pete's tails. Holy God!' Anderson shivered a bit. 'Never again. And what do you think of the groom?'

Rollo's eyes narrowed, the way they often did these days, as if he'd be very glad to see less and less of a lot of things, Bernard Whitworth being one of them. 'He should go far,' he said. 'I suppose Theo's the sort of girl who could, as the books say, have had any man she wanted?' He paused enquiringly.

'Has had till now, from what I hear. Look old man . . .' Anderson laid a plump hand, the signet ring one, on Rollo's knee. 'What you don't realise about women is . . .'

The groom, whose speech had drawn a well-judged blend of laughter, tears and short hurrahs from those nearest, dearest, most polite or most impressionable, was now conducting his bride around the choicest clusters of guests. These were composed largely of Sir Basil Folding's colleagues, would-be colleagues and wives, with a sprinkling of sons, stepsons, daughters even, just starting out in life. In fact the upper branches of the civil service were fully, if not over-fully represented, whereas the academic contingent, apart from one or two eminent figures, distinguished for services rendered from time to time to Her Majesty's government, notably during the war, was confined to those whom Lady Folding referred to as the children's friends. Abigail, in a muslin scalloped picture hat and a dress inspired by *Giselle*, along with Oberall in his only suit, could and indeed did – much to the major-domo's disappointment – claim to be the only royalty present. Such presence, so frequently announced, did not, needless to say, pass without comment from Lady Folding and other ancient denizens of *Debrett*.

'Hallo Theo,' Mary said warmly, as the bridal pair approached. 'Congratulations.'

'Thank you.' Theo in hand-sewn *décolleté* brocade looked becomingly flushed and dazed. 'I'm so glad you could come,' she said almost automatically. 'Have you had any cake?'

Mary grinned.

And Theo grinned back. 'Do you know,' she said, 'I've gone and torn the Brussels lace. Does it show?'

'Of course not.' Though it did a bit.

'Oh Bernard,' Theo drew him nearer, 'you haven't met Pete yet, have you? Pete Mason my permanent medical adviser.'

They shook hands.

'I think . . . Pete hesitated. 'Didn't you have rooms in the tower once?'

Bernard's eyes, the inscrutable sort, walled off by stout lenses and even stouter rims and rods of tortoiseshell, remained focused on a point just above Pete's right shoulder.

'You must excuse us,' he said moments later, with the hint of a bow. 'I didn't think anyone could have quite lost touch with so many relations as my wife,' he paused here tenderly, 'seems to have done. And now I'm afraid they're all simply dying to be resurrected.' He smiled his best curtain-call smile.

'See you later,' Theo said, being led gently off.

'I don't know,' Pete rubbed his chin, as chins are rubbed on such occasions. 'If it weren't for the voice and those glasses, I could have sworn . . .' He looked round, wondering still, but by this time Bernard was fully concealed by a feathered toque and a bulging floral silk dress. 'Oh, well,' he shrugged it off, 'I wonder what's happened to Anderson?'

'Not too far from the bar, if you ask me,' Mary said.

Pete went off to see.

And Mary made her way to the windows, hoping there might be fewer half-eaten trifles there, and even possibly one or two ashtrays. She had only just found a bit of pillar jutting out enough at one point to take a glass, when somebody touched her arm. The glass fell on the carpet, and, turning sharply, she trod on it.

'Dear oh dear,' Daniel said. 'Never mind. I dare say the management can well afford it.' He kicked what he could under the velvet curtains. 'There we are. And now, can I get you another?'

Mary, too confused to reply, went on looking at the carpet, rubbing the drink in with her shoe. Since that postcard and the long, letterless vacation that followed, she had gradually stopped expecting Daniel to turn up, though even now she hadn't quite lost the trick of spotting him in the distance, faltering, veering off, cursing herself for being such a fool.

'Ah, here he is.' Daniel beckoned up more champagne. 'To the happy pair?' The two brims clinked awkwardly.

'Theo's looking very nice, isn't she?' Mary said, taking a quick swallow.

'She's not the only one.' He smiled at her, the same old smile.

Mary drank a bit more. 'And what's been happening to you?' she said.

'Oh, much the same.' He brushed a hand across his chest. 'Still alive, as you see. That thesis was rather a grind.'

'I suppose,' Mary was beginning to come to, 'you had to do the best part of it in Rome?'

'Most of it, yes.' His eyes shone on, teasing, unabashed.

'I – er got married, you know.'

'Yes.' He frowned a bit. 'I did hear. I hope you're happy.'

'Why not?'

'Why not indeed.' He glanced at her gravely.

She did not glance back.

'I have your wedding present, by the way,' he went on, smooth again. 'It's a little too fragile to post. You must look in some time, both of you, to collect it.'

'Where are you now?' she said.

'Oh, back in the seats familiar,' he chuckled. 'Halls where we have supp'd of old. And among the grass shall find,' he murmured on, not quite to himself, 'the golden dice wherewith we play'd of yore.'

Mary continued fairly calm. 'But surely,' she said, 'the college can't house you indefinitely?'

'It looks very much as if they'll have to,' he said, almost smug.

'You mean . . .'

But Daniel was looking round the room now, peering across the hats, the flat formations of smoke. 'It's not four yet, is it?' he said, turning back to his glass.

'Half-past, actually.'

'Are you sure?' He seemed quite put out. 'I'm due to lecture in Greenwich at five. Never do it.' He looked ill all of a sudden, very ill.

'The tube's quite near,' Mary said, wishing she could drive him to Greenwich, or even better cancel the whole thing.

'Tube?' He raised a wan smile. 'Out of the question, I'm afraid, with a pack of lantern slides.'

'Well,' she said gently, 'you'd better slip off before they start getting out the confetti. Perhaps you'll come and see us some time. We're in the book under Flew, Tobias Flew.'

'Of course I shall.' He squeezed her hand, as though it belonged to him.

'Happy darling?' Theo said, half an hour later in the back of the hired limousine, her hand resting a little drunkenly on Bernard's shoulder.

'It went off pretty well on the whole,' he admitted. 'Apart from that fool of a cousin. You'd think at least the commissionaires could have stopped him. Just a minute.' Dislodging her with a brisk pat, he leant forward and tapped sharply on the glass partition.

The driver drove on.

Bernard tapped gain, pushed with his palms, tapped, pushed, rattled and thumped.

'Not Air France,' he called out, still scrabbling at the glass. The driver touched his cap without reducing speed.

'No, *Not* Air France!' Bernard shouted.

The partition suddenly slid away.

'Aer Lingus,' he spluttered into the stiff, scarred neck.

'Aer Lingus, sir?' The voice expressed not so much astonishment as quiet disdain.

'As if,' Bernard reseated himself irritably, 'the Mediterranean were the only sea.'

CHAPTER TEN

Mary was up on the hill, in the kitchen, which had always been green, dark green capped by yearly layers of flaking white. It was now a uniformly mistaken light blue, her first and last attempt to come to any long-term plans with the house. She was at this moment making coffee for herself and Paracleta Noonan, the fifty-year-old maid from Ireland. Paracleta was disconcertingly short and fat, a congenital achondroplastic, Pete had once suggested, though on the whole he favoured hormonal imbalance superimposed on severe childhood rickets. In domestic service from the age of twelve, Paracleta had been living for the past five years in the slums of Belfast, looking after her dead sister's children and their father, a chronic tubercular drunk, never quite off the dole. These children, Brendan aged nine and Kathleen aged seven, were, as she often said, her cross, a much scrubbed, kissed and decorated cross, contemplated from all angles through her waking hours. It was entirely to provide them with a better chance in life – air, that is, not saturated with the products of the gas works, longer sums for Brendan, more intricate folk-dancing steps for Kathleen – that she had replied to Mary's advertisement in the *Northern Whig*. The family had now been installed for six weeks. Two bedrooms, a sitting room and a playroom had been prepared for them, but they lived in the kitchen and slept all three in one bed.

Brendan, narrow-faced with furtive blue eyes, was, as Paracleta said, small for his age and very highly strung. He was also mentally retarded. Kathleen, even smaller for her age, was a pert spindly doll with fine orange hair, shampooed and set nightly by Paracleta, and a squint which the county Eye Hospital had undertaken to deal with in due course, as had the Eye Hospital in Belfast. Both children were, after much persuasion, attending the local village school, arriving with Paracleta after morning prayers and being absent altogether on liturgical or national feast-days. For this was an Anglican school. All the same, Brendan could almost read now, though, as Paracleta was quick to point out, the sums were shorter altogether, and, even if Kathleen could print her name, one embroidery afternoon a week hardly made up for there being no dancing classes. There again she had to admit that neither the Marist Brothers College nor the Convent of the Sacred Heart were what you might call handy. Nor were they free. In fact the everyday advantages of her religion were not what they had been. Little Flower raffles and rallies, Legion of Mary excursions, slight reductions in second-grade currants, not to mention the flags, the processions down enemy streets – all these were sadly lacking. Indeed, as she was just beginning to realise, there was nothing to dress the children up for. The nearest Catholic church, a chaste little monument, erected in classical style by a few prosperous Newmanites in the fastidious heyday of the district, was hardly congenial. In fact, one way and another, trips to town were becoming an almost daily necessity. Familiar altars and oleographs were springing up all round the house and the children had recently been enrolled in

Catholic packs of Cubs and Brownies many miles off.

This being Saturday morning, Mary was wondering just what plans had been made for the weekend.

'Such children, God bless us,' Paracleta said from the yard.

It occurred to Mary that Brendan might once again have mistaken the waste-paper basket for the chamber pot.

'Are you all right for lunch?' she called, as the coffee boiled up.

Paracleta appeared with a pile of children's clothes off the line, clothes all too obviously designed not to wash well. 'How the time flies,' she said, dumping them down on the draining board. 'Ah yes,' she took a look in the larder, 'those sausages will have to do us. I'm not saying they aren't pork sausages, mind you, but I'd be surprised, all the same, if there was a speck of pork between them. Little Kathleen wouldn't touch hers yesterday. Would you believe it, a child of that age knowing the difference. Poor little mite.' She plugged in the iron.

The children did not eat meat, fish, fruit and vegetables. They did not drink milk. Since the arrival of a jar containing a 'buttermilk plant' from cousins in County Tyrone, there had been less trouble about the bread.

'We may be having one or two guests for dinner tomorrow,' Mary said, getting out the sugar and spoons.

'Dinner, is it?' Paracleta wiped her hands on her frayed, splitting overall. Such an overall could only be obtained from a certain Belfast drapery store. Any more readily available replacements had been politely refused. 'I promised the children we'd be at the swings tomorrow,' she said quite flat.

'But this won't be till the evening.' It wasn't the dinner or even the floors so much as Paracleta's plans that worried Mary. 'Which swings?' she said.

'Don't you know the swings?' Paracleta privately considered

that both her employers were heading straight for the mad-
house. Pete she allowed for, as a professor, but Mary's
round-about advances and rapid retreats she pitied and despised.
Armed from the start with the habitual 'what would madam
like me to do next?' and 'thank *you* sir' for the last-minute
ironing of an evening shirt, she had, and who could blame her,
very soon taken the upper hand. 'Round behind the station,
where else,' she said.

Mary nodded, seeing she would have to drive them there.

'Bran-dinn!' The voice rose to a plaintive squeal.

The kitchen door crashed open on Kathleen, white with
rage, followed by Brendan, whose tearstains were all the clearer
for having, as it turned out, hitched a lift on the back of a coal
lorry.

'He laft me, Mammy. He laft me,' Kathleen sobbed away in
Paracleta's arms. 'And he's aten ma ribbin.'

'I did not,' Brendan said sullenly.

This was the first time they had walked back alone from
school.

Grabbing one mug of coffee, a banana and a half-empty
bottle of wine, Mary hurried off back to the sitting room.

A couple of hours later the children, along with three play-
mates recruited by Paracleta at the village post office, were
riding the bamboos on the front lawn. At first Mary had suggested that they play anywhere but on the front lawn, but
Paracleta's handclappings and shrill repetitions of their names
all round the house had proved even more disturbing. And
Pete had said nonsense, let them play where they want to. For
Pete liked the children. He liked almost everyone who made no
attempt to alter his appearance, or interrupt the intricate vigils
he now kept every night.

Mary still tried to work during the day. Screened from the

lawn by a sofa piled high with standard works of reference, she was sitting as usual on the floor, making notes, punctuated by the now unforgettable cries of street games still extant in the neighbourhood of the Belfast gas works, especially those associated with swinging round lamp-posts on a rope. Only here they used the telephone pole. A hysterical outburst from the collie dog at this stage hardly bothered her. This dog, suffering no doubt from lack of self-discipline and regular employment, was obliged to make its own excitement. At such times it had in the long run proved wisest to act as if it lived somewhere else. But a spurt of metallic rapping on the french windows was going a little too far. Mary's head appeared slowly above the sofa.

Daniel lowered his stick, smiling nervously.

'It's all right, just a game,' she said, opening up with a grunt or two at the dog, now lying on its back, paws supplicating but unrepentant.

'I see. It's as well to know these things in advance.' Daniel gave the dog a tentative pat, which passed without acknowledgement. 'I think he quite likes me. Don't you?'

'Of course. He only really goes for people in hats. Don't let him in, though, will you.'

'No.' Daniel shut the window firmly. 'I wasn't thinking of doing so.'

Mary took the cushion off the floor, cleared a space for Daniel, and perched herself on the far arm of the sofa.

'I hope you don't mind my dropping in like this, the back way too.' Daniel sat down, books between them. 'I was just having lunch with Fred Finch. Do you know him?'

'No, I don't think so.'

'Lives a mile or so up the lane, at least his wife does, when she's here. A buxom Slav,' he grinned, 'with a way all her own.

As a matter of fact she spends most of her time up and down the beaches of the Mediterranean. Slavs are, I'm told, very fond of the seaside. Anyhow she's just back for the winter now. I dare say you'll meet her some time. Poor old Finch.'

'Why poor old Finch?'

'Oh nothing.' He smiled discreetly. 'His wife's a highly temperamental woman, that's all.'

The street games seemed, from the sound of it, to be taking an ugly turn.

'Surely none of those belong to you, do they?' he said, shrinking a bit.

Mary outlined the more appealing aspects of the situation. 'Usually,' she explained, 'Pete takes them to the cinema on Saturdays, or the baths. They won't go near the river, but they like the baths. Then there's Woolies, the main branch, but that gets a bit expensive. I'm sorry about the games, but Pete's out on an all-day job at the labs, and I'd been trying to work.'

'I hope I didn't disturb you,' he said politely.

'Oh no, not at all. I was . . . er, wondering when we'd see you.'

'I've been a bit caught up in college politics,' he said, 'but it's all settled now, all settled. Ha!' He suddenly clapped his thigh, like a punter who's pulled it off at last.

'So they're going to keep you on?'

'Well, it's only a lectureship at the moment, but I think we might say that the ultimate object is well within reach.' He looked very pleased.

And Mary looked pleased too. 'Would you like a drink to celebrate?' she said. 'Or tea, perhaps?'

Daniel never touched tea. He was, however, prepared to try a little Spanish brandy to get down the goulash he'd had up the lane.

Over the second glass a silence, more wary than sympathetic, came over them. The children were all presumably at high tea in the kitchen. Anyhow they had left the lawn.

'Would you like to go for a walk?' Mary said at last. 'We could miss out the view, and Percival's Plinth and the Mafeking Pinnacle.' The district, though little prone to pilgrims nowadays, on account of the steep hill, the two buses a day and the absence of any public house, was well stocked with poets' hummocks, philosophers' fishponds, economists' arboreta and other overgrown memorials to private enterprise, few worth recording and none in the least scandalous.

'There's a way through the woods,' she added. 'They're at their best now.'

Daniel agreed that this was just the time of year for walking through woods.

They set out under a high winged sky, with a catch of bonfire smoke in the air. And coming to the crossroads they turned off, shuffling and crackling into the woods. Mary led the way, slowly at first, holding back the brambles with Daniel's stick. Now and then they paused over a fungus, a beech-husk, an imaginary squirrel. But as the wood deepened and the path grew doubtful, Mary went faster, head down, tripping and stumbling, suckers and roots springing back behind her. And always Daniel behind her too, his harsh jerky breath in her ears. Breaking through to an old clearing she stood quite still. Then, planting the stick like a flag, she turned to face him, laughing, a laugh she hardly knew. Daniel, white-lipped and bleeding a bit from one temple, caught her wrists roughly. And the stick slipped back.

Lying there, looking up through the infinite criss-cross of dying leaves, she became increasingly aware of the tree stump digging into her spine. And then the dog arrived panting and dribbling into their faces, like a guardian angel back on duty, a little late but back all the same. They stood up, brushing themselves. Daniel took most of the leaves out of Mary's hair. And they walked back through a thinner wood, hand in hand till they reached the road, then side by side, with the dog trotting busily behind them.

They used the front door this time and Daniel went straight upstairs with a clothes brush. Oddly enough the children were not in the bathroom. When he came down, Pete had just got back and Mary introduced them.

'I thought I was going to miss you altogether,' Daniel said. 'Perhaps you'll have dinner with me in college some night soon.'

'I'd like to very much,' Pete said. 'Won't you have a drink?'

'Thank you. Just a quick one though. I have to be getting back.'

'By the way,' Pete turned to Mary. 'Rollo can come. I saw him this morning. I don't suppose,' he was back at Daniel, 'you'd be free to eat with us tomorrow night?'

'I'd love to,' Daniel said, very simple and sweet.

'You don't know any nice young girls, do you?' Mary said.

'One or two,' he smiled, catching her eye.

'It's just that our other guest,' here Pete winked heavily at Mary, 'is a little bashful.'

Daniel promised to see what he could do. And, after another round of Spanish brandy, he asked for the time.

'Good Lord, is it really?' he said. 'Would you mind if I rang for a taxi?'

'Nonsense,' Mary said. 'I'll drive you in . . . or Pete will, won't you, dear?'

'I'm sorry,' Pete said. 'Any other time, but I'm afraid the dip-switch isn't working at the moment.'

'Couldn't you fix it?' she said quickly.

'Well,' Pete stiffened a bit, 'if I could find the insulating tape . . .'

'Please don't bother. I'm sure I can get a taxi.' Daniel moved towards the door.

'The bus has just gone up the road,' Pete said. 'It turns there, should be back in five minutes.'

Daniel took the bus.

And when Mary got back to the kitchen, to see about supper, she found Paracleta solemnly seated over her missal.

'Children in bed already?' she said brightly.

'Indeed they are.' The plump pink face was all worked up, puckered and bulging with woe. 'And there they'll stay, the little monkeys. Did you ever hear the like?'

From the sibylline flood which followed Mary gathered that the children had been led off by the other children to look for conkers in the woods. And that Paracleta had had some difficulty in finding them.

'That fella Tim's been writing again,' Paracleta concluded, referring to the children's father. 'Says he's thinking of getting work in England.'

'But he's not fit to work, is he?'

'Not on the roads, he isn't. Might manage a spot of gardening though,' she suggested.

'No one,' Mary said firmly, 'can afford a full-time gardener these days.'

Paracleta was back again at the afternoon.

'You never saw them at all, in the woods?'

'No.' Mary started looking for eggs. 'I can't say I did.'

CHAPTER ELEVEN

Rollo, never employed on enterprises to which he might debit his travelling expenses, had arrived on the six o'clock bus. Since then he had been explaining to Mary in the sitting room the consequences of having been obliged to eat savoury rice for lunch. Pete was still out testing the dip-switch mechanism against the garage doors.

'Savoury,' Rollo choked sourly. 'Exciting article of food.'

'You don't know Daniel Frost, do you?' Mary said quite casually.

'I believe I've heard of him.' Rollo sounded as if the news were none too good, though if it had been he would have sounded much the same.

'Well, he's coming to supper tonight. And just in case you don't get on –' Rollo rarely got on – 'he's bringing a girlfriend for you.'

'Oh, he is, is he?' Rollo frowned suspiciously. 'What age?' he said, as if the whole matter were of the utmost indifference to him.

'Last term at school?' Mary suggested temptingly.

'Not that I mind if he brings a web-eyed widow along. Only some impossibilities are a bit more intriguing than others.'

'I see.' Mary laughed, finding it handiest on the whole to dismiss the range of Rollo's manias as mist mostly, fastidious coils of mist, with the odd desperate peak or two of fun.

Daniel, wearing a scarlet rosebud in his buttonhole, arrived in the hired car shared between those members of his senior common room whose public appearances were most in demand. With him was one of his latest batch of history pupils, a tall, proud-looking girl with a slight cast in one eye. She was called Arabella.

The dinner passed off well enough. Mary carved and poured the wine, Pete assisting intermittently on request. Paracleta, back from the swings, had taken the children to Benediction, more as a matter of principle this time than policy, for Paracleta liked waiting at table when people came. Mary did not like her doing so. Years of four-course family meals, not speaking, eating up everything, keeping her elbows in, had long since removed dining rooms, especially her own, from the list of places where entertainment might reasonably be expected. And if she hankered after fork suppers, pub sandwiches, chips in the park, it was largely under the impression that the informal approach was more revealing, more sympathetic. Being, as she was, too demanding as yet to appreciate the finesse of the formal mask.

Daniel, well stocked with recent academic intrigues, took large helpings of whatever came near him, mashing and slicing it all as he talked, forking it up in between times surprisingly fast. Rollo dealt hesitantly with a little of everything unlikely to cause further fermentation, making occasional highly reticent advances to Arabella, who ate nothing.

As Mary removed the cheese, leaving the brandy bottle at Pete's elbow, she caught Daniel's eye, which is after all what such occasions are for. The economics of castle building continued as before, according to Daniel, for the benefit of Pete, while Arabella, having just disclaimed all knowledge of Beatrix Potter, went on studying her fingernails.

'Shall we . . .?' Mary rattled the door handle invitingly.

Arabella did not look up.

Mary coughed. 'Arabella,' she said, 'perhaps . . . if you're ready . . . There's coffee next door.'

Arabella got out somehow, blushing hard.

'I'm sorry,' Mary said, closing the door after them, seeing that she and Arabella might just as well have stayed where they were; only sooner or later moves had to be made. 'Would you like to go upstairs?'

Arabella shook her head.

When Mary got back to the sitting room with the coffee, the guest was up by the bookshelves, like a bird flown in, resting there, before the next wild scrabble at the window glass.

'Milk? Sugar?'

Arabella did not look round.

'Crème de menthe?'

'I hate parties,' Arabella said.

'Oh dear.' Mary put the glass penguin containing crème de menthe back behind the eight-day keyless clock. She'd been trying to get rid of both penguin and clock for a long time. 'Ritual can be reassuring,' she suggested, pouring out two cups of coffee.

'I'm sorry.' Arabella rubbed a knuckle sharply across each eye. 'It's those exams.' She took her cup. 'I'll never pass them.'

Mary clattered spoons crossly.

'Do you have to pass them?' she said.

'I suppose not, really.' Arabella gave a wry little laugh, the sort of laugh Mary had used often enough. 'Nobody cares what I do, except Daniel of course.'

'Daniel?'

'Yes. He's a wonderful tutor.' She was almost happy again. 'And so understanding about people too.' She paused. They both tried the coffee. 'As any good historian must be nowadays,' she went on demurely. 'Don't you agree?'

'I don't really know. Of course,' Mary looked at her sharply, 'there's nothing like being understood.'

A last spurt of merriment from the dining room gave way to a lot of scraping, presumably of chairs on floor, the walls of the house being the sort designed to conduct sound rather than heat.

'May we come in?' Rollo said, peering round the door. 'I presume we're not interrupting any true life stories,' he added hopefully.

Pete was just behind with the brandy.

'As it happens we were just exchanging recipes for fruit jelly,' Mary said, with a cheerful wink at Arabella. And she went out then to get more coffee. On her way back, she stopped in the hallway, seeing Daniel coming down the stairs.

'Hallo,' he said softly, catching her arm.

'Hallo,' she kissed his cheek. 'Mind, you'll upset the tray in a minute,' she laughed. 'You know your pupil thinks you're wonderful.' She turned towards the sitting room.

'Not quite my type,' he murmured, grave and masterful, holding the door back for her.

Pete and Rollo were talking about Anderson. Daniel, who knew nothing about Anderson, joined Arabella at the bookshelves.

'You might have a look at this,' he said, handing her the *Collected Works of Tennyson* open some way through 'The Princess'. 'A great poet,' he said. 'A very great poet.' Leaving the book in her hands, he sat down next to Rollo, with whom it was becoming increasingly clear he had less and less in common. Their backgrounds were, as it happened, what is called not dissimilar, only Rollo was not at all interested in his background, whereas Daniel, more conscious, less certain maybe of how far he had come from his own small industrial town, felt obliged to make every step gold. The saga of his growing years conveyed to the impressionable not only the relentless struggle of a rare spirit against sickness, poverty and ignorance, but also delight, unfailing delight in places and people, all too easily dismissed by the undiscerning as drab or just plain dull. That bridge, for instance, he used to cross on his way to school was not just a metal bridge, once used for coal trucks, but a miniature architectural triumph, quite enchanting on a misty day. With people his touch was even more remarkable. He had by now quite a collection of people, lesser vessels mostly whose chips and cracks he knew and loved, kept, as it were together by occasional coats of his own special brand of glue. For Daniel was passionately interested in people. He drew them out, on the not unnatural assumption that most people are only too anxious to be drawn out. Not Rollo, though. Feeling at this stage possibly that any reaction would do, Daniel (his chair slightly higher than Rollo's) tried a new approach.

'Do you know Greece?' he said.

'I'm afraid not. Come to think of it,' Rollo examined him blandly, 'I suppose that in certain circles Athens might well be regarded as the Mecca of the modern world.'

Daniel's eyes flickered a bit. 'I can't say that had occurred to me.' He turned to Mary. 'I'd give anything to get to Rhodes one day,' he said, all gold again.

'Rhodes? That's the one with the butterflies, isn't it?' She smiled at him, filling his glass and Rollo's, sitting then on the floor beside Rollo, whispering, 'How's the indigestion?'

And Pete wanted to know whether Daniel spoke Greek.

'Alas no, not modern Greek.'

'I presume all the islands provide much the same amenities for the determined traveller,' Rollo suggested, clearly not trying to get over anything.

'As a mere medievalist,' Daniel smiled modestly, 'I should say Rhodes is unique.' And he went on to explain, principally to Pete, the absorbing interest of the island to one concerned with the heyday of the Knights of Malta, the founding and functioning of the Hospitals of St John. Arabella left the bookshelves, to listen in. And Mary put on her only jazz record, quite quietly for Rollo.

One record could not unfortunately lead quite quietly to another, the choice of records being largely confined to the more tortured compositions of the nineteenth century. So the Knights of Malta gave way to the gramophone, and Rollo, taking advantage of the self-conscious silences such entertainment tends to impose, read the *News of the World*. Pete seemed to be sleeping, though at the more martial moments he would conduct vigorously, like Anderson only more so. Daniel just sat, tapping a bit, and Arabella sat too, not tapping. Mary smoked, filled glasses, sat and got up and smoked, changed the record, filled glasses again, not liking any of it any more. As a final touch she tried the 'Gute Nacht' from the *Winterreise*, not liking that either, deciding then and there that music was not to be used as a kind of emotional shorthand.

As it turned out, Pete's eyes being more bloodshot than ever, because of his intricate vigils and all the smoke, Mary drove the guests home.

On the way in, Daniel, at the back with Arabella, talked about poetry, as he mostly did this time of night especially after a party. He began with the relative merits of Wordsworth and Shelley. He preferred Shelley, backing this up with a sizeable passage of Elizabethan-type dramatic verse, which no one made any attempt to identify. As they sped on down the hill, he conjured up that wild west wind, a deep autumnal tone, sweet though in sadness. For Daniel could produce quotations to suit almost any occasion. His favourite sources were Shakespeare, Tennyson, Arnold, Keats, and Shelley of course, Housman and Gilbert and Sullivan. There were always a few more lines than you might expect, and his repertoire was wide enough to allow for a good many evenings spent in the same company. Living poets were not included in the canon, possibly because most of his colleagues made no attempt to cultivate this particular branch of the game, skilled though they were in seasoning their most casual encounters with wise melodious sayings.

Arabella's college annexe was just locking up. As the car slowed down, various couples, not quite prepared to part for the night, stirred in their shallow shop doorways and padlocked alleys, startled by the undipped headlights. Mary switched everything off.

'Is Arabella what you'd call a promising student?' she said to Daniel, as they moved on again, making for his college, Rollo's bed-sittingroom being not by any means on the way.

Daniel shook his head sadly. 'Far too unstable, I'm afraid. You see, she's an only child and the parents are divorced. Poor Arabella.' He might well have been referring to a deformed pekinese, which he had just trodden on, not entirely by accident. 'I'm very fond of her,' he added.

At the college gates, the front entrance this time, Mary got out to see to one of the sidelights. And Daniel invited Rollo to dine with him some night soon, this being so to speak his trump card. He then joined Mary, joggling away at the offside wing.

'All right now?' he said gently, placing a hand over hers.

'Of course,' she laughed, straightening up with a fumbled squeeze at his nearest finger.

'May I ring you?'

She nodded. 'Mornings are best,' she murmured, regretting it straight off.

'In the morning, then.' He turned quickly into the lodge.

'I'm not at all sure that parties bring out the best in people,' Mary said, driving off again with Rollo beside her.

He felt under the dashboard, still trying to find out where the draught was coming from.

'I'm sorry you didn't fall for Arabella,' she went on. 'Though it looks as if she's rather wrapped up in Daniel at the moment.'

Rollo snorted a bit. 'That young man, my dear,' he said, 'would be perfectly happy if he never saw another woman for the rest of his life.'

She did not enlighten him.

CHAPTER TWELVE

Abigail's flat in London was a larger version of her former accommodation. Apart from a rickety antique desk bearing two scrolled silver inkpots, a crested leather blotter and a copy of the *Almanach de Gotha*, there was little indication, in the sitting room at any rate, that she no longer lived alone. The boutique was a good deal more elegant though, almost a Petit Trianon, any hint of frivolity in the Florentine mirrors or pot-pourri pots being well offset by a large icon featuring a very gaunt Madonna and Child and an equally large portrait of Abigail in red chalk, presented to her by the artist – an elderly Spanish optician – at the close of a Bond Street exhibition entitled 'Beauty in the Bone'. A few of Abigail's own compositions, inner skyscapes with misty crags and spiral steps, and planets, always planets, had also been framed and hung, along with a set of hand-tinted photographs featuring flaxen-haired lace-collared boy princes posed two by two in miniature horse carriages, enshrined in worn plush and ormolu. The bookshelves, designed to display china, were kept fairly steady by a dark set of metaphysical treatises in German, old type. Above were lighter books on diet, Mexican sun gods, travel and self-analysis, though, as Abigail was just explaining to

Theo, neither of the Oberalls had time for much light reading
these days. In fact, what with no domestic help and Nillie's
secretary arriving at nine every morning, there had hardly been
a moment to spare, not even for their very dearest friends. This
morning the secretary had flu and Nillie had gone to the health
food stores for wheat germ and seaweed soup.

'You see,' she said. 'Nillie has been doing a bit of translating
recently, and he finds he can only get through it by dictating as
he goes along. Of course the translating is only temporary, but
it does help a bit. It's very hard, you know, for Nillie, at his age,
to get the right sort of job.'

She did not add that Nillie, at his age, had fully expected to
be provided with the right sort of job. Such provision had so far
been confined to a pensionable vacancy in the London by
Night department of the Rubel Travel Organisation, along with
the use of a desk and chair in their West Croydon branch.
Guide cap, desk and chair remained unclaimed. Certain shares
of Abigail's had been extracted instead from an ancient trust to
allow for the setting-up of the flat. And from time to time
Abigail worked in a very secluded flower shop. This was called
staying with friends in the country, as indeed it would have
been, if more friends had placed first-class travel tickets or
chauffeur-driven cars at their disposal. And if more of those
friends' houses had been properly run, run that is on princely
lines. For since his marriage Oberall had grown increasingly
concerned that persons of substance, with some slight claim to
taste, should not only accept but support him at his own valu-
ation. If this rarely happened, it was not Abigail's fault. Having
renounced a whole cupboardful of slacks, jumpers and sandals
for one hand-ruched skirt, two low-cut silk blouses and a pair of
embroidered slippers, she pitted her prince against the world.
And though this barely reconditioned flat was not quite the

palace she had pictured, the robes had to be scrubbed, turned, patched and pressed, the gold given back to the dentist some-how, there was always a little China tea in the biscuit tin along with a small ancestral shovel. And above all there was Nillie, who knew how to admire her. He also shared her interest in invisible forces. These they explored together several nights a week, attending lectures, borrowing manuals, practising exercises, Nillie always a little in advance, knowing longer words in more languages, Nillie indeed steadily expanding his esoteric vocabulary, with an eye to next month's rent. For if a beautiful princess might be deemed to display flowers elegantly, might not a wise prince assist the bewildered, but otherwise well-endowed, to deeper, richer, rarer planes of life?

'You'd sometimes think,' Abigail sounded quite wistful, 'that no one had ever heard of Heidelberg.'

'Except perhaps as a breeding ground for GIs,' Theo laughed. 'Why? Did Nillie get his degrees at Heidelberg?'

'Well, not degrees exactly. He went on there after the cavalry school. In those days apparently you could just study whatever interested you. Nillie was mostly concerned with metempsychosis at the time.'

'I see.'

'He had several treatises printed.'

'Yes.'

'Still,' Abigail smiled her mysterious smile, 'there are one or two little Oberall galleons due in fairly soon now.'

'You mean that job at the German Embassy,' Theo suggested, trying to remember just which little Oberall galleons had already been written off.

'That too, of course.' Abigail stared into her gilt-edged cof-fee cup. 'Though it very much looks as if anything from that quarter will have to be quite unofficial. Because of certain

links . . .' Those links referred to an elderly cousin, an ardent
monarchist, who was in the habit of being removed two or
three times a year from naturally fortified islands or hilltops on
which he was making a stand, trying to be king.

Theo put down her glass of milk on a copy of the *Bhagavadgita*.

'You know,' she said, 'Bernard can't get himself fixed up
properly either.'

'But I thought he was getting on so well in that publicity
department.'

'I'm afraid that's rather a dead end really.' Theo then
launched into an abridged version of her husband's nightly complaints. It transpired that Bernard having, on the strength of
introductions from Theo's father, offered his services to industry,
was now anxious to withdraw them. He was thinking of taking
up Plato again. Plato in London, though, with all possible perks
attached. Or, as Theo preferred to put it, he'd made up his mind
to have one more shot at the academic life. 'And then a fellowship,' she concluded. 'After all, Bernard is essentially a scholar,
though he's not too keen to admit it just yet.'

'What about your medicine?' Abigail said. 'I do feel it's such
a waste you're not practising after all these years.' Although a
good many Oberall indispositions had been much assisted by
prescriptions from Theo, Abigail sometimes wondered just how
long it took a qualified non-practitioner to get quite out of
touch.

'I can always go back to it later,' Theo said. 'Just now Bernard
likes his meals at the right time, all that sort of thing. And we
can't afford any help. Which means one of these wonderful
part-time jobs, like lining up X-rays or blood donors or chamber
pots at the infant welfare clinic.' She smiled. 'Anyhow, I seem
to be pregnant.'

Abigail did not ask for details. If she considered babies at all, it was as miniature essences of her more sentimental moods. At these times she might refer to some little creature, a beautiful baby girl for Nillie, but any such intimations very soon shifted on to the pros and cons of iron and calcium injections. For Abigail regarded her body as far too ethereal for reproduction. And so indeed it seemed, though oddly enough she had never been ill, classifiably ill that is, such commonplaces being confined by and large to the more robust-looking.

Theo took up a small curling square of plain whitish knitting. 'And how is Raphael getting on?' she said.

Abigail bowed a bit, spreading out both palms, as if the existence of Raphael were a physical fact she had learnt to support, if not as yet to embrace. It must be admitted that Raphael had been more or less sprung on her, ripping her fairy web with the sordid claws of life, though not, as it turned out, utterly destroying it – thanks to the tracking down of a certain naval man, a swimmer too, retired to bird-watching in a Hampstead attic, who had finally been persuaded to take over Oberall's wife. Not until these two then had definitely taken up residence on the Continent, could Abigail make any attempt to regard the role of stepmother as one she might possibly play. And not, for that matter, until his own devoted long-suffering mother had taken to living with a complete stranger, running a guesthouse under their joint Christian names on the worst side of Lake Como, could Raphael himself see his way to acknowledging the existence of Abigail. As things were now, he dined at the flat quite frequently, and was even talking of resuming the rank and style of Oberall, which at sixteen, just off the Burlington Arcade, he had most bitterly renounced.

'I'm afraid that poor boy has had very bad luck with his tutors,' Abigail said. 'We were up there last weekend, staying with Mary . . .'

'Were you really? I haven't seen Mary for ages, not since I borrowed Pete's gown to take my degree. How are they getting?'

'Well, I must say dear, it was all pretty dismal. Pete wasn't there, of course, and the place was bitterly cold. You know what those concrete houses are, with no proper carpets either. Nillie got the most terrible fibrositis; it's only just beginning to wear off. None of the fires were working and I don't believe the beds had even been aired.' Abigail breathed a bit. 'It's all very well playing the penniless student, but, after all, if one can afford to live comfortably, it does seem rather absurd . . .' She broke off to examine the frayed beading on one of her glove-like slippers.

'What's happened to Pete?'

'Oh, he's got a job in Wales now. Something to do with coal dust. He comes up when he can, you know that sort of passe-partout arrangement, as Nillie calls it. Apparently Mary didn't take to Wales at all.'

'So she's up in that house on her own?'

'Well, there was an Irish woman there, some kind of a cook-general with two dreadful children, but I don't think they're staying long. Actually I did most of the cooking. Nillie had very bad typhoid as a child you know, and the adhesions just don't allow him to take liberties with his food. There again Mary hasn't the faintest idea about food, lives on cornflakes and Nescafé, as far as I can see. No wonder she's so nervous, can hardly answer the telephone, even hides, if you please, from the milkman.'

'What on earth does she do all day? Some course?'

'I don't think so. She reads a lot. French mostly. Nillie says that's always a bad sign.'

'A bad sign of what?'

Abigail wasn't quite sure. 'It's not that mere escapism is in itself more harmful than most forms of . . .' she began, ripping more beads off the slipper.

'But the French go too far?' Theo suggested.

'That is possible. Nillie and I never read novels, as you know, except one or two of the Russians. They are, somehow . . .' Abigail knitted her shapely brows, 'altogether . . .'

'Larger?'

This seemed to do.

'Does Mary ever see anyone up there? Theo wanted to know.

'There was a little dinner party on the Saturday, for Raphael. And a young historian. You remember Daniel, don't you, Daniel Frost?'

On re-examining her knitting in the underground, Theo found she had dropped so many stitches that it hardly seemed worth going on. She thought of Bernard, having dinner out again, of the curtains she might shorten during the afternoon. 'My wife,' she muttered sharply at the Nu Playline brassière, 'is a mere domestic drudge these days. Used to be so gay too, so full of ideas.'

CHAPTER THIRTEEN

The same day, some hours later, Mary had just drawn the curtains in the sitting room and settled down to write to South America.

Dearest Daddy and Mamma,

Thank you for your letters. Forgive me for not replying straight away, but there has been rather a lot to arrange. As you know I have been very busy with French literature all this year. Unfortunately, for the particular research I have in mind, a good many essential documents are to be found only in the Bibliothèque Nationale. I have an introduction from one of the professors here, a Semantics expert, who has offered to arrange everything in the way of student facilities for me, including accommodation at one of the colleges in the Cité Universitaire. This is, as it were, the residential section of the Sorbonne, with separate colleges for men and women, much as here, though qualifications for admission are somewhat less parochial. I think it would be more convenient in every way to be out there, than to take rooms on my own, or lodge with some so-called family, serving up sauces every night. It is also much cheaper because of all the subsidies that go with studying anything in France nowadays. I know how you feel about Paris, Daddy, but after all you were there quite a time yourself, and those 'diseased specimens of humanity' are to be found in any town surely. They can't all be locked up. There is, you must admit, a special colour index, a *justesse d'âme*, if you like, which only Paris can provide. You may not need it later, but that's a very different thing. I shall be working under one of the professors at the Sorbonne, also attending lectures there, and hope to get back speaking French nearly as well as you do. *On verra-rra-rra-rra-n'est-ce pas?*

There may, by the way, be some difficulty in getting my allowance transferred. You know how absurdly interfering the English are about these things. Perhaps the Paris office could help, if I really got stuck. I shall certainly look up M. Poire or is it Poivre? And the baroness, Mamma, if she's still there. We are subletting the house furnished to some Americans, not the Palm Beach sort; in fact the rent will only just about cover their winter fuel. But then they won't be splashing out rye on the rocks every night, nor leaving their children to express themselves in Swiss chocolate all over the walls. I know how you feel about letting anything, Daddy, but our furniture, except of course Mamma's revolving bookcase from last Christmas, had suffered a fair amount of wear and tear before we even saw it. And the rent will help to keep things ticking over here. Pete is to have the car in Wales; that will mean the battery being properly charged during the winter, much better really than dismantling it altogether. As you say, most garages are potentially criminal institutions. I have arranged all the insurance, as you suggested, and shall of course see that everything is properly covered whilst I'm away.

Pete will probably come over to Paris for Christmas, if he can be spared that is. I'm glad you understand about Cardiff. It really isn't the sort of place to settle down in, and if we were to try founding a family again, I should have to keep in touch with the hospital here, could not very well be travelling up and down all the time. Anyhow we shall see about that later; it's wisest, they say, to wait a bit longer for the glands to get their balance again.

No more news from the Nuffield Research people yet about Pete, but everyone gets back here sooner or later, if they're any good, that is, and if they really want to. When I've done with the Bibliothèque Nationale, we might perhaps have another look for that house, get on with that healthy normal life you have in mind. A smaller house might be more sensible . . .

(Or no bloody house at all, she thought.) I shouldn't think it will make much difference whether E. is elected Vice-President or not. It's not as if she's at all likely to be ignored at this stage. If there were any latter-day saints, I suppose you could call her one – such shrewd fanatical self-assertion without the least hint of grace. Admirable, as all flames are, but somehow never radiant.

Jake had his stitches out yesterday. I hope he'll leave motorbikes alone from now on.

Mary signed and scratched all over her head, deciding to leave the rest of the page to be filled in later. She lit another cigarette and started on a smaller pad of paper.

To Whom it May Concern
Paracleta Noonan has been in complete charge of our

household for the past two years. During this time her unwavering devotion to the task at hand has been most memorable. She is now returning to Belfast, to ensure more suitable education for her two adopted children than this somewhat isolated neighbourhood can provide. I only hope she will meet with such appreciation as she so steadfastly deserves.

This clearly wouldn't do. Nor would anything else. She turned to the next page on the pad.

Dear Professor le Mantec,

Thank you very much for your letter and the forms. I realise that my qualifications for writing a biography of Max Jacob are, as you say, somewhat slender as yet. They will, I trust, fill out. I do see too that the period in question is rather remote from your chosen arena, but you will, I'm sure, appreciate its appeal to the less meticulous, or should I say less disciplined mind. Neo-Celtic Catholic dilettantism is not, I agree, the soundest approach to the French language. But we cannot all be sound. And surely you, from your long-standing acquaintance with Proust, must admit that there is something to be said for starting at the wrong end and working backwards? I should very much like to come to tea on Friday and shall have the forms filled in by them.

Mary was not at all sure this would do either. She started again.

Darling,

Is there any chance of your getting away this weekend? It looks as if everything will be fixed up here rather sooner than I thought. And there is Jake and the gramophone to collect. I quite see you'd need the car for a kennel, hope it's going all right now.

Jake has had the stitches out, most of them. I'll try for the smaller ones later. The Cincinnati Statisticians want to move in next week, and they're prepared to pay some of the rent in dollars, which might help, if I get cut off for going to live in 'nothing but a bedouin brothel', as Daddy calls it. I know you think it would be quite a good thing if I did get cut off, but really darling, I don't want to be serving all day and night in a Moo-Cow milk bar just yet. I might, of course, teach English in Paris, but there again you need qualifications and some slight notion of grammar. Anyhow I've more or less fixed up accommodation in one of the student hostels. After these last months, it will be good to hear feet along the corridors, even the hide boots of vicars' daughters off on their hitch-hiking weekends.

Paracleta and the children left this morning. The bus moved off while I was still readdressing circulars for the postman. Silly, really, the way 'significant events' always get messed up. Paracleta seemed determined to send a Christmas pudding to Paris, so you'd better be there to eat it.

I should be glad, I suppose, that you're getting to like Cardiff more and more. It's funny they don't mind your slicing up rat's liver instead of miner's lung. Or does everyone on the unit have their own little sideline, like the radiologist with his chain-smoking rabbits? You're right, of course, about getting away from here, for a while at any rate, though this little section of the 'hot-house' is more of a hardening-off frame just now – none of the radiators work any better than last year. The Americans won't be too pleased. Maybe after a few months in the 14th arrondissement Cardiff will seem quite a haven. We might get a little farmhouse or something near the hospital. It was those greasy lace curtains, and sharing the oil cooker with those student nurses, that got me down. And of course the black bath and the no-smoking library. It's all very well not minding in the least where you sleep, but couldn't you possibly find something a bit more cheerful for the winter, with a landlady who'd look after you properly? You should be able to manage, you and Jake, a bit better than the Lascars. Now don't say there's my father talking, and I'm very spoilt and you can manage quite OK thanks very much. 'Cos it simply ain't so.

You left three brand new biggest and best volumes of Jane Austen here last time. It seems odd for you in Cardiff with the rat's livers and those lace curtains to start collecting Jane Austen. Do you like her? All right, all right, I've a very destructive mind. Anyhow please try to be back this weekend. (*It's my birthday*, she wanted to add, but did not, self-indulgence being all very well, but which self, when?) I shall miss you and Jake (she put instead, regretting the Learish endearments that had punctuated their correspondence so readily four years ago).

Then she got the dog its supper, herself another pint mug of Nescafé and returned to the cushion on the floor with a large cash register. This recorded much late-night lamentation, interspersed with quotations from whatever she happened to be reading at the time. Since discovering an insertion in darker ink, with different t's and s's, reading 'not every weakness is aimiable' (sic), she had thought more seriously than usual of dumping it all in the canal.

In Paris (she wrote) I shall have mathematical pocket books only, keep the ooze out. Meanwhile this little phase might as well be rounded off in keeping with the rest. D. has telephoned every day this week, wants to see me anytime I've a moment to spare. A moment to spare! Of course it's all because of Paris. Perversity is so obvious really, all the turns laid down. It's no wonder we all start off trying to walk straight. Anything to avoid the old A B C that we just twitch, contract, relax, quite automatically. Maybe we do, but at least we can each cultivate our own set of delayed responses. What the hell am I going to do in Paris anyway, but sit in some numbered cell all day waiting for the post? Not as if that's ever going to deliver a gay little Greetings Telegram. 'All fixed up now, darling. What size ring?' Just how queer is he, I wonder. It's all very well being the only woman someone can go to bed with, their salvation etc. etc., but that's not going to help him get on in this big bad world. That New Year's Eve party, for instance – D. staggering to his feet with that look in his eye, for me, oh yes, just for me. 'I resolve to be more straightforward in future.' Good God!

Met Finch in the lane this morning, very brave and sad. He wants to make D. his executor, can't get hold of him though. Could I get hold of him? *Could I get hold of him??* Poor Finch, he looked like a bit of old cardboard the bonfire didn't quite reach. I suppose dear Yanya must have found out about the little woman in Purley. Anyhow he's all set for a last look at the Aegean, a last slip off through the porthole probably, along with the little lady from P?

Mare guidem certo est omnibus I think he said. Why the Aegean though? I should have thought the Thames estuary would have been more thorough somehow. Sidling off a mudbank in the fog. That's the way surely . . .

And then the telephone rang. It was Daniel. He sounded rather drunk and wanted to see her as soon as possible. Mary said she'd like to see him too and could he come up and that Paracleta and the children had gone. He said of course he'd come up straightaway and rang off.

Shortly after 2 a.m. there was a low tapping at the french windows. Mary tied up her dressing-gown cord, switched off the Schubert C Major Quintet, now playing for the fourth time, and went towards the curtains.

'Friend.' The voice was a little hoarse, but otherwise quite familiar. She let him in.

'I saw the light,' he said. 'Sorry to be so late, but the car broke down on the by-pass and I was hours getting a lift.' Pete put down a canvas toolbag, full of unwashed shirts and socks.

'I brought you these,' he said, tugging out a long bent parcel. 'Flowers. It is your birthday, isn't it?'

'Well almost, darling.' Mary kissed him, going on into the kitchen, where the dog had brought down the saucepan rack in his baffled anxiety to defend the house.

'I was just hoping you'd come,' she said, putting on the water for eggs.

CHAPTER FOURTEEN

The pipes were at their worst in the mornings. From six a.m. till eight the whole building creaked and groaned in giant labour. Then the electric polishers took over, three to a floor, with three great women behind them. By this time it was advisable to be down in the basement canteen and attached to the breakfast queue. Cooking or other domestic appliances were not allowed in the bedrooms. There was a gas ring on each floor, just outside the lavatories. Coffee could be made here, but the main thing in the mornings was to avoid the great women. In three months Mary had managed, by a system of stiffening nods and rising bribes, to keep these women more or less at bay. But for their health's sake, or perhaps just for the sheer novelty of it, they changed floors too often for any system to be altogether successful. Once cornered, the cross-examination followed a fairly standard pattern.

Mademoiselle knows, of course, that cooking is absolutely forbidden upstairs. Only water. Nothing but water. Mademoiselle seems to be looking very tired this morning. Madame. Excuse me. My poor head; since that operation it crackles all day long. And the husband is in England? That's a good way off. And the children? Ah, no children. Madame is so young still. And this little pot-plant? It looks so sad. Nothing but a muddy old branch after all. Poor thing. Perhaps it had better be taken away. No? And the empty tins? Not empty. Excuse me. It is not good to smoke like that. Very expensive too, English cigarettes. And the old newspapers? But of course they are old. Look at the date. Today is . . . And all these scratches on the lovely floor. The machine can do nothing, absolutely nothing against scratches this deep. Might Mademoiselle not get herself some slippers in the sales? Do they not have slippers in England? Really the room must be kept properly. What would the Directrice say? Washing clothes in the basin too. Mademoiselle, knows, of course, that washing clothes in the basin is absolutely . . .

At breakfast Mary took care not to sit anywhere near the girl called Judith, who lived along her corridor and reminded her of Arabella: the girl called Zazetta, a former room-mate: the student of engineering, called something like Pogo, who had once taken her to the cinema. She pretended to read in the queue, got two bowls of coffee at once, balanced them down to the quietest corner and opened up the book again, feeling rather sick.

The canteen was full of young men and women eating off tartan china. Those in the brightest check shirts, the blackest sweaters, the tightest jeans, were English, aiming mostly at teaching diplomas. They spoke French in public. The native French speakers, a smaller more dubious collection, preferred American. Once off the basement steps, in fact from 10 a.m. onwards, breakfast eaten, laundry collected, pigeon-holes examined, the two groups had little connection. Such amenities as the common-room, reading-room, music-room, dartboard and netball field were used, if at all, by the English. The others relaxed elsewhere. Presumably they studied elsewhere too, for

they all carried perforated packs of student cards entitling them
to balanced meals and built-in beds. If those who ate the balanced meals and those who slept in the built-in beds were not
always those whose photos had once been clipped to the cards,
there were, on the whole, enough ladles of pea purée, enough
brown blankets to go round. And as long as the nationalities
represented 'out at the Cité, oh here, yes there for the moment
anyway' kept more or less to their own blocks, there was little
blood drawn. If nightly orgies were rumoured in the Maison
Hellénique or the Maison de Maroc (*mon Dieu quel mélange là-
bas – attendez* . . .) those bedded in the red-brick structure
designed to further relations between England and France slept
chastely enough. Trafficking between the male and female residential sections of the building, depending largely on the
temperance of the auxiliary night porter, was 'how d'you say the
lowest ever'. Inseparable couples soon found themselves looking for fresh keys elsewhere. And if most of the inmates slept
night after night behind the same number on the same door,
alone, or along with an allocated comrade at a slightly reduced
monthly rent, this was because no better alternative had, as yet,
presented itself.

After breakfast Mary stood about in the hall, waiting for the
small irreproachable day-and-most-nights porter to sort out the
post, along with his large irreproachable wife and ten-year-old
son in shantung shirt, bow-tie and velvet shorts. The winter
sports posters were down. Jazz clubs, Russian film shows, ice
hockey rinks, the miming group, the rose window of Chartres
still extended a cordial welcome to all. The pigeon-hole marked
M received a small yellow envelope edged in black. It was
addressed to Signorina Z. Martelli, and carried a Garibaldi
stamp. Mary had once shared a room with Signorina Z.
Martelli, or Zazetta, or just Zaza if you like. It was only after

referring in the fourth application (typed) to unspecified immoral advances on the part of Miss Martelli that she had managed to get a room to herself. Even now there were moments when this room too would suddenly seem to be sprayed all over with varnish remover and wild carnation scent.

Seeing that the great women had now gathered for refreshments at the far end of the corridor, and that her bed was still unmade, Mary removed the stockings from the rail of the washbasin, propped up the *Laissez tout cela s.v.p.* notice on the desk, got her music case and coat, and went down again and out towards the Métro. The morning rush was passing off. She got herself one of the seats reserved for the mutilated, still feeling sick. To sit down anywhere once away from the room was getting more and more difficult, owing largely to the bland Latin assumption that any woman not on the move must be looking for a bit of sex. Like a monkey gibbering after a nut. And perhaps just because in a way it was so and yet so very much not so that way, it had all got quite out of hand. In fact she could hardly cross a park now without keeping her head down, clenching, unclenching each finger in turn, muttering away. Anyhow, as she told herself during these eccentric promenades, the parks were frozen, not for sitting in, now that the best birds had gone. That left the cafés . . . *pardon, mademoiselle, c'est à vous les gants, le sac à main?* Extra, always extra to sit down. And the cinema, *pardon, mademoiselle, c'est à vous* . . . and no smoking. And the libraries no smoking again. And, of course, the student canteens.

Once out of the Métro Mary had coffee at the counter of the nearest café. Then she joined the queue at the Bibliothèque Nationale. Half an hour later she left the queue, bought a newspaper, went back to the café, had more coffee at the same counter, pretending to read the newspaper, still feeling sick.

Then she set off for the nearest student canteen, hoping for soup and a seat by the window. Although it was barely quarter to twelve the queues already filled three flights of stairs and were just fanning out on to the pavement. She went on to another café, sat down inside near the football machine, had a glass of hot wine, would have had several, if the woman in black adding up in the corner had not looked so disapproving. On her way back to the Métro she spent some time in the foreign section of a large bookshop well equipped with mirrors. When she came out she had with her a second-hand American paperback, unpaid for. Every ten days or so she was liable to have one of these with her, because of the hustling, touch not, taste not, handle not, counting house air of it all, and because of the mirrors. Once back in her room, she lay on the bed, read the paperback for an hour or so, then spent the afternoon copying out lists of references relating to various aspects of French poetry.

At 4.30 the afternoon post arrived. At 4.35 she went down to the pigeon-holes. This time there were two letters, both for her. She opened the one from Pete first. It said that he and Jake were fine and how was she getting on. Getting the best out of Paris? It said that everyone on the unit was still very busy and that there wasn't much chance of his making up that Christmas leave just yet. Maybe in the spring.

The other, from Daniel, had been posted in Brussels and read as follows:

My dearest,
    I trust you will have gathered by now why I never replied to your letters. God knows it wasn't easy. But I felt somehow obliged to let you go your own chosen way without any hindrance from me. I still hope you may meet, or

indeed have met, someone more worthy of you than I could ever claim to be. Just in case this is not so, or if you have any feeling for me left, would you think of coming to Brussels this Saturday? I shall be waiting for you in my old muffler in the lounge of the Hotel Metropole from six p.m. on. I would have come through Paris to find you myself, if it had not been for some wretched lectures I was misguided enough to undertake in this city of Moloch. And on Monday, snowstorms permitting, I must take my free seat to Lausanne in the pink Buick of a kindly local merchant, to pick up the Simplon–Orient for those long-awaited Isles of Greece. They too come under the heading of earning one's living alas! If you do find my long silence quite unpardonable, I shall of course understand. Meanwhile, as the great *Lakiste* said 'I take my little porringer and eat my supper here.' Let us meet while we may.

                              Love as ever,
                                      D.

Mary put all this into her only Craven A cigarette tin, emptied a week after coming to Paris and kept ever since for this purpose. Pete's went into one of several Senior Service tins. Then she went out to the nearest grocer for bread, wine and gruyère cheese. On the way she composed messages to the Hotel Metropole. First a telegram.

                    6 O'CLOCK   M.

Then a postcard.

Sorry, can't make it. Have a good time in Greece.

Then bits of a letter.

> Must it be the Metropole? Ghent or Bruges or even a
> hut in the Ardennes would have been a bit more roman-
> tic, damn you. Anyhow it's all a long way off and no pink
> Buicks about. It would, I suppose, be far too complicated
> for you to pick up the Simplon–Orient here. It does come
> here, starts here, doesn't it? Women seem almost diaboli-
> cally designed at times for waiting and would it be
> weeping? Spinning? I mean I'm not feeling too good.

It was odd, she thought, once past the post office, still on
strike, how little anything mattered once you tried saying how
much it did.

After bread and cheese at the desk, and wine and a bit of
washing in the built-in basin, she spent the evening composing
more messages to the Metropole. By ten-thirty she had printed
YOU BLOODY FOOL some way through *Childe Harold* and was
reading La Fontaine. At eleven someone knocked at the door.
It was the girl called Judith, bringing in water, hot milk, a mug
and a small bag of lump sugar.

'How nice.' Mary got off the bed, making for the grocery
and china drawer of the built-in cupboard. 'Well,' she said,
prising open a new tin of Nescafé, 'had a good day?'

Judith, curled up by now on the bed, was fingering her long
fair hair, film-star hair, though it wasn't cut that way. She
looked oddly transparent, or perhaps just tired.

'Hell as usual,' she said.

'Couldn't you try another school?'

'They're all the same. It was hard enough getting into this
one. I might pick up a few private pupils some time, but they
probably wouldn't even cover the travelling expenses.' She

wetted a finger, glumly assessing two fresh ladders in her stockings. 'It's not as if anyone wants to get acquainted with selected
passages from Thomas Browne or Howard Spring,' she went
on. 'A working GI vocabulary is all they're after. Pretty
fluent most of them, as it is, to judge from the number of fish-
net nylons about. One wanted to know today whether I was
too poor to buy lipstick, or did my boyfriend prefer it that
way.'

Judith, an orphan, brought up by a sister on the stage (this
sister recently married and settled in Sevenoaks), supported
herself in Paris by teaching English to girls between the ages of
twelve and fifteen resident in the neighbourhood of the
Bastille. At nineteen, tall, boyishly set and jointed, skimpily
smart in her sister's cast-off clothes, she was already too lucid a
waif to attract most would-be protectors.

'How about you?' she said.

'Oh, working.' Mary stirred in the milk.

'Max Jacob?'

'Good Lord no.' She laughed. 'When anyone takes care to
state in writing what a horror they have of *le genre biographie his-
torique*, you can hardly start analysing their school reports.
Anyhow there's quite an industry already. You know those tender little film scripts . . . Max Jacob, *l'homme qui faisait penser à
Dieu* . . . The last time I saw Max it was raining, bitter implacable rain. Of course neither he nor I realised that this was to
be . . . And so on till those last days in the internment camp. *Sa
Mort édifiante*. The memorial service at Saint Bênoit . . . *Et
Max, notre Max, pouvait-il vraiment mourir?* You know what lyrical heights can be reached on such occasions. And then, of
course, the more sober-minded find themselves obliged to ask
themselves whether the time has now come to take the old
fake really seriously. So you see it's all fully covered. As for the

letters, I can't imagine the most plausible Ph.D. student hunting down half of them, let alone being allowed to photostat the more moving passages.'

'You sound a bit sore about it,' Judith said, not entirely won over by Mary's grand manner.

They both tried the coffee.

'I suppose that's because I'm not a plausible Ph.D. student,' Mary said. 'As a matter of fact I can't get any "material" in this country. The relatives either have everything locked up or burnt because it's so shameful, or they want to be bribed. And I've no idea where the bidding starts, or how to bid at all for that matter. I mean it's bad enough getting the right sort of ending to a thank you for having me letter. As for those ageing literary gentlemen, *les meilleurs amis*, they just can't believe that any healthy girl, especially coming from England, could possibly be interested in anything but sex. And they're all so squat and knowing and nasty. Still,' she smiled, 'I suppose it's about time women stopped wanting to whitewash everything. It must be some sort of domestic instinct, like keeping the cupboards clean. Alas, alas,' she chanted in mock Yeatsian accents, 'the incurable virginity of soul.'

Judith looked suitably impressed.

'All the same,' Mary went on solemnly, 'Max Jacob will have his chapter . . . *Tout*,' she took a deep breath, '*m'est indifférent sauf l'amité et la Prière . . . et sans doute l'Art.*' She had two ways of speaking French. One was very slow and very English. This served for most casual encounters. The other very fast, very French, either well rehearsed, or well provided with pregnant pauses, was designed for rarer, more intimate impressions.

'Have you got a title for the book yet?' Judith said.

'I don't know really. Might call it "The Lure of Lists" perhaps. There's nothing more soothing than copying out things under different headings. Though of course it's more fun if you can get someone to tick them off for you as you go along.'

'Did that professor come back from America?'

'No.'

'So you're still not going to any lectures?'

'No.'

'I must say I couldn't manage without somewhere to go, in the mornings anyway. Nobody cares whether you live or die in this place. Except dear Fanfan, of course.' Judith was referring to her room-mate, a Mauritian law student, who attended what she called statutory dancing classes six nights a week, returning in time for breakfast. Between these classes Fanfan slept. 'She'd just love to have everything sealed up for weeks,' Judith added sourly. 'A real old-fashioned fumigation, with herself and pink curlers included.'

'There, there,' Mary laughed, thinking of those pink curlers. Domestic pink was a terrible colour. 'All the same,' she said, 'if they did lay on Sunday socials here, I don't suppose you'd attend. What's happened to that nice Czech?'

'Pole actually,' Judith said. 'The Fair Isle sweater gets shorter every day.'

'Perhaps they're the fashion in Poland.'

'Perhaps.'

Mary got out the wine again, and more cigarettes. 'It's all very well,' she said, rinsing the mugs, 'you saving yourself for some tubercular laird, but I must say I can't quite see you rubbing down gun dogs, combing sporrans, parcelling up Causeries for the London Library indefinitely.'

'I don't know.' Judith stared dreamily at her sister's Minnehaha pantomime slippers. 'I love the country.'

'Anyhow,' Mary handed over half a mug of wine, 'lairds don't live round here.'

'No, I suppose not.' Judith now began tracing patterns on the bedspread.

'Drink up.'

Judith drank. 'There was another abortion down the corridor yesterday,' she said.

'Was there?' Mary frowned a bit. 'How do you know?'

'The stretcher got stuck in the lift and the girl got hysterics. In spite of all the gin she'd had.'

'Why gin?'

'I don't know, really.'

'Is that what usually happens?'

'Well, the last one threw herself downstairs and broke a leg.'

'Oh . . . I suppose they usually get taken to the infirmary?'

'Actually I think they're handed on to the nuns. No anaesthetics.'

'I see . . . All in all,' Mary smiled, just, 'one must be best off as a Muslim. By the way, are you doing anything this weekend?'

'Doing anything?' It might have been a beheaded waxwork talking.

'I mean you could be mixing goulash for some World Youth Rally, couldn't you?'

'Look here Mary, it's all very well –'

'All right, all right. Now then,' she drained her mug, 'I take it we have both come across Americans with large cars?'

Judith nodded gloomily.

'I take it we have both decided to manage without large cars, or even little cars in future?'

Judith nodded again.

'Right. You see,' she smiled quite kindly, 'the trouble with looking after you is that it mostly means my catching measles twice. Anyhow it looks as if we've both got well over the free transport stage. So now. On Saturday evening we shall go to a music hall. And eat properly afterwards. On me, because I'm quite rich now. And then,' she went on smoothly, 'on Sunday morning we shall not hear Mass at the Russian Orthodox church. We shall . . . well anyhow we shall have lunch on the other side with a baroness, an old school friend of my mother's, now taken to designing belts and knitting jackets for pets. She's a fine cook. We shall then go to a Ravel concert. And after that . . . well after that we shall drink Muscadet somewhere. We shall not, at any point, think of taking a stroll in a frozen wood with lemonade afterwards, and not too long for the next train back. Is that so?'

Judith smiled.

'I think you need cheering up,' Mary said. 'Pity about the transport, isn't it? The beet fields should be at their best this time of year. And the *auberges*, *à la chandelle*, *au coin du feu* . . . And,' she added just for the fun of it, 'La Rôtisserie Ardennaise or the Metropole grill.'

CHAPTER FIFTEEN

Two months later Anderson and Rollo were drinking champagne in the Ritz bar. It had been Anderson's idea to fly to Paris for the weekend, on the pretext of showing Rollo that good times were still to be had; there was no need for despair. Since their arrival the previous evening, they had, between them, spent fifty pounds. And Rollo was regretting every handful of his share.

'Do you see that?' Anderson pointed his cigarette at a group standing by the bar. 'Benjamin Britten,' he beamed triumphantly. 'Didn't I tell you that anyone worth meeting came here sooner or later?'

'Perhaps I should have bought an autograph album, instead of that rubber doll,' Rollo said. 'Might have got a fingerprint or two off Marilyn Monroe.'

'My dear fellow,' Anderson sighed irritably. 'You're very hard to please. First you want to see Paris through the eyes of Katherine Mansfield. All right, so we go to the flower market and the ferret shops and the cemetery. I know the taxi-driver jibbed a bit at the cemetery, but there are several gates and naturally he thought we might slip out through another one.'

'We could have walked there, couldn't we?'

'Walked? Not while I'm your interpreter. And anyhow just how many more courtyards and windowboxes do you want to see? Didn't I hear you say in that last traffic jam that it was none of your nostalgia anyway, and what about a bit of that famous good living? Of course you have to pay for it. That's what money's for. The point is, it's all here. Get anything here,' he leant back happily, 'if you know your way around.'

'We didn't get much last night, did we?'

'Things have changed a bit,' Anderson admitted. 'I dare say that's not the best district any more. We'll have to make enquiries.'

'You can count me out,' Rollo muttered, peering with mild interest at a newly arrived couple about to settle some tables off. The woman, small, trim and tailored à l'anglaise, carried her fifty-odd years of unwavering femininity with discreet self-assurance. Creased from the plane, still flushed from the hairdresser's, crowned with a turret of swan's feathers, touched off here and there by black net, she might well be assumed not to have wasted a moment so far. Her escort, that much taller, wiser, weightier altogether, embodied the temperate distinction of one in whom a just blending of blood and brain had proved steadily successful.

'It's nice to see our country decently represented for once,' Rollo said.

Anderson eased himself round a bit. 'Good Lord,' he said. 'The Foldings. Excuse me a moment, would you?' He pushed back his chair. 'The old boy can be quite helpful at times,' he added, squeezing himself out with a solemn wink.

Rollo took the opportunity to order himself a large bottle of tonic water. he was just starting on it when Anderson came lumbering back saying 'well that's that', rubbing his hands, happy as ever. 'You see what I mean about this place. From six to eight this evening the company of one of Britain's more promis-ing younger composers, and should I say her most hermetic diarist would be much appreciated at a cocktail party *pour encourager les diplomats*.'

'What about the bookshop?' Rollo said.

'Now, now. Don't fret.' Anderson patted his shoulder man-fully. 'We'll find it, all right. there can't be more than one shop round there specialising in sweets got up to look like fruit. I tell you the whole window is stacked with frosted *vivandières*, marzi-pan baskets, angelica boughs, all bursting with cherries and so forth. All you have to do is walk right in and ask for a scoop or two of wild strawberries.'

'And then,' Rollo sniffed at the last of the tonic water, 'and then I dare say they hand you over to a gang of fuzzy-wuzzies in the back yard . . . Monsieur want preety pictures of my sister. Rightoh. I geef him preety pictures, verry preety. *Un, deux, trois*.' He shuddered.

Anderson flickered petulantly at his lighter. 'I sometimes wonder,' he said, 'why you bother to live at all.'

'As a matter of fact "Ole Man River" was about the first song I think I ever really appreciated. And now,' he sniffed at his glass again, studying the label on the tonic water, 'like poor Tom Kitten up the chimney, I find that one flue seems to lead to another.'

'What you need is another glass of champagne,' Anderson said.

Rollo rebuckled his trouser band, straightened his coral cashmere sweater and reached for his lightweight coat.

'The strain of seeing eye to eye with one's friends can lead to a chronic squint,' he said.

Anderson made signs for the bill.

*

In spite of careful calculations, Mary arrived far too soon. The buses at the Cité had been held up by a student demonstration, the entrance to the Métro cordoned off by police. Two Arabs were said to have stabbed one another dead. After half an hour's wandering through the suburbs she had waved for a taxi. The driver had opened the front door. It had not, of course, been a taxi at all, but it had been going in approximately the right direction, at least so its driver said. He said at the second set of traffic lights that she must have dinner with him, or at least a drink. He knew just the place. He also drove very fast, had a grey wig, gold-rimmed spectacles and pointed black shoes. Once across the river he had steered with one hand. On jumping out at the fifth set of lights Mary had run down the nearest alley, click-clack on the cobbles in her cocktail shoes, stepping up at last straight on to the avenue she wanted. And the right end of it too. The lift was mostly mirror, and the white polo-neck sweater, even under a coat, looked more like a white polo-neck sweater than ever. Once more she wondered whether it could possibly pass as evening wear. And when the maid came to take the coat away in the shining hall of the shining flat, she was quite sure it could not. She tucked it inside her skirt, pulled it out again, grinned apologetically at the maid, said it was rather cold tonight wasn't it, and went on in. A few pointed questions from her hostess, an old friend of Pete's father, were hardly encouraging. Words such as research, Sorbonne, just a few months, fell like so many olive pips in the crested silver ashtrays. Her host, an even older friend of Pete's father, seemed more solicitous. Such information on student life as she saw fit to provide was received with discreet, tolerant, slightly flirtatious amusement. And then he handed her over to the chaste, silken knot of wives entitled to be there and to drink and to watch their husbands drink.

Mary was just explaining to the last of these how she ran a pan-Celtic revivalist press in an unused section of the Métro, and was only present on the understanding that her enterprise received the official recognition it required to carry on, when she saw Theo come in.

'I was beginning to think you might have been carried off all of a sudden,' she said some minutes later, wedged between Theo's armchair and the radiogram.

'So was I.' Theo, obviously pregnant, laughed a bit. 'My mother goes quite crazy in these beauty salons. And then when she gets all the stuff home, she can never remember which goes on first.'

'How's Bernard?'

'Oh, all right, making quite a name for himself.' She sounded a shade too offhand altogether. 'He's up north on some philosopher's spree at the moment. That's how I come to be here . . . taking a last look at *la vie* before we start advertising for a cot. Of course,' she scratched some fluff off her black moujik-style smock, 'this is hardly the time for the Faubourg S. Honoré. As a matter of fact my mother seems to be getting much more of a kick out of it than I am.' She looked up across the room at her mother, a long high-chinned look, which tried but by no means succeeded in taking everything into account.

Lady Folding, in black too now, anniversary jewels and long gloves on, tautly transfigured by her afternoon's adventures, was absorbed in what could only be classed as sparkling conversation.

'Who's that talking to her?' Mary said, noting black hair, blue eyes again. Noting also mandarin mask, wary faintly patronising glance, sparse chopping gestures. All in all thick, rooted, split somehow but pretty implacable.

'That,' Theo said, 'is Dermot McNeill, brilliant French

scholar, fanatical Scot, and oddly enough an up-and-coming member of Her Majesty's Foreign Service. Not quite the usual dapper young diplomat, is he?'

Mary smiled vaguely.

'My father admires him,' Theo went on, 'with the mild qualification that he'd rip you open if you got in his way.'

'Oh?' Mary watched him, wondering, remembering various articles he'd written, trying to connect them with a pin-stripe suit.

'And how about you?' Theo said. 'Do you like Paris? You're looking awfully thin, you know. A little too pale and interesting.'

'Well, as a matter of fact I haven't been too well.' Mary leant across the radiogram, extending a ring of tomato juice into a spiked sun. 'Another miscarriage,' she concluded.

'Oh . . . Daniel?'

She nodded.

'Do you mind?'

'On and off.' Mary was beginning to wish she'd never mentioned it.

'What about Pete?'

'Pete? He doesn't know Why should he?'

Theo started plucking at the golden sheaf of corn embroidered on one of her pockets. 'Look here, Mary,' she said suddenly, 'you know what I think of Daniel.'

'Yes, I know what you think of Daniel. I think much the same, so we must be right, mustn't we?' Mary smiled, raising her glass. 'Let's drink to the gullible,' she said, 'the clay feet fetishists. Subtle clay is sweeter, but solid clay is sounder. We therefore did not deem it meeter to stick to the latter.'

'But you can't go on like this,' Theo said. 'I mean why don't you come back? You could stay with us, if you like, and then perhaps when you're feeling a bit –'

'Good Lord!' Mary was staring at the door. 'There's Anderson, if you please. We might almost be back in the Kardomah. I'll just see . . .' She started squeezing herself out. 'Perhaps I can get him over this side, though it's rather far from the drink.'

She waited near the window while Anderson confessed to an elderly French gentleman, equipped with a flesh-coloured hearing aid, that he himself unfortunately knew very little about the famous birds of Wales, but had as it happened had the honour of composing several little marches much favoured by *La Garde galloise*.

'Hallo ducky.' He turned at last. 'How nice to see you?' He patted her arm affectionately. 'I felt sure you'd be squatting in some sheikh's tent by now, stirring away at the camel soup.'

'Did you really?' Mary accepted a cigarette. 'And what are *you* doing over here? Selling anthems?'

'Dear me no. I'm educating Rollo.'

'Rollo? Is he here?'

Anderson shook his head like an old circus bear. 'Poor Rollo. I'm afraid he's retired to his lonely bed with a miniature edition of Trollope. Trollope, I ask you! Here we are in the glittering heart of Europe on a Saturday night and Rollo –' He shot out a hand at the passing tray of drink. '*Merci ma belle,*' he bowed to the maid. '*Ravisante,*' he murmured over her departing shoulder. 'There now,' he presented Mary with a fresh glass. 'Drink up. You're coming out with me tonight, aren't you? What's the best place these days?'

'Best place for what?'

'You know, I sometimes wonder if you're quite all there.'

'All where?' At this point Mary knew for sure that the brilliant French scholar, fanatical Scot had only one arm.

'Now listen to me.' Anderson said, short and sharp. 'Would

you please stop acting the little girl lost. It really doesn't suit you . . . We'll leave now, if you like,' he added coaxingly.

Mary took her bag off the radiator. 'How long are you staying?' she said.

'Only tonight. Rollo would never miss Sunday afternoon by his own gas fire.'

'Well, give him my love, won't you?' She held out her hand.

Anderson shook it automatically. And before he'd quite realised what had happened, Mary was several groups away talking to someone else. She had, in her hurry, bumped into Dermot McNeill, spilling most of his drink.

'Never mind. You hold this.' He gave her the glass, then mopped up the pin-stripes a bit, waving aside all apologies with a large navy-blue handkerchief. 'Drink we have always with us,' he said. 'But who are you?'

'Friend of a friend,' she whispered, seeing their hostess approaching.

'Dermot dear!' They were neatly separated. 'You simply must meet a charming old gentleman from Oslo, who admires your work tremendously. He says he really can't believe you're the man he's thinking of. You look so young and cheerful.'

Dermot smiled not too painfully, allowing himself to be led off with a faint shrug implying almost anything.

On getting back to Theo, Mary found her chatting with one of the wives about the disgraceful behaviour of the local babysitters.

'Goodbye dear,' she said. 'I've got to go now. Write to me, won't you, about the baby and everything.'

'But Mary – '

'No, no. Don't move.' Mary pressed her back. 'It's just that I've rather lost the art of keeping up appearances.'

She found her coat in one of the bedrooms, under a pile of

stoles and furs, and had just about worked out the latch when her host turned up.

'What's this? Not leaving us already, are you?' he said.

'I'm sorry.' Mary lowered her hand guiltily. 'I'm afraid I must. I – er, didn't want to disturb anyone, so would you please say good-night to your wife for me. And thank you.' She'd got her hand back on the latch, but had to take it off again to be helped on with her coat. 'Let me know if you ever come over my side, on a tour of inspection or anything,' she said.

'Of course,' he smiled, 'of course. Give my regards to Rupert when you see him. And try not to overwork.' He gave her shoulders the sort of squeeze he presumably thought they might be expecting, not the fatherly sort. 'Now then, easy does it.' He took over the latch himself then, not quite so tolerant, not quite so amused any more.

Mary cursed in the lift, went on cursing and miming down the avenues till she reached the quays. No one bothered her. Most were already eating or drinking somewhere by now, those out alone possessed by their own impossibilities. On the Pont des Arts she stopped because, well just because she liked it there, this light on water, most of all. The *bateaux mouches*, those monstrous little idols to avarice, were still suspended. The washing was all unstrung on the barges, easels packed up, anglers gone, lovers and ragmen merged at last, as it might be home. She moved along, more or less bound if anywhere for St Germain-des-Prés. And there she sat, for the first time in many months, outside the Deux Magots, drinking vermouth, watching people pass. It was the women she watched mostly – hopeless, haggard male impersonators, each enslaved to some neurotic little god. Somehow it seemed unthinkable they should survive.

'We might as well sit here.'

Mary felt her throat tighten, shut off. Some great bird started flapping about in her chest. She did not look round.

'Of course there's the Reine Blanche.'

'And the Pergola.' This voice she could not for the moment identify.

'Ah well, the night is young. The orchard walls are neither high nor hard to climb. What about Martin? Do you think he's stumbled on a soulmate already?'

The other twittered nervously. 'Not under a fiver,' he said, 'unless it's an Arab.'

'What it is,' sighed his companion, 'to be back in the north. *Ich träumte von bunten Blumen*,' he thrilled sadly, '*so wie sie wohl bluhen im Mai*.'

'*Vous désirez, messieurs?*' The waiter, remonstrating with a peanut seller, spun his tray straight into Mary's lap. '*Oh! Pardon, pardon, pardon . . .*'

'You haven't got a handkerchief, have you Daniel?' she said.

Daniel produced three. Raphael de Groot stood by, fingering a bunch of monogrammed silk which he was clearly hoping would not be required.

'I think,' he said, as they came to the sticky stage, 'I'd better take a look round for Martin. He can't be far off. We might meet later, perhaps?'

'Just as you like.' Daniel sounded a little put out. 'We're all friends here, you know.'

'Nevertheless,' Raphael backed away, 'if you'll excuse me . . .'

Daniel scowled after him, then drew out a chair for Mary. 'Poor Raphael. Such a problem child,' he said.

'That's what you like, isn't it?' Mary started laying out her cigarettes to dry.

'Is it?' He grinned the old impudent grin. 'I must say Paris

doesn't seem to have made you any sweeter. Still, never mind,'
he took her hand. 'What's it to be?'

'Coffee, please.'

'Coffee? Dear oh dear, you women.'

'Coffee and cognac, then.'

'That's better. It's not as if we meet every day.' He signalled
the waiter, who came straight up, winking and grinning, no
doubt assuming his tip not lost after all.

Mary noted at this point that Daniel spoke Linguaphone
French. Somehow this reminded her how he wore expanding
bracelets to keep up his shirt sleeves, and socks with patterns
going all the way up them. None of this helped much.

'And how was Greece?' she said.

'Wonderful.' His voice trembled slightly, but then Daniel
could turn the most slug-ridden cabbage into a celestial veg-
etable. 'I didn't get further than Athens this time,' he
admitted. 'Too many old friends there, all dying for a bit of
moral support. And, of course,' he grinned again, 'all only too
pleased to put their intimate experience of the country at my
disposal.'

'Was Raphael with you?'

'Oh yeth,' he said. 'Wafael came too.'

'And what about the Knights?'

'The Knights?' He laughed sharply. 'They go marching on . . .
You know,' he leant forward, very grave now, skeletal, intent,
'sometimes I wonder if there'll ever be time enough. You see,
there's no one else who has any idea of what needs to be done.
Some sub-equatorial professor thinks he has, but he'll never do
it. Never. Hasn't the training, for one thing. Can't even write
decent English. Nothing but *vide* this and that.'

Mary watched him coldly. 'I'm sorry I couldn't come to
Brussels this time,' she said. 'I got ill.'

'Oh dear, I'm sorry. All better now? As a matter of fact, I had a nasty turn on the Lycabet myself. Almost got anointed by the monks up there. Still, it looks as if they'll have to postpone the ceremony a while yet.'

'Yes,' Mary said, 'I dare say they will.'

They sat for some moments, drank, sat on, silent, pretending to be terribly interested in everything going on round about.

'I wonder what's happened to Raphael,' Daniel said at last. 'And Martin. Do you remember Martin Freemantle? Used to live above me in college, till he ran away to sculpt. We came across him on the boat back, sleeping on his very own crate of Parian marble. He's a sweet boy really. A bit intense, but delightfully naive at times, for one so tall. He considers women, by the way,' he glanced at her teasingly, 'as an unfortunate necessity.'

'Really . . . I sometimes wonder if women weren't designed for quite another planet. That's not him, is it?'

Mary pointed out a long bespectacled figure in gabardine raincoat and creased grey flannels loping gloomily round the newspaper kiosk. He looked like a very expensive version of Pete, only paler, sharper round the mouth and eyes, hungrier altogether.

Daniel waved his stick invitingly. The young man nodded, turned away, looked back again and, seeing the stick still going, came cautiously up, by no means too keen to settle in this particular spot.

'Come along, Martin. Take a seat.' Daniel shifted his chair nearer Mary's. 'Did you have any luck?'

Martin's eyebrows shot up. 'I've no idea what you mean,' he said.

'Now, now. Don't get alarmed. My friend here would be the first to agree that women have their limitations.' He introduced them. Neither looked up. 'Isn't that right though, Mary?' Daniel went on, high and bright. 'You don't support the great earth mother, do you? Ever loving night and morning, pay as you breed, till death do us part.'

'I don't support anything,' Mary said, feeling suddenly sick. It was all very well to imagine these scenes, but till now she'd never quite believed in them.

Daniel, flushed and oddly exalted, started drumming softly on the table top.

'I think I'd better go now,' she said. 'Goodbye Daniel.' She would have touched him, but could not.

'Tomorrow,' he muttered, still drumming, his eyes fixed and glittering like a doll's. 'I'll ring you tomorrow.'

'I'm afraid I shan't be there.' She turned away, fumbling through chairs and shoulders, treading down dog leads and camera straps.

'Just a minute.' Martin caught her at the kerb. 'You've forgotten this.' He held out the handbag.

'Oh . . . thank you.'

They stood on there at the corner, waiting for the lights to change.

'May I see you home?' he said, glancing down at her face, her hands tight on the bag.

'It's quite a long way.' She swallowed and coughed a bit, clearing her throat. 'And the Métro's not working.'

'That's all right. I'd rather like a walk.'

And as they went he talked about his mother and sister, his schooldays, marble, the Minoan face.

CHAPTER SIXTEEN

It was November, early in the afternoon. Mary was walking through the grounds of the Cité Universitaire, grounds designed to make ample allowance for outdoor exercise. There was quite a parade of vegetation still, some green, some brown, all neatly sheared, knotted and spiked. In fact the place looked more like an open prison than ever. And the odd inmates she came across were those she had always come across, using these paths about this time of day. At the entrance to her old quarters, she took out a headscarf and a pair of dark glasses. With these on she got through the hall, past the porter, up the stairs, chanting the Argentine national anthem steadily under her breath. Round the last bend she smacked straight into leopardskin, bore on, ripping it back, clutching at twin pulps of coffee lace, drowning in wild carnation scent. It was Signorina Z. Martelli on her way to a tea dance.

'Sshh!' Mary grabbed her glasses and scrambled up, frowning with disgust. 'It was too tight anyway . . . This is a game,' she look down threateningly, 'a nasty rough English game called prisoner's base. You'd better hide.' And she strode on down the corridor followed by what may well have been a traditional orange-boat curse.

Judith was in. She had taken over Mary's room on the strength of a well-timed family history of tuberculosis. The shoulder-high sheets of red paper, pinned up round the walls to hide the stains, had given way to a patchwork of postcards from the Museum of Modern Art. The bed was covered with striped towelling and, instead of the avocado pear pip on matchsticks in a marmalade jar, there was a leather-bound triptych displaying enlarged snapshots of a bald baby before, during and after its bath.

'What do you think of my new niece?' Judith said, getting out mugs for coffee.

'Oh, is that who it is.' Mary was sitting on the towelling. 'She looks very solid, not the sort of thing anyone could ignore. I mean I'm sure she's very sweet. Have you seen her yet?'

Judith shook her head. 'No free flights to Sevenoaks,' she said. 'Anyhow they're pretty crowded there now. No room for a spinster aunt. Still,' she spooned out the Nescafé, 'I don't suppose my sister would object to a cheap nanny in the family. Who would?' She started stirring briskly. 'And how was Sicily? You caused quite a scandal here, you know, rushing off like that.' She knelt across the bed, pulling down a gaily covered dictionary of argot from the bookshelf. 'They even went so far as to get a circular printed.' And she shook out a concertinaed leaflet into Mary's lap.

'"Any student",' Mary read, '"enlisting in archaeological or similar expeditions is requested to inform the office at least one month in advance of their proposed date of departure. And to settle all outstanding accounts. Otherwise he or she cannot expect to be readmitted and will, in addition, be liable for the full monthly rent, until such time as their rooms may be reassigned to others."'

'Dear oh dear.' She handed it back. 'And all because I forgot to pay the laundry bill. Do you know that laundry bill followed us all round the mountains, by donkey mostly and of course the odd motorbike. The archaeology seems to have upset them a bit, doesn't it? Perhaps a little social survey would have gone down better . . . Mosaic Man – Units in the Making. Or the Teutonic Tripod – Taormina turns again to Greece. Post-war significance of same.'

Judith looked at her blankly.

'Sorry,' Mary said. 'We've been celebrating. You see, I'm getting married again.'

'To Martin?'

'That's right. Sicily is a very feminine country. At least, I'm not so sure about Palermo – that's another little Athens – and the other seaside resorts. But the mountains, mountains and sea. *Che bellezza* once again. Some people,' she smiled, 'are very responsive to landscape. Especially sculptors.'

'But I thought . . .' Judith paused doubtfully. 'Well, when you went off, there was no question of anything like that, was there?'

'No,' Mary said. 'No question at all. Just an archaeological expedition, to . . . pass the summer, shall we say. Suits me. Suits Martin, though he would keep harping on my getting myself a peasant lover. I must admit,' she waved her mug pontifically, 'a certain lack of precedent is always attractive, a challenge to womanhood, all that nonsense. Though it isn't nonsense at all, unfortunately.' She got out her cigarettes and a picture box of little wax matches. 'Pretty, aren't they?' She lit up, watching the flame die down, slowly circling it out. 'It's very sad, but I'm getting to think nice, normal anything doesn't much appeal to me any more . . . unless it's very young.' She took another quick look at the niece. 'Like puppies. It must be quite common, this grand refusal, sidling off rather. A profound dislike, distrust maybe of anything obvious. Perhaps it's just the old craving to be damned in style.'

'The little things in life have always meant a lot to me,' Judith said.

'Oh yes,' Mary smiled at her, very gracious, undeceived. 'Odd socks stiff on the line, milk tops pecked by the birds. And just how long would you go on looking at them once the telephone rang? It seems to me that if some things matter so much more than others, well, it's no good going into ecstasies over the others, is it? I mean it's very misleading.'

Judith wasn't so sure.

'It was a great relief,' Mary went on, 'to be definitely off the telephone for a while. And having an escort was a nice change too, especially in Palermo. Fair hair, always fair hair, the infallible catalyst. Just that bit more remote I suppose, like a black Madonna. It's very odd, mind you, the way they behave with all those Madonnas looking on. But there we are, you can't take a stroll through a set of cloisters without dressing up as a war widow or a Pan American art student.'

'That's all very well,' Judith glanced at her, flushing a bit, 'but you can always get escorts. You don't have to marry them.'

'Can you really though, make use of anyone for long? Sooner or later you own them or they own you. Anyhow the whole system would take a much fatter address book than I've ever had. Never had one at all, actually. Have you?'

'Well, yes. By the way,' Judith started rummaging in one of the built-in drawers, 'I kept the last lot of mail for you.'

'Oh?' Mary put it aside, including the telegram, but not the heavily sellotaped airmail envelope. This she squashed into her handbag. 'I'm afraid my father considers the Mediterranean most unhealthy,' she said. 'In fact he was not prepared to support the archaeological expedition any longer.'

'What about the divorce and everything?'

'Oh that.' She smiled a bit. 'He seems quite convinced that the whole Maso family is most unhealthy, syphilitic I should say. You see I never managed to get a photograph of Pete with his hair combed. Anyhow it turns out that my father would not be averse to my marrying a bricklayer, provided he was clean, upstanding and so forth.'

'Why a bricklayer?'

'Oh, I don't know. Just his term, possibly for someone honest, hard-working and penniless. Penniless principally.' She fingered the telegram uneasily.

'That came yesterday,' Judith said.

'Do you mind?' Mary ripped it open.

CAN HARDLY OFFER CONGRATULATIONS INEXPRESSIBLY
PERTURBED CHOICE UNDERSTANDABLE BUT UTTERLY
UNWORTHY TRUST THIS REACHES YOU PLEASE RING ON
ARRIVAL — D

Mary screwed it up.

'Anything serious?'

She shook her head. 'You can hardly imagine,' she said lightly, 'what a performance it is getting divorced. Martin and I had to hang about for hours this morning bouncing up and down on the appointed double bed waiting for the detective to turn up. And then the statement . . . Mr Freemantle and I are very much in love with one another . . . Fantastic face-saving terminology . . . Don't worry we won't say anything nasty. Snip, snip, snip. Doesn't hurt much, does it? Give and take. Just a little, mind, here and there, so's it won't notice. And don't you dare ask why.' She stared out of the window at more windows on the far side of the netball pitch, all part of the same institution.

'It's the glib freemasonry of gilt-edged sentiment that's so depressing, knowing you can't break it, ever. Because it's the sort of safety most people want.'

'Couldn't you have done the divorcing?' Judith said.

Mary grinned like a clown on closing night. 'The most tolerant people can clamp down all of a sudden,' she said. 'Usually when you're least expecting it. Forgive the little tirade, by the way. There's not much you can get by with in English any more, other than "Fine thanks, and you?" I suppose that's largely why we came here . . . *pour jeter les haut cris*, well timed, of course, appropriately placed. *Le coup de grâce, le cri de coeur.* What else, after all?' She was looking at the floor now; a good deal less scratched than it used to be. 'Though there's always poise, isn't there? Poise, wit and tact. Those are about the only full-grown feminine virtues in demand nowadays.'

'Do you really think so?'

'Blessed are the awkward,' Mary said all on one note, 'for they shall be trodden straight.' She shifted round to examine the bookshelf. 'Do you find German more profitable than French?'

'Well, not exactly.' Judith seemed a little embarrassed. 'It's just that I've been helping Jaro with some translating . . . Benn mostly,' she added modestly, 'Gottfried Benn.'

'Jaro? Was that the nice Czech?'

'Pole actually,' Judith said.

'And how's he getting on?'

'All right. Much nicer than I thought. People often are, aren't they? I . . . er, knitted him another sweater. He's quite a poet, you know,' Judith tugged out a bright blue file, without upsetting the stack of school exercises waiting to be corrected. 'I get one most mornings,' she said, unhinging a handful of creased typescript.

'In Polish?'

'Oh no. German mostly, German and French.'

Mary read a bit. 'Rather like Rilke, aren't they?' she said cautiously. 'I mean a lot of *ur-* this and that?'

'Do you think so? I can't say I see much resemblance myself.'

'I suppose,' Mary went on thumbing through the sheets as fast as she dared, 'you can say pretty well anything in German too, only it's rather harder to swallow . . . Still,' she handed them back with a smile, 'he's got a lot of fine feelings, hasn't he?'

Judith looked at her doubtfully.

'And when's the wedding?' Mary said.

'Wedding?' The file snapped back on the typescript. 'Whose wedding?'

'Well, my German is not very advanced, but he does want to marry you, doesn't he?'

'Oh yes, I dare say he does.'

'I'm all for making things as simple as possible,' Mary said. 'If you're living with someone, for instance, you might as well marry them, if that's what they want. After all, it's only a matter of signing in the right space.'

'But I'm not living with Jaro.'

'Oh, you're not? I see. Still the old game of tip and run, is it? Just one kiss and you have to be off. To what? Another midnight session with *The Oxford Book of German Verse*, all lined up for tomorrow's walk in the park. You shouldn't knit for anyone,' she said severely, 'unless you're prepared to go to bed with them.'

Judith did not reply.

'I'm sorry, dear.' Mary waved placatingly. 'Don't mind me. It's only that I'd very much like to see you set up somehow. High-minded young women make everything so much more complicated.'

'But you got married in a church, didn't you?'

'Oh yes, indeed I did. Nice little girl doing the obvious thing. But I see now it might be a good deal more sacred to hold someone's hand on a railway bridge, than to walk down the aisle with them. Either it's all part of a pattern or it isn't. You can't just pick out the cosy pieces to please the relations.'

'Isn't that more or less what you were suggesting I should do?'

'Good Lord no.' Mary turned back to the bookshelf. 'Look at all these, now. And the postcards. How to make yourself thoroughly miserable in ten easy lessons. No wonder you look so pasty, as my mother used to say, lying on your bed reading French novels all day.'

'Mostly German at the moment.'

'That's worse still. Not even an entr'acte to cheer you up. Now Martin and I,' she lay back on the towelling, 'are going to get right away from all that. Not that Martin was ever there much. He reads rather slowly. And most men live in compartments anyway. Any section not in use simply doesn't exist. Unless, of course, someone suddenly rifles it.'

'And then what?'

'And then they call in the neighbours for moral support, or the doctors, or the police. Anyhow, as I was saying, Martin and I are going to live in the country.'

'Here?'

'I wish it were, but I'm afraid my father wouldn't dream of acquiring property in such a decadent country as France. Even England strikes him as somewhat unappetising.'

'Well, there's always the dollar area.'

'Oh no. Cheap. Cheap and stuffy and all that iced water can only lead to cancer of the throat.'

'I see. But weren't you going to forget about him? Start some sort of a school, wasn't it, in Sicily?'

'That's right. So we were. But it turns out that Martin would very much like a home somewhere. You see he's a bit tired of trinket sculpture, the sort of knick-knacks you can shift by taxi from one lodging house to the next. So it looks as if we'll have to settle down in style now . . . busts round the courtyard, half-hewn torsos wrestling under the elms. There might even be a cave for Cerberus or a cliff for prophets and warriors. And one of those garden walls to back up some terracotta plaques on the seasons, or mythical beasts.'

'It sounds like a life's work.'

'Yes, it does rather, doesn't it? Everything will be for sale of course. And other sculptors can come and work there. A sort of communal studio and open-air gallery up on the moors some-where,' she hesitated. 'Not Scotland or Wales or Yorkshire. They're a bit too remote.'

'What about you?' Judith said. 'You and Max Jacob?'

Mary laughed. 'If there's one sure way of ruining a beautiful new life, it's to drag all the old mess into it. I shall spend my time driving jeep-loads of rare boulders up and down the avenue, pumping water, baking bread, rearing a large handsome family.'

'So you're going to have a family too?'

Martin would like a family.'

'Well . . . that's nice.'

'Is it?' Mary took off her watch and shook it sharply. 'I must be going soon,' she said. 'Have you got that case anywhere?'

Judith pulled out a withered carpet bag from under the bed. It contained a dusty assortment of empty wine bottles, coat-hangers and cooking apparatus.

'Dear me.' Mary scratched a bit more off one of the peeling P & O labels. 'If my father could see it now. His favourite bag, loved and cherished these forty years.' She got out the bottles first. 'Would you mind very much if I left the contents here?

You should get something back on the bottles and . . . well there's not much missing from the spirit stove.' She started laying out sections of charred tin. 'A spirit stove is always handy, isn't it?'

'You remind me of my sister,' Judith said, 'trying to get rid of her Hedda Gabler muff.'

Mary looked at the row of metal bits a little ruefully. 'It's odd how anxious one can be at times, to bestow rubbish,' she said, stuffing bottles back between the coat-hangers.

'No, look here. Please don't bother. I could do with the odd francs.'

'Could you? Good.' She got the bottles out again, two at a time, disliking them more than ever.

'How long are you staying?'

'Not staying,' Mary said. 'Martin's got sinusitis. It started in Rome, when I wanted to stop on there, and he didn't. Anyhow he won't go near a doctor till we get to London. I can't blame him. But all the same . . . rushing through Paris like this . . . Greet detective, buy six tablets codeine, two litres wine, collect bag, board train. It might almost be Cardiff, apart from the wine, which was pretty nasty – that dyed stuff.'

'Still, it was nice seeing you again.'

'Nice seeing you . . . Oh well,' she snapped up her handbag, put back the headscarf and the dark glasses, 'off we go again. Be nice to the Czech though, won't you? There's not that much choice after all.'

'I'll do my best.' Judith stood by the door, hugging her thin crossed arms, tentatively self-sufficient like a winter birch.

'You know,' Mary said, suddenly seeing her there, 'you're a nymph. That's it. A wan, impalpable nymph. And I never thought of it before. You'll be all right. Nymphs always are.'

'And you?'

'Oh, I'm a defrocked goddess.'

'That sounds very romantic.'

'Yes, very.'

'Say yes,' Mary muttered to herself at the head of the stairs, 'yes, yes, yes, no-o, yes . . .'

She forgot the carpet bag.

CHAPTER SEVENTEEN

'Quite like old times,' Rollo said, drawing out the nearest chair at a corner table in the Kardomah.

'You're looking very elegant,' Mary said, sitting down in it, with the music case beside her.

'Am I?' He pulled out his primrose tweed tie, examining the horizontal fringe as if it were a sample-size secret weapon someone had palmed off on him. 'Present from Sark,' he said.

Mary smiled. 'I can't quite see you in Sark.'

'Can't you?' He looked at her severely. 'As a reluctant, though not, if I may say so, entirely unimaginative member of the moderately moneyed classes, I took my mother to Sark for the last three weeks of July. Nothing wrong with that, is there?'

'Oh no,' she said. 'Nothing at all.'

'We can't all take the star flight to Istanbul whenever we feel a bit chilly.'

'Of course not.'

'And what brings you back to these drab little lanes?' He waved again at the distant flotilla of waitresses, like a man ten days on a raft. 'Is the yacht in dry dock at present, or did a posse of drunken bandits set fire to the villa?'

'Oh, do shut up, Rollo. Please. Treacle tart is not the only honest pudding in the world, you know. As it happens I've been down in Somerset for the past year and a half, acting as builder's provider. And for the past two weeks I've been laid out in a local nursing home, reading the Bible.'

Rollo fell suspiciously silent, as he always did at the least mention of famous literature, especially anything foreign.

'I tried to get in touch with you,' she went on, 'but they said your whole row had been pulled down.'

'Oh yes,' he sighed gloomily. 'I'm being driven up in the world. Two rooms now, two rooms, kitchen and bath. A proper little apartment. Or what is commonly described as living according to one's means. There's no getting away from it as far as I can see. Any more rises and I'll find myself in a mansion flat with every post bringing in fresh folders on the family pension scheme . . . Did you have your appendix out, by the way?'

Mary shook her head. 'Just one more attempt to lead a healthy, normal life,' she said. 'The last apparently for which this particular department is prepared to take the consequences. Though I don't quite see what consequences, they'd be taking anyway.' She turned aside, asking for and receiving the ashtray from the next table. 'I was thinking it might be as well to have the whole contraption removed. It's not much assistance one way and another.'

'Oh, I shouldn't do that, if I were you.' Rollo spotted a waitress a little off route adjusting her cuffs. He made a two-fingered sign which she seemed to accept as a compliment.

'I can't think what's happened to the nice girls nowadays,' he said, gazing wistfully in the direction of the service screens. 'They can't all be taking short courses in Spanish or gliding, can they?'

'Don't know, really. Have you seen Pete at all?' Mary said.

'Pete?' He shook his head, suddenly seized by a yawn. 'I'm afraid Cardiff's a bit off my track,' he said, coming to piece by piece.

'You know he got married again, almost straight away, to a nurse.'

'Ah . . .' Rollo smoothed out the glass over the plastic lace mats. 'Here we are. Sugar?'

'I gather she's not exactly glamorous, but very fond of Jane Austen.' Mary started the usual hunt for saccharine tablets. 'They've got Paracleta with them,' she said. 'And the children. And Jake, of course. Jake's got kidney trouble, I believe.'

'Ha!' Rollo swivelled his cup round, lipstick side out. 'That'll limit the old boy's activities a bit, won't it?'

'You never liked Jake much, did you?'

'Oh, I don't know. He wasn't the sort of dog you could dismiss in a hurry.' Here Rollo boxed air a bit, warding off tongues and paws all round. He did things like this, when he felt at home.

'And how is Anderson getting on?' she said. 'I haven't seen him since Paris . . . wasn't too sure how he'd get on with Martin and all that. You know how it is. Friends are so often part of a setting. They may do their best to break it up, but they can't very well be transferred.'

'Did you have one bun or two?' Rollo said, pencil in hand.

'No buns. Is it possible, do you think,' Mary leant across the table, chin in hand, 'that sculptors mostly go on sculpting because they can only lay their hands on one stone at a time? Martin seems to have turned over entirely to architecture and landscape gardening.'

'Oh?' Rollo looked up politely. 'I suppose there's quite an opening for that sort of thing in Somerset?'

'Maybe. Operations have so far been confined to the domain. You must come down and see it all some time. The house is nearly finished now . . . Lovely house,' she added flatly. 'Right up on the moors.'

Rollo did not reply.

'What is it, dear?' she said, seeing the buns had been crossed off long ago.

'Nothing. Not quite my line of country, that's all.'

'Nor mine.' she admitted. 'But Martin gets restless in towns.'

'It seems to me that if certain territories are noticeably less populated than others, there must be some very good reason for it.'

'Wine . . .' Mary was picking at the luncheon menu now. 'Wine, laughter, friends. That's about the lot, isn't it? All we have to fall back on?'

'Yes, yes.' Rollo nodded, like a bird on a spring. 'Sooner or later the peaks begin to pall. Isn't it about time you produced a little pamphlet?' He smiled at her encouragingly. 'Against the Grain, or My Life and Loves on the Outskirts of Town.'

'You're a swine.'

'Of course,' he said. 'Of course.' He got out a sixpenny tip. 'In recognition of his long, much-tried capacity as singing master, Mr Jute's presence is now requested from time to time at major sporting events. This afternoon,' he continued modestly, 'is devoted to the final heats of the under-sixteen interschool diving championships . . . at the municipal baths. Would you care to accompany me?'

'Not quite my line,' she said.

'Even I am beginning to find it somewhat unproductive.' Rollo sighed, pummelling his fishing hat, folding it neatly in half, wrapping *The Times* round it. 'You wait,' he said fiercely. 'You'll find your old friend drug-running yet.'

'What on earth have you been reading?'

'A *Child's Garden of Verse*,' he said.

When Rollo had gone, Mary got out the letter to South America, started two nights back in the nursing home.

Tomorrow (she continued) I hope to be discharged. If all goes well, I shall be spending a quiet weekend with the Foldings before going back. They've settled about eleven miles from here to enjoy their retirement, though from what I hear it looks very much as if she's much the more settled of the two. As you say, Daddy, no man worth his salt wants to sleep out his life in an armchair. And Basil can't be much over sixty yet. Still, as you know, it's an old English custom to start laying down asparagus beds at the peak of a life unremittingly devoted to public service. I believe their house is quite old, probably full of weeping stones, if you'll forgive my mentioning these unfortunate objects once again. They've been patching the place up, though not, I imagine, to anything like the extent of your enterprise in Somerset.

Martin has been on the job non-stop since I've been in here. There has, I gather, been an inevitable hitch in the proposed plan for the outhouses. Anyhow Martin is busy drawing up a detailed plan of the whole issue, along with diagrams, so you will be able to see for yourself exactly what needs to be done.

Thank you, Daddy, for approving the 3 x 1½ inch joists in the hemlock. 6 x 4 in Oregon pine are only used in churches nowadays. The same goes for the square drain-pipes and the Penrhyn Bangor slates. The latter, by the way, could never be handled by any of our local men, if they ever wanted work in this country again. We are, of course, using solid brass fittings throughout and have made quite sure that every foot of new timber is guaranteed kiln-dried and treated against –

She took up a smaller pad.

Darling,
    Just out of that Hall of Mirth, thank God. I'm coming

to think the music of the spheres could hardly continue without the steadying influence of a night nurse's knitting needles. Thank you for the flowers. The wrapping came in handy too, for those paper fans I was making to cover all the cigarette stubs in the grate. And the evening cascara pills.

I do wish you'd thought again though, about stripping those outhouses. They weren't that far gone surely. And I was getting quite used to the laurels. Those roots will need a chain gang on day and night shifts for the next six months. And then you'll have to start growing something else there, to keep the gales down.

I met the bank manager – no, *not* his assistant – outside Smith's this morning. Having enquired after my health, and yours, and the weather down in Somerset, he said of course I did know, didn't I, that the building account was now £3,000 overdrawn. I said I hadn't quite realised the exact figure, but it did look as if the end was well within sight. He was glad to hear this, for my sake, and thought it should be beautiful there in the summer. He also wondered if it were just possible that the last draft from South America might have gone astray. I said one never knew. Things were a little tricky out there at present, arrangements apt to be delayed . . .

You do realise, don't you, that Papa could go on quibbling over the cost of a barrow-load of ¾ inch gravel till he died. There is nothing he likes more than getting the very best of everything assembled according to his own impossible specifications at less than cost price. You've never seen that light in his eye when there's half a gallon of turps missing from the annual wholesale consignment to do up the shutters at home. Do you wonder we get those wads of instructions every day? We're just setting up another little outpost of the empire, that's all. He'd have us copying out bills of lading for the next five years, then find some slip in the adding up and refuse to pay. Probably start a great lawsuit too over a chipped bathroom tile, and round the whole thing off by tying up the property for seven non-existent generations.

A beautiful house is OK, all you say, but not built like this. Art Treasure – there's a faulty connection, if ever there was one. Sorry dear, I'm a bit touchy, as you know, about money getting mixed up with everything – not signed on yet at the Labour Exchange, nothing grand like that. But I do wish you'd left those outhouses alone. Back on the Sunday express. Will you meet me with would-it-be laurel leaves in your hair?

This time the waitress insisted on clearing the table for lunch.

Mary went out. It was more than two hours before the bus left for the Foldings. She got her bag from the chemist, who'd been keeping it because she'd bought iron pills there. She left the bag, along with the music case, at the bus station. And then she set off for the principal bookshop, on the faint assumption that, in times like these, it might be open from dawn to dusk. She went several hundred yards out of her way to avoid the corner on which she had last seen Pete, after sharing out the books and records – books since moved from shelf to tea-chest to shelf again, records which had warped in store and never been played since . . . All right, you take the car for Jake. I'll have the fridge, might need it some time . . . The car had got smashed up on Snowdon on some sabbatical expedition. In spite of numerous handmade additions, it was never an alpine car. But the fridge, recently installed in Somerset, went on and on, one of the silent sort, designed to last a lifetime.

The principal bookshop was only allowing people out. That left the pubs and the park. She would have liked a drink very much, but for all their liberated armoury, women are still a long way from getting themselves a quiet drink over the counter. At least they may get one, but the second demands a large book or a studied vacuity quite out of keeping with any good reason for being there at all. She took the road to the park, used mainly by army lorries to get up a bit of speed on the quiet. It was a pale, disowned October day. The slight ache of being up and about again added that touch of poignancy without which movement, except by appointment, soon becomes irrelevant. Just past the third knot of lime-roots buckling the old flags, patched here and there by concrete slabs – for this arterial bypass had been a lime walk once – she spotted someone veering towards her in the wake of a small yellow dog. There were only four limes between them, before she was quite sure who it was.

'Hallo,' he said, running the old hand through the old hair. 'This is Blanche.' Daniel, a pinched shrunken Daniel with a sore on his lip, hauled in the lead. 'She's got eczema, I'm afraid.'

'Oh.' Mary edged back a little. 'And how many legs?'

'Three,' he said. 'Three and a quarter. She was run over right on our doorstep one night. So we took her in, didn't we, Blanche?' He prodded the squirming yellow rump with the tip of his hickory stick.

'Surprising how she gets about really, with all that weight.'

'Yes,' Mary said. 'And no hair.'

They stood for a while watching the dog wriggling on its back.

'What are you doing here?' he said.

'Just looking around.'

'Have you had lunch?'

'No, not yet.'

'Well, come along then. The little house is just round the corner, rice pudding on the hob.' He took her arm, dropping it almost straight away to deal with the reluctant Blanche. 'Eleanor's in bed, taking things quietly,' he went on, as soon as they were all moving in approximately the same direction. 'You never met her, did you?'

'No. I never met her.'

Eleanor was the only daughter of the President of Daniel's college. They had been married two years last Primrose Day in the college chapel. Mary had not been invited to the wedding.

The little house was not far away.

'One of the few irreproachable investments,' Daniel said, bundling Blanche down the basement steps, 'from which the college draws its princely revenue.' He unlocked the powder-blue front door.

The house was pie-faced, Georgian semi-detached style, very demure. For this little lane was one highly prized by university folk. Inside the feminine touch, more gilt than chrome, held discreet tasteful sway. Mary, who had till now numbered Eleanor amongst the customary academic accessories – all cat clubs, sun-hats and marigold chutney – providing Daniel with a pre-shrunk guaranteed-100 per cent virgin wool backcloth, was quite surprised.

They trod steadily up three narrow flights of burgundy stair-carpeting, Daniel first, taking care to explain that the carpeting had not been paid for yet.

'Here we are, my sweet,' he said, ushering Mary into the bedroom. 'I've brought you a visitor.'

Eleanor was lying curled up on the large double bed in a blood-red kimono, with *Vogue* and *Harper's Bazaar* on her knees, and assorted works of Mrs Gaskell and Miss Martineau piled up on the chiffonier behind her. Small, dark and feline, she looked very much at home.

'This is Mary,' he said.

'Really?' She held out a pale lacquered hand. 'How nice. I've heard so much about you.'

Mary brushed palms warily.

'How are you?' she said, backing towards the freshly enam-elled jardinière.

'Oh, I'm fine. Just following our funny little doctor's orders . . . for the sake of the next generation.' She turned to Daniel. 'Is Blanche all right, dearest? She didn't have very long out. You know the vet said she must have air often.'

'I assure you, my love, she's had plenty of air. Hasn't she, Mary?'

Mary went on examining the jardinière.

'Can I get you anything?,' he went on gently. 'More coffee? Lemonade?' He ran his finger round the brim of the lemonade jug, finding a chip there, frowning slightly.

'Not just now.' She passed one pale lacquered hand across her forehead. 'I think that wretched migraine must be coming on again.'

'Oh no, dearest. I'm sure it's not. Have you taken those pills?'

She smiled bravely. 'See that Blanche has her dinner dearest, won't you? The rabbit is out in the meat safe, and you'll find her bowl behind the begonias. Such a greedy little dog, but we can't let her starve, can we?'

'No,' Daniel said, hand on the doorknob, 'we can't do that.'

Mary stepped forward, at her most Girl-Guidish. 'What about another hot bottle?'

'Thank you,' Eleanor smiled at her sweetly, 'but Daniel gave me this little pad for my birthday.' She held up a pink quilted square on a flex. 'Such a nice surprise.'

'Yes,' Mary said. 'Lovely.' She took another look at the wardrobe mirror. Now that the sun had come out on the dust, it was quite clearly a question mark initialled D.F. that was on it. She thought of her father . . . *do you call this clean* . . .

'Perhaps Mary could help me with the rabbit?' Daniel called from the landing.

'Behind the begonias, wasn't it?' Mary said to Eleanor, smiling hard, retreating from blood-red kimono to half-shut door.

At the foot of the first flight down she paused to hear out the faint but increasingly familiar *Heiligen Dankgesan* (Beethoven Opus 132), one of the great works which a close analysis of the suicide rate among certain communities could hardly afford to dismiss. 'Wireless?' she said, pointing at one of the two closed doors.

Daniel shrugged back, smiling a bit. 'No talking on the stairs,' he murmured, beckoning her down.

'And now,' he said, shutting the kitchen door firmly behind them, 'what about a little salami? And . . . let's see,' he opened the over door, 'ah yes, rice pudding . . . a stingless pleasure.'

'Who's the music lover?' she said.

'Dear me. How suspicious you women are. If you must know, our one and only guest-room harbours a lodger. Though I must say it can be rather a strain.' He started laying out floral crockery clipped and glued but all ancient, all elegant. 'Do you remember Arabella?'

Mary did.

'Well, she's installed at present, though I'm not at all sure we can stand it much longer. Last week I seriously considered investing in a stomach pump.'

'Oh?'

'After all, no one wants a suicide on their hands.' His voice rose sharply. 'In their own house too.'

'No, I suppose not.'

'Poor girl, she will take everything so seriously.' He was quieter now, almost indifferent. 'Quite attractive, too, don't you think, in her way?' He started rubbing up some gnarled cutlery. 'And all the makings, mind you, of a scholar, if only she'd steady down a bit. But really, I just can't bring myself to apply for any further extensions. She seems to have some sort of a phobia about exams, rather like those little boys who will keep climbing on to the highest springboard and never never dive.'

'Sooner or later they mostly hold their noses and jump,' she said, 'from what is known, I suppose, as the sheer pressure of public opinion. But couldn't you find her a young man instead?'

'*Non cuivis homine contingit adire Corinthum,*' he got down the breadboard. 'Or should one say Paris?'

Mary, who had been leaning against the dresser, suddenly slid into the dog-basket.

'All right?' He helped her gently up on to a small painted stool, the sort of stool that is mostly used for getting things down off shelves.

'Just a bit giddy,' she said, gripping the table. This wobbled too. 'You haven't a drink anywhere, have you?'

Daniel knelt at the doors of the dresser, examining various gritty decanters. 'It very much looks as if my ration has run out,' he said. 'We could always go down the lane, of course. Would you like that?'

'Yes,' she smiled. 'Like Blanche, I seem to need plenty of air.'

'Come to think of it, perhaps we'd better take Blanche too.' He unhooked Blanche's lead from the bunch of cloths and aprons hanging up behind the door and stood there swinging it slowly in front of where Mary was looking.

'Why not?' she said, rising unsteadily, eyes fixed on the clip

of the lead glinting a bit, still swinging slowly . . . 'Why not?'
And the next moment she was down the hall at the front door
fumbling with all sorts of bolts and chains.

'There, there.' He reached over her shoulder, flicking back a
small brass knob. 'The rest are merely decorative.'

There was no one drinking in the lounge bar, no one that is
that they knew. After the second brandy Mary found that her
knees no longer vibrated whenever her heels left the floor.
'Fantasies,' she muttered firmly, watching Daniel making his
way to the door marked GENTS. 'Nothing but fantasies.' The
door swung shut. She attached the lead and dog to the nearest
table-leg and lay back in her chair, eyes closed, tuning in to the
rinsing of pint mugs, the click and rumble of bar billiards coming from the next room.

'Remember me?' Beer breathed hard all of a sudden all over
her. 'Your old friend, Little Boy Blue?'

'Yes,' she said, holding her breath, seeing there was nowhere
to shrink to. 'Oh yes.' Though she didn't.

'Raphael . . . Raphael von und zu Oberall,' he bowed drunkenly, 'at your or anyone else's service . . . Still bearing up, you
see.' He stood to attention, saluting the hunting prints, then
crumpled again, one hand on the table, the other fondling the
bristles on his chin. 'A little the worse for wear,' he giggled
thickly, 'though that just about sums us all up sooner or later.'
He giggled again. 'What do you say?'

At this point Blanche, trodden out of a deep sleep, started
yapping hysterically.

'Not mine.' Mary yanked at the lead, clucking and hissing,
throwing down crisps.

'No. Of course not. I know this creature.' Raphael toed a few
crisps a bit further off. 'The last and longest word in creatures.
Belongs to the landlady, doesn't it? Not allowed out without its

keeper. Are you, my precious?' He spat and missed.

Mary took another quick look at the Gents. 'Its keeper will be along presently,' she said.

'Oh he will, will he. Do you mind then, if I sit down?' He sat down, crossing his legs, hitching up his trousers where the creases might have been. And then he collapsed across the table, sobbing 'the bloody bastard, oh the bloody bastard', pounding stubs and tickets out of the ashtray, sobbing 'the swine, the f——ing swine. My God. If only you knew . . .'

Daniel did not reappear. Mary, following the barman's instructions, found him round the back, pacing among the bins and crates, much as an entomologist might pace among counters of joke beetles and butterfly brooches. It was the first time she had ever seen him waiting for anyone.

'Ah, there you are,' he said. 'Forgive my slipping out like that, but one can't go near a pub in this place any more without getting belched at by some lunatic.'

They started walking out of the yard, not back down the lane, but the other way, towards the principal bookshop and Daniel's college, with Blanche.

'You know, I've done more for that boy . . .' He swung his stick at the publican's elderly labrador. 'Grrr . . . you brute, you.' They moved on. 'I've nursed that tender little specimen day and night for five years. And what does it do? Goes and gets itself a third. And a bad third at that. Just can't lay off the drink, that's all. It's in the blood, I suppose.' This time Blanche clearly had to stop, so they stopped, looking at her on and off. 'The whole petty dynasty is rotten,' he said. 'Always was. And I thought' – here he almost laughed out loud – 'I thought he might even pull off a fellowship. Kept telling him that. Now, of course, he hasn't a chance, yet he goes on hanging about here drinking his head off. Heaven knows what he does it on. I

shouldn't have thought that particular branch of the family
had any rights left to dispose of.'

'So you've abandoned him to his own devices, is that it?' she
said, once they'd got going again.

'They can't all tag along,' he said, almost whining, leaning
more than ever on the stick. 'I'm not Atlas, am I?'

'Oh no, not Atlas . . . more of a Pied Piper,' she suggested, so
as he didn't have to hear. 'I was wondering whether Blanche
could get as far as the bus station. I'm spending the weekend in
the country.'

'In the country?' He smiled at her, the old smile. 'I should
have thought you'd had more than enough of the country,' he
said, brushing her cheek affectionately. 'What about looking in
at college, just for a moment? I've some mail to collect. And
there's a nice fire going. No pupils till four. So you and I could
sit and talk. You do know, don't you,' his voice was deep and
tender now, as at 2 a.m. on the telephone, 'my feelings towards
you are quite unaltered.'

They were passing the Methodist chapel, his head just under
the J of VOTE FOR JIGGS splashed up on the wall in cardinal red.

'I don't expect to meet anyone like you ever again,' she said
gravely. 'But surely you've more than enough on your hands
without counting me.'

'I always count you.'

'Well then, would you please see me to the bus station?'

'Is there only one bus?'

'Yes, only one.'

Parting, she remembered (chugging past the sports grounds,
bags on the rack), is all we know of heaven and all we need of
hell.

CHAPTER EIGHTEEN

The Foldings' house was old stone, sprawling, neatly tended, not surprising in any way. By the time Mary arrived, the apple picking was in full swing. That is to say Theo was up the ladder with a jelly-bag wired to the carpet-sweeper stick, Bernard below with a baby-scales basket, filled from the bag and then emptied into a bright green, rubber-wheeled wheelbarrow. The baby, a tow-headed, dark-eyed, latest Joan of Arc little girl, a perfect ball-game mascot with her thick knit sweater and scarlet jeans, was sitting in the wheelbarrow, tasting the last scarred Coxes, while Sir Basil Folding KCMG, MBE, sorted out keeping and non-keeping cookers into small conical heaps.

Mary, who had picked apples before, went inside to help with the tea. She had never managed to get very far with Lady Folding, but this did not prevent her admiring the teapot, buttering the scones, generally making herself likeable. A little discreet card-playing on such topics as the Freemantle family, or the new establishment in Somerset, might have been more successful if Mary had tried to play properly, which she did not. Some games are less amusing than others, but all the same the fact that she handled the pack at all was something in her favour.

The Masons, Lady Folding felt bound to admit, had some rather odd connections after all, hadn't they? Of course people did say the strangest things. She had heard that one of the Mason aunts, living in Maidenhead, wasn't it, kept a brother locked up in the boathouse. Could that be possible? Mary had no idea. By the time the cake forks had been distributed, the medals and other engraved mementoes in the show cabinet duly admired, they were getting on splendidly. Lady Folding thought it a great pity that Theodora and Mary saw so little of one another. She was also very sorry she hadn't been able to call in at the nursing home. But what with her back and Basil being away all the week with the car – he sat on so many committees that she just couldn't think what to do with the calendars – Still he did love being here really, his own home at last. Theodora was the moody one nowadays. She couldn't think why. Had Mary noticed how moody Theodora was? Oh well, she would. Of course it wasn't easy with the baby in London. Country air was so much better for little people. She was always telling them that. But then there was Bernard's work to think of. Mary hadn't by any chance seen him last week? No, they didn't have television either. Her eyes had been very troublesome lately. All the same it was such a comfort to know that Bernard was getting on well at last. And why Theodora with that lovely child shouldn't be as happy as the day was long she simply couldn't imagine. All this talk about taking a job too. Did Mary have a job? No, of course not. It was sad in a way to think of all that training gone to waste, but sooner or later didn't every woman realise that a well-run home was its own reward? As for those day nurseries, in her time no self-respecting girl would have dreamt of dumping their only daughter on a sandpit full of germs. Still, mothers mustn't interfere. Perhaps though if Mary could have a quiet chat some time with Theodora . . . was that everything now? Oh dear the lemon . . . she wouldn't mind? How sweet of her . . . just behind the bottled plums.

Tea put an end to apple picking for the day. Sir Basil, who had the privilege of drinking his two cups through the window, went back to his sorting, seeing that the gardener had just dropped in to have a look round and might be prepared to give advice. The gardener's wife dropped in soon after, equipped with a plastic apron advertising the better-known cocktails, prepared to lend a hand with the tea things, though this was Saturday and there was a football match going on. Since last harvest festival – it can't take all night to dispose of three marrows – she preferred not to let her husband walk home on his own.

Mary went upstairs with Theo to help bath the baby, now at the stage of getting everything into the water, especially watches.

'She's fallen in love with Queen Victoria,' Theo said, propping the red shoe upside down on the towel rail to drain. 'The last time out in Kensington Gardens she knelt before her for half an hour, clinging to the railings, screaming with rage whenever I tried to move her on. In fact she screamed so loud that an elderly gentleman let his best kite drop into the pond.' She skimmed off the larger scraps of sponge and tightened the taps.

Mary looked on from the driest corner. She followed the damp imperious little head, the chunky fist scrubbing tiles with a nailbrush, legs staunchly astride, all of a piece, wanton, inviolate. 'Rather nice, all the same, isn't she?'

'Might be worse.' Theo scooped her out of the water, whipped on a toga of towelling and started rubbing away before the sudden change might be recorded, though it was recorded nonetheless. 'Bit of a Whitworth sometimes, aren't you darling?' She made another pass at the ears. 'They all hate being touched.'

'Will you have any more?'

'I don't know.' Theo grabbed a safety-pin disappearing down the overflow. 'People do, don't they?' She put the watch back in the toothmug, and the toothmug on top of the bathroom cabinet.

'Can I do anything?'

'Well, if you'd just keep her away from the shaving cream.'

Mary put her into the laundry basket, while Theo mopped up a bit. 'I hear Bernard is doing well,' she said.

'Oh yes. He's supplementing his teaching now with life and times in ancient Greece. Question Time in the Agora. Tonight the Acropolis, Socrates speaks first. It all goes down very well, apparently . . .' She turned towards the laundry basket. Mary, gathering up the last shreds of soluble napkin and the rest of the matches, followed her into the nursery. 'What shall I do with these?' she said.

'Oh . . . in here.' Theo held out a plastic chamber pot lined with peppermints. 'Free play,' she said, smiling a little scarily. 'Once is nothing like enough.'

'Does she feed herself yet?'

'You'll see.' Theo rolled up the high chair and spread out the mackintosh sheets. Then she brought up a tray with the supper on it.

They came at last to figs, pensive fistfuls of figs.

'I hear you're thinking of taking a job,' Mary said.

'Yes.' Theo was sitting on the window-ledge, looking out over the dark lawn. 'I'm afraid my natural instincts are rather few and far between. I mean,' she flushed slightly, 'it's all very well being a glorified servant, but an unglorified one . . .' She was tracing now on the window pane, little pin-man saints bending down to pick up things.

'No one to see what you do?'

She nodded. 'I suppose so. Perhaps it all comes of getting so used to seeing your name pinned up on a list somewhere. I must say I thought medicine was pretty repetitive, but scouring a bath out night after night really saps one's self-esteem.'

'Some men,' Mary smiled a bit, 'are said to be so good about the house. I met Daniel this morning, quite by chance . . . and Eleanor.'

'Did you really?' Theo stopped looking out over the lawn. 'And what do you think of her, Eleanor?'

'I'd say he's met his match this time.'

'Yes,' Theo grinned happily. 'That's what I'd say too.'

Mary was looking at the miniature wash-basin, set in hand-painted tiles featuring fish – something, she thought, that might well have been installed in Somerset. 'Isn't it amazing,' she said, going back to the morning, and Daniel and Eleanor, 'what quiet little murders some people get away with.'

'Yes.'

The figs were coming to an end. Mary was thinking of broaching one or two problems connected with living in Somerset, when Lady Folding tapped at the door and came straight in, mustering the last tentative minutes with the importunate rapacity of one whose days are always planned.

'Are we not asleep yet?' is what she said.

Theo, seeing the inevitable approach of family ritual, with all its vicarious observances, suggested that if Mary liked to go downstairs, she would probably find Bernard in the study, first door on the left past the umbrella stand.

Bernard was sitting at the leather-topped desk in front of an ancient typewriter, with a pile of heavily scored proofs under the Anglepoise lamp. Mary noted with some satisfaction that in another five years he would probably be bald.

He was talking about his work. 'You know,' he stretched back, tipping the padded hide, one hand practising simple scales, the other rolling the red pencil, 'sometimes the circuit cuts out altogether. One's fingers just won't connect. I can see I'll have to get a secretary soon, or a tape recorder.' He looked at her curiously, very thick glasses and all. 'It's hard to know which of the two would be the most rewarding in my particular case.'

'Nice place to sit in,' she said, glancing along the built-in shelves of political history, cut short here and there by hints on hedging, happy plumbing, bee keeping . . .

'Oh yes, quite the stage set,' Bernard said. 'I have permission to make use of it during the afternoon, though I must confess I find the atmosphere somewhat paralysing.'

'Perhaps it's not quite all it seems.' She leant back off the coal box, picking out a stained copy of Stendhal's *De l'Amour*, closely annotated, as it turned out, in green ink. She mentioned this, putting the book back in its space.

'I dare say a good deal of pruning went on at one time.' He yawned emphatically. 'You know the Folding family motto – *Beyond retreat, above reproach*. It takes a lot of living up to, doesn't it?' At this he left the chair and started pacing up and down in front of the curtained bay windows.

Mary stayed sitting on the coal box. 'What are you at now?' she said.

'Oh, just a little skit on Diogenes, the bottom of whose tub, as some have already had occasion to observe, would not bear too close an examination.'

'What about that new Plato?'

'Numerology,' he scoffed. 'Nothing but numerology. About the lowest form of hackwork you could think of. That's what Theo simply won't understand.' He turned, gripping the desk, rocking slowly to and fro on it, as if it were all he had. 'Women are such absurd idealists . . . suckling babies in a basement, whilst I eke out a little more light on Wittgenstein, the last clause to Kant. That's what she'd really like.' He rocked on. 'As if it weren't more than enough to churn out some reach-me-down version of the whole bloody make-believe term after term.'

'Rather more noughts than crosses,' she said, for something to say.

'That's it.' He stopped rocking, leaning towards her, very excited. 'That's it exactly! How did you know?'

'I didn't,' she said quickly. 'Don't know anything, never have.'

'Oh no,' he smiled, 'of course not.' He started edging round the desk, still smiling. 'It looks as if you and I move on much the same tramlines,' he said softly, his hand on her shoulder.

'Do you really think so?' she leant back nearer the bookshelves.

'A drink might be nice,' she said then, patting his free hand in a there there now sort of way. He moved a bit closer.

'I won't be a minute.' She swivelled off the coal box, ducking for the door. 'Must just find my cigarettes.'

She did not come down again until Sir Basil had left his loft for the night and drinks had appeared in the sitting room. Bernard, coldly attentive to the point of indifference, offered her sherry and cigarettes from a silver box and a light from a silver lighter and a brass Indian ashtray, before resuming his dissertation on post-war rural economy. Towards his father-in-law he maintained, on the whole, the deferential, slightly truculent approach of a bright sixth-former. The two of them seemed to be very interested in what they were saying, though there was, as in so many masculine exchanges, the hint of an impasse, a sudden crunching of cog on cog, facts dangling absurdly irrelevant. Meanwhile transmission continued. And Mary drank sherry and smoked and appeared to be listening, though what she heard, three times running, was the front-door bell. The third time they must have heard it too. Anyhow Sir Basil, with a meticulous glance at the grandfather clock, excused himself on the fine hushed note of one now alas obliged to conduct important business elsewhere.

Mary got up to examine the family miniatures over the mantelpiece, while Bernard ran silently through the contents of his wallet.

'Only sherry?' Theo said, coming in before, but not very long before the possibilities of miniatures and wallets had quite run out.

'Not too bad this time,' Bernard said, picking up the decanter, swirling it round in the tasselled light of the standard lamp, considering its colour.

Theo turned to unhook her sequinned shawl from the piano key. A little drawn, but bravely reassembled from the day's scrub and scatter, she looked game enough for the first half of the evening. 'Guess who came on the bus,' she said.

Bernard gave the decanter a last quick swirl before putting it back on the lacquered tray. 'The gardener's nephew on leave from the NAAFI,' he suggested. 'Or could it be the latest delegate from the Privy Council, disguised as a vacuum salesman? Country life is so full of delightful surprises, like running out of milk, or excavating the septic tank.'

'Well, this time it happens to be Dermot.' Theo turned to Mary. 'Do you remember that party? Dermot McNeill?'

Mary did.

'I presume he's now in the study,' Bernard said, 'engaged in a quick little conference on behalf of the Orkney Republic. Or would it be France again? Some new alliance? Free trips for the boys?'

'I've no idea.' Theo helped herself to some more sherry.

And so did Mary. 'What happened to his arm, by the way?' she said.

'I'm not sure, really. I believe it got ripped off in the Métro by some mob of hysterical women determined to get in or out. He never mentions it.'

Bernard was whistling softly through his teeth. 'Staying the night, I suppose,' he said casually. 'Did you bring those records along?'

'I did . . . for Mary. I thought she might like them.'

'Mary?' Ah yes, of course.' He nodded, largely to himself. 'Another thwarted Francophile. *Sonnez la cloche*,' he minced. '*Messieurs, mesdames, le dîner est servi.*'

Dinner passed without incident. Dermot McNeill, forking up boiled fowl strategically, provided his end of the table with a moving oration on the death of Robespierre, including the gouging of bullets out of the shattered jaw. He spoke well, with all the sardonic elaboration, even bland distortion now and then, of one determined at all costs to distract himself.

Lady Folding enquired after his aunt, who used to work with her on the Red Cross. Bernard toyed with great wines – they were drinking Cypriot white – while Mary up the other end was cross-examined on public rights of way in Somerset. Sir Basil had, it appeared, recently taken to sitting on a board committed to the fostering and furthering of National Parks.

'. . . and then, of course,' she concluded hopefully, 'there's a lot of moor, not used much for anything. People could walk all over that, if they wanted to.'

'Not a keen rambler, are you?' he said.

'No, not a keen rambler.'

There was port then for the gentlemen, washing up for the ladies, the gardener's wife being obliged to see to her husband's supper, before lending a hand at the village hall on behalf of the Countrywomen's Association.

After the coffee and cocoa liqueur – a present from the Lebanese Legation – their host retired to his study, admitting, under jocular family pressure, that he was now engaged in writing his memoirs. Only a very small volume though, nothing personal. Just his slant on one or two of the more notable problems of recent years.

'So that's that, then,' Theo said, as he left the room. 'Now we'll never know.'

'Know what, dear?' Lady Folding blinked at her innocently, if persistent ignorance drawing near the last, bleary post may pass for innocence. As it may.

Theo started plumping up the hand-thonged leather pouffe, a present from a cousin in Kenya. 'All right, Mother, it's not a play,' she said.

'A play? Of course it's not a play. Whoever thought it was?' Because of her back and her eyes too – she had grown old here all alone one day – Lady Folding retired soon after, leaving the young people to enjoy themselves in their own way.

They went out to the pub, to find the semi-finals of the local darts championship well under way and not a free stool in the place. No draught bitter either. But having come, they stayed. And after the second round Dermot and Bernard were well under way too, exchanging passages from *Paradise Lost*, Dermot as if these words were the only ones he wanted just then, Bernard as if to prove that he had once wanted them too, every bit as much. Theo and Mary listened on and off, nodding and smiling, getting their glasses filled – women watching men. Eventually they were all able to sit down, and at closing time Dermot bought a bottle of whisky.

Past the church, down the high-walled lane smelling of pigs and straw, Bernard and Theo kept some way ahead, discussing who was to go back to London and how and when. Dermot took Mary's arm. 'Hear the voice of the bard,' he whispered, and then, all down the lane –

> '*O saw ye bonnie Lesley*
> *As she gaed o'er the Border?*
> *She's gane, like Alexander,*
> *To spread her conquests farther.*'

'Come on,' he said, 'Sing! Why don't you sing?'

'Can't sing,' she said.

He went on fitfully till they reached the low iron gates glinting in the moonlight.

'Shall we shut them?' Mary stood fingering the lumpy paint, still sticky here and there.

'Point of view,' he said, and they left them open. 'Not a bad night.' They stepped up on to the frosty grass, kicking apples as they went. 'Owls about.'

'Yes,' she said. 'And mice maybe.'

Back in the sitting room Bernard produced the records.

'Review pickings,' he said, 'palmed off on me by someone who suddenly finds himself allergic to the French language. Here you are? He put them all down beside Dermot. 'No Viking two-steps from the Outer Hebrides, I'm afraid.'

'Thank God for that.' Dermot, whose patriotic outbursts were confined to a few highly discriminating compatriots, started shuffling through the shiny covers. '*Phèdre*,' he said finally. 'Let us hear *Phèdre*.'

'That'll suit you too, won't it Mary?' Bernard turned back to Dermot. 'Mary here is always getting herself locked up in country places.'

'Oh?'

'Whilst Bernard,' Mary collected herself slowly, 'thinks he

can cover the whole countryside on tramlines.'

And that, for the moment, was that. Bernard took charge of
the gramophone which, like the Stendhal, had not been used
for a long time. After the first side Theo remembered once
again that she'd have to be up early in the morning. This time
she said so.

'And what about you, Mary? You must be pretty done in.
First night up and all that.'

Mary who had, earlier in the evening, felt cast in lead, with
certain areas still molten, said she was doing fine actually,
wouldn't be long though and that whisky was far more soothing than Ovaltine. The gramophone started up again. Bernard
pointed out various cuts and defects in interpretation. Dermot,
as one long accustomed to all manner of blots on an intimate
landscape, nodded indifferently, whilst Mary, who had not
heard *Phèdre* before and could follow about half of it, said
nothing. They played all four sides . . .

'*Et la mort à mes yeux dérobant la clarté. Rend au jour qu'ils
souillaient toute* . . .' Dermot paused, eyes closed, '*sa pureté.*' He
bowed his head. He spoke perfect French.

'Pity she had to hiss it like that,' Bernard said.

And then for the first time Dermot looked at Mary. A grand
and glorious conspiracy had been growing steadily between
them, a conspiracy to get rid of Bernard. Bernard, of course,
knew this.

'What about a little *Bateau ivre* for light relief?' he said.
'Barrault at his Romeo and Juliet best. Or Brassens now, the modern Villon? . . . Oh well, far be it from me to disturb the spiritual
communion. You know where your room is, don't you Dermot?'

'Yes, thank you. Won't you have a drop more whisky before
you go?' Dermot held up the bottle. 'A rather shrunken
nightcap?'

'No thanks, not for me.' Bernard moved to the door. 'Work, you know. My knocking, or should one say tapping hour.'

'I envy you.' Dermot divided the rest of the bottle between his glass and Mary's. 'Good-night then,' he said.

'Good-night.' Bernard switched out the main light. 'I don't suppose you'll forget the others.' He laughed, not a very pleasant laugh, and left the room.

'*Un plus noble dessein m'amène devant vous,*' Dermot said cheerfully.

And they drank to that.

'You kiss very well,' he admitted a little while later. 'Must have had a lot of practice.'

'Intuition,' she murmured. And then 'I must go', several times, wondering how drunk he was.

'You'll come and see me, later,' he insisted.

'No, not tonight. Soon,' she said. 'Soon', in case he might change his mind.

CHAPTER NINETEEN

Sunday morning it was raining, with not enough news-papers to go round. Once up there was no getting away from anyone, if you were looking for newspapers that is, and coffee. Sir Basil had his own mug up in the loft, where he was prudently employed assembling apple trays, never at a loss for long.

Bernard and Dermot had the papers and the coffee pot in the sitting room, Bernard expostulating at every other column, Dermot fitting epigrams into the more spacious advertisements. Mary was helping Theo; at least she wanted to talk to her, rather than stay on in the sitting room once the coffee was gone. But first there were milk of magnesia pills and beauty grains to be scraped off the carpet, toilet rolls to be fished out of all three lavatory bowls, and then the artichokes to be got ready for soup. Lady Folding was very proud of her artichoke soup. So Mary didn't do much talking to Theo. She gathered, in the lull of helping the baby pick currants out of the flour bin, that Bernard would probably be taking the family car to London that evening. If he did, and if Mary really had to get back so soon, he could certainly give her a lift to the station. She also gathered that Theo didn't think Dermot was going straight back to London. That he'd been married something like twenty years. They hardly knew his wife, in fact Theo had only met her once. Yes, she was quite good-looking, adamantine, according to Bernard, though she reminded Theo of one of those wooden figureheads, goddesses was it, they used to have on the prows of boats. And then it was that Lady Folding decided it might be nice to have bread sauce, just for a change.

During lunch it became pretty clear that Bernard was not going to get the car after all, seeing that it would be wanted in the morning for visiting National Parks. So Bernard decided to wait till the morning too, it being quite impossible, he said, to hold a paper clip between your teeth, let alone prepare a lecture, on the Sunday night train. Theo was clearly pleased he was staying, for marriage had so shaped her life that Bernard present on any terms seemed better than Bernard gone.

Various plans having been made, kindly greetings given and taken, last-minute alternatives politely suggested and more politely declined, Dermot and Mary left on the afternoon bus. Apart from a family party up the front and one or two old men in greasy caps, along with their small bundles screwed up in newspaper, they had it to themselves. There was another bus later, time enough for the ramblers to unpack the honey and eggs, rinse out the Thermoses, stuff autumn leaves into clay vases, before another week's work began. The baby wanted to come too, clung to the unwound window, great eyes fixed on the luggage rack, and was carried off as the driver climbed in, bucking like a rabbit.

'Have you any children?' Mary said, soon after they'd got going. It was the first time she had spoken to him that day.

'Several,' he said. 'Nothing much else to have after all, is there?'

'No, I suppose not.'

Perhaps it was then, about then anyway, that Mary knew she was lost. She had, of course, wanted to be lost for a very long time, but this was fog, all-absorbing fog, where the least word, gesture, silence even, looms unretrievable. For love, perfect or imperfect, far from casting out fear, may well be built upon it, if the need is great enough and the balance too fine, too intricate and strange for ordinary use. Looking back, for she was of course to look back, it was only here in the bus that he'd told her anything she'd wanted to know, anything about himself that is, the usual signposts people look for trying to find their way about.

He was forty-one. He lived in Putney. Yes, on the river. Any water was better than none. His father had been gassed on the Somme, fighting for England, yes dear old England God bless her. His mother had brought him up. It hadn't been easy, no, scholarship boy. She'd died too, soon after he'd got to the university. Not Glasgow. Edinburgh. History and French, nice polished pursuits. He had married young. His wife and children were in the country at present, not very far away, no. Staying with the family, her family. He found her family a little depressing these days. He worked in London mostly, that was correct. Not his favourite city by any means, but then his job was not what you might call designed to emphasise the liberty of the individual. Just now he was taking a week off, one of the three. Yes, only three. He was spending it here in the library. How slow they could be at times. You'd almost think the whole staff did nothing but joy-ride on that underground railway of theirs. Not French this time, no. Political History. The ways and means of certain Lord Advocates of Scotland during the latter years of that far from illustrious regime.

And that then was all he told her by way of biography. Mary, hunting for cigarettes (he did not smoke, never had), came upon photographs of the house in Somerset, taken by Martin to prove to her father what had been or should still be done. If it hadn't been for the way things were, the way Dermot was prin- cipally, she might well have asked him down to stay some weekend. But they'd clearly passed that stage long ago. So she showed him one of the photographs, saying that this was where she lived and that it was quite a nice place to live, still vaguely hoping, though not believing, he might get there one day.

'Every shade of money,' he suggested, at which she could only agree.

The fog crept closer. Just rain from the look of it, with the bus picking up, putting down, throbbing on. It was quite a new bus, so they could hear one another perfectly well.

'You'll have a drink,' he said, as the last frenzied sweep of machinery shuddered to its stopping place, dead on time, and the family party got its small ones out first and the old men tightened their bundles. The bus station clock said a quarter to four and the fast train to Somerset left at six.

They left her bag at the bus station and walked to his hotel, private and commercial, with a very narrow entrance and a washpail and scrubbing brush abandoned in the hall. He had his key with him.

'Not bad here,' he said, hanging up the coats. 'I could have got myself a guest-room in one of the colleges. But it looks as if,' he came to her then, 'that might have been most mistaken . . . Better get those things off,' he added softly. 'I won't be a moment.'

Mary sat on the brass bedstead, looking out on the dripping leaves, the old wall topped with broken glass. And then she put her last 10-lire piece in the gas meter and started to undress, wondering why it was all wrong once again, whether it would ever be right.

He came back with a long bottle of Kirsch, uncorked. She

couldn't imagine where he'd got it from on a Sunday afternoon.

'This should keep the damp out,' he said. And it did.

Mary missed the last train. Later on down the road over beer – she drank cider – and sandwiches, she told him she thought there might be another train in an hour or so. They did not check up on this. She told him she wasn't English at all really, father Swiss, mother Irish, brought up in grand hotels round the world, parents now living in Buenos Aires. She also said that her husband was very fond of Greece and was always encouraging her to take a lover. This partly because some excuse seemed necessary and partly because it was true and perhaps he might like to know. Perhaps he might also like to know that she'd been married before, to a mathematical mind. And that she'd tried living in Paris, but couldn't quite take it. He said he couldn't quite take it either. One of these days he'd be writing a book on certain aspects of the French mentality entitled *A B C . . . et puis glissade*. And she laughed a little uncomfortably, feeling he might always have everything worked out well in advance. For he had also said *c'est le premier pas qui conte*.

They drank till the pub closed, and back in the hotel bedroom (washpail and scrubbing brush on the landing now) he drank more, while she sat back feeling a bit giddy. Then the telephone rang.

'Hallo,' he said. 'Yes. I'm afraid I am,' in a voice which was not the voice of a man talking to men. 'Of course I shall . . . Goodbye.' And he rang off, very neat and nonchalant.

'I see you're well looked after here,' she said. He did not disagree. 'You know,' she went on, smiling too, 'I really must get back to Somerset somehow. We're off the telephone after ten. Now you wouldn't leave anyone hanging about all night, would you, wondering whether you'd get smashed up?'

'It happens to all of us,' he said.

There was, he knew, one sure way of keeping her, and he kept her.

It was not the knocking that wakened them. They'd been lying there silent for quite a while, listening to the rain. By the time Dermot had got himself ready to unlock the door, tea and toast had been left outside the mat. Tea and toast for two though, which was, come to think of it, almost as odd as that bottle of Kirsch, considering that this was England and a most respectable neighbourhood. Dermot didn't touch the marmalade. So Mary didn't touch it either. Marmalade boiled down all of a sudden to the essence of cosy frivolity. And there was certainly nothing cosy or frivolous about the two of them there just then.

He shaved, while she felt her chin. It didn't hurt much if she kept her mouth shut, but was pretty sticky over a wide area, and would, she imagined, form a crust.

'There's a very tough bit just here,' he said, stroking his jaw, staring into the wash-basin mirror, as if it might possibly splinter all over if he stared hard enough. 'No help for it, I'm afraid,' he concluded, reaching for the towel.

'It's all right. I like it that way.' And soon she was stroking his hair again, straightening his tie. 'All the same,' she said, tucking in the empty sleeve, 'you seem to know well enough how to take your revenge.' For this was so. It was also the one thing she never meant to say, the one thing that mattered most.

'What strange ideas you have,' he said.

They walked out past the steam laundry, along by the canal – a waste limb of it that nobody ever mentioned in the guidebooks. The shell of a punt, with the cushions still in it, lay rotting in the reeds, and higher up one grey swan floated unseeing among the buckled tyres and rings of scum. It wasn't raining any more, not much anyway. Now and then trucks changed gear in the distance, factories hooted, trains whistled down the line.

'*Noël sur la terre,*' he said drily.

'I know.' She wished more than ever he didn't have to feel that way, didn't have to insist that she felt it too. 'But isn't it our fault? I mean –' she stepped back quickly. The boy on the racing bike swerved on up the tow path, flags flying, bells ringing, terrier dripping and panting after him. 'That boy now,' she drew up again, 'he can't hear you, never will. What if we've been picking up the wrong words all the time, dismissing the ones in large print along with the picture blocks?'

'That rather depends on what you're looking for,' he said. 'Sooner or later you'll take what you want.' And further on, a little more eagerly, across the steaming wheels of the train to Somerset. 'Give me a ring some time, won't you?'

'I will,' she said.

CHAPTER TWENTY

Martin was busy with the outhouses. When Martin was busy with anything, he thought about it all the time. And would talk about it too, if any talking was going on. In fact he didn't much notice people, unless they happened to be in his light. If beautiful then, he wanted them, momentarily; if useful he made use of them; and if members of his family, he did his best to make them see things his way. His way was a long established one: rolling pastures, with one or two noble chimneystacks down the valley: wilderness won over, disguised rather as cultivated space. For he loved elegance and silence and deep green grass. And now there was money, on certain terms, to have all this, to own it, for he needed to feel quite sure it would never be taken from him. The terms were not his terms, the money not his either, but then old Gallen was pretty soft after all, if you knew how to handle him. And Martin knew how to handle him. They were all the same, weren't they, those rich Victorian papas? You just told them what they wanted to hear in their own language, playing up the only daughter, much-loved most generous utterly indispensable father side in the first and last paragraphs, with an occasional, very occasional hint that the only daughter might be carried off

to Tibet if things were made too difficult. These then were the
lines he'd been working on. If they hadn't been quite so successful as he'd hoped, there were several others he might try,
only he hadn't got round to thinking about these others yet. It
was not so much the money he wanted, as his childhood safely
restored on a somewhat sounder basis than the original. For he
had lost it all very suddenly – family, house and lands.
Admittedly the family were not dead, the shaky old house was
still standing, the lands still grazed; but the ties had been cut
without any warning and all the lofts and lanes of his childhood
sold up, not for a song so much as a banana farm, while he was
still at school. Now he wanted them back. For in England,
married, with maybe a family one day of his own, his mind
worked that way. In Greece, stripped of such pieties, it had all
been much simpler – no house and lands, no silver candle-
sticks, no security. But grants ran out. and now he was getting
on for thirty. So what could be wiser and sounder and safer
than a house in the country, his own country, wife and children,
something to fall back upon. Something he'd always wanted, in
a way. A perfect setting for his work too, if he was ever to do
anything really worth while.

Mary wanted it perfect too, on and off, each new mess at any
rate cleared up as quickly as possible. For the setting was far
from complete, and it had all been going on for a very long
time. It was true that the crates of Parian marble made an excel-
lent carpentry bench. Martin was sure that he'd sculpt all the
better for having mastered the ins and outs of the building
trade. And weren't those oval windows, with their little venti-
lation disks, far more beautiful in the long run than a tangle of
wire labelled Freedom, or Man in Chains?

Mary was up in her room at the elm desk she had drawn to
scale, looking out through the panes of glass she had traced,

seen cut, packed into the car with 5 per cent discount for cash, on to the evening moors. The room was long, low, lined with open bookshelves, just as she'd wanted it, and she knew exactly how much each strip of the native oak flooring had cost. At least she had copied out the figures twice, in case her father might decide to pretend that the first set had never reached him. At this particular moment she would gladly have traded the whole property for the St John Ambulance hut on Putney Bridge.

> Dearest Daddy,
>   I hope you're dead by Christmas . . .

She started again.

> Dearest Daddy,
>   Thank you for your letters of the 26th/7th/8th. This is to wish you a very happy birthday. I do see that the drought . . .

She got up to examine her chin. It was still peeling. The chin story – party, drink, borrowed make-up, probably some sort of allergy, and something wrong with the telephone line – had not gone down very well. It wouldn't have been quite so bad, Martin said, if she'd enjoyed it. But just out of the nursing home, getting beaten up like that. It all seemed a little pointless to him. Perhaps it should be explained here that they had an arrangement, Martin and Mary, the sort of arrangement almost any young man would gladly get his future wife to sign. It was all most reasonable, and, needless to say, it had never worked. So far only Martin had made use of it. His comings and goings were quite sudden on the whole, pretty brief and followed by great guilt. On such occasions Mary stayed in, pretending not to mind, though she did mind, very much, seeing that she'd nothing much else to think about then, up there on the moors, other than what he was doing and how, and with whom. She'd agreed to the moors in the first place largely because they seemed far enough from the sort of streets Martin might want to pace at night. Unfortunately this pacing of streets, driving off rather in the car – a long-awaited, much-corresponded-over replacement from South America – to the nearest park benches and guards barracks, made a lot, indeed all the difference when it came to Martin's sculpting. And it was always coming to that. It was not so much the actual driving off that worried her as the nightly threat that he might drive off, if thwarted in any way. After the first year, she even found herself encouraging him to go, partly because she liked reading at night, not talking about her father and the house and lands, but more, much more because she could hardly help it, such twists being part of the pattern of living like this, going on wanting what she couldn't get. And what she wanted, presumably, was some slight acknowledgement that the way she happened to be made might be pleasing rather than practical. At the time, unfortunately, that such associations might well have been laid, Martin's attention had been confined to the shower-house and shrubberies of his public school, one of the more militant variety.

Still, they had their arrangement. Since her return, long bath and longer sleep, a touchy truce had wavered between them, on the understanding, his of course, that she would never do anything so silly again. He was in fact very hurt, being, as he saw it, his wife's sole protector, not only against her father, but against herself. Bearing this in mind, insisting on it whenever there might be any doubt, he felt worthier altogether. And indeed at the time he was not far wrong, though the protection referred to was hardly fortifying, except by way of a walling-off, which looked like being quite impenetrable, unless they ran out of materials before very long.

Mary left the mirror, having noted, apart from the chin, the appearance of certain scaly patches here and there, indicative, she presumed, of some deep inner conflict. Or could it be vitamin deficiency? She returned, not to the letter, but to Racine. She'd never much looked at him before: too grand, too Greek perhaps, too many capital letters anyway. But this was no longer so. She had even come to copying out lines, leaning them off by heart, like a schoolgirl. And she'd screwed them up then and poked them into the new boiler, so as not to block up the drains.

This was Wednesday, nine days got through on Racine and nine bottles of Rhine wine. On Friday, 8 a.m., she took the car to London, on the pretext of a medical check-up, and also to get the gramophone repaired. From the Leicester Square Lyons after several coffees and several more cigarettes, she rang Whitehall. There were several connections to be got through. Dermot said he was quite busy, yes, but sounded pleased.

They met outside the National Gallery and had lunch in a little oyster bar he knew, just off the Strand. It was all very nice, except that Mary found by the time it arrived that she couldn't swallow anything.

'I should have thought you'd have booked a room here for the afternoon,' he said, as they walked back past the Charing Cross Hotel.

She said it would have been a good idea and that she was very sorry it hadn't occurred to her. Coming into Trafalgar Square they met a friend of his. Mary, having been introduced, stood aside looking into a bookshop window.

'Perhaps you'd rather not meet any of my friends in

future,' he said, as they went on down Whitehall.

He was back in the office by a quarter to three and she spent the afternoon reading in St James's Park, since he had suggested they might meet again soon after six, in a certain wine house he knew, if she could spare the time, that was. It wasn't too windy round by the fountains. If Mary hadn't been bothered by her watch, which kept stopping, it could have been a most enjoyable afternoon.

He was half an hour late, getting his hair cut. It seemed to her almost irrelevant that he should have hair at all, except in so far as it was black and his. She had, on the way from the park, bought herself an eyebrow pencil, tried it out in a telephone kiosk, rubbed it all off again, well aware that it wasn't her mind that interested him, nor was it for that matter her eyebrows. As things were, with a little mishandling he could destroy her. And she him possibly, though this was far less likely.

Meanwhile he talked and she agreed. Occasionally they gripped hands. The drinks were a long time coming.

'Good God, this country,' he said, bringing the last lot over, himself. 'Your change, sir. Thank *you*, sir. First come first served, you know . . . The whole place reeks of scented disinfectant.'

He had, apparently, still two weeks leave left, and there was just a chance of getting to Paris, all expenses paid. He wasn't the only man for the job, but he'd do his best to convince the authorities that this was so. Mary said she thought she'd be able to get away all right, that she could do as she liked, really. And he told her where they'd have dinner on the first night. She didn't know where this was, but smiled all the same, as if it were just the place she'd been thinking of, though it did occur to her that he might have invented it. For there was a mischievous note in his voice sometimes, suggesting that any plans for the future were not to be taken too seriously. Soon after eight he decided he'd have to be getting back, so she offered to drive him to Putney.

'A chaste life, from the look of it,' he said a little sceptically, glancing round at the books and the unrepaired gramophone on the back seat.

'Simple rural pleasures,' she said.

He had a car too, made to measure, but he couldn't afford to run it this year, what with the rent and the school fees going up. He had a son at school in Scotland. Quite a good school, but the governors seemed to be more than a little intoxicated by the possibilities of insurance. Long sickness scheme; short sickness scheme; loss of school hours scheme; laundry scheme. What about a collarbone scheme, compulsory betting on the part of all parents and guardians again the shrinkage of football boots? And all for Latin, and Greek of course. And Scotland. So far his son seemed a good deal more interested in football than anything else. He said that parents and guardians were once again requested to note that the fees were still less than double those charged twenty-five years ago. He also said that money was bread and wine, body and blood, whichever way you looked at it. *Chacun pour soi et le bon Dieu pour tous.* And what could be more estimable than a heart of gold? She wished once again that she'd kept those photographs to herself. It was a bit late now to start explaining how she'd come by a house in Somerset with all those pillars and anti-downdraught chimney pots. Nor was there any explaining the ostrich-skin handbag, now lying under the clutch pedal, except that she'd hoped it would last for years. She touched his knee – his clothes were essentially dark and worn, with just enough buttons to go round. There was nothing redundant about him, except perhaps the gold chronometer on his wrist.

'Down here,' he said. And they drew up, by mutual consent, in a cul-de-sac alongside the river, not very far from where he lived, not very far either from other cars drawn up with their lights switched off. The river ran high past the jetty, molten in the orange light coming from Putney Bridge.

'You don't happen to know the owner of that, do you?' she said, looking out at the cabin boat anchored there, a little arc in midstream with its huge happy eye.

'No, I'm afraid not.' And later, 'You're sure you'll be all right now, going back?'

'Yes,' she said. 'I'll be all right.'

CHAPTER TWENTY-ONE

There were several Fridays much the same. He was going abroad soon after Christmas, for six months or so. Promotion? Possibly, but how long, oh Lord, how long. She didn't want to stay in this country for ever, did she? No, of course not. He said that he had three lives – public, scholastic and emotional – and that twenty-four hours in the day was nothing like enough. He hadn't quite realised till now what a net he was in. He was not ambitious, no, just liked looking on, only one must admit that some views could be rather more stimulating than others. The prospect of Paris grew more remote.

On one occasion he was setting down an epigram on a scrap of paper (she had none), arising out of the prospect of Paris growing more remote. On handing it over he suggested that she might perhaps take a look at the other side too. It was in red type: regretting that any further cheques drawn on this account . . .

She sent him money, all she could raise from the building overdraft, anonymously of course, to further his historical researches. People did do that occasionally, after all, didn't they? She had a friend, she explained to the bank manager, whose daughter needed an urgent operation. Only one man in the country could do it, not the man her friend's daughter would get by sitting in the outpatients' department. Not that her friend's daughter *could* sit anyhow; it had already got far beyond that. And would they kindly not mention any of this to her husband, who did not always see eye to eye with her in such matters . . . She gathered from the bank that he'd got it all right and didn't much mind his paying for the drinks after that. One pays for rarity, he said, which was a little ambiguous.

He was often ambiguous, using words largely to set off some series of chain reactions depending on their emotional hold over the company present. The better read the company, the more fun it could all be, though he didn't have any fun really, this being one of the last games left for those who read a lot. And Mary, who had had a good deal of this type of entertainment before, B+ variety admittedly from Daniel, was still hoping it might be dismissed as a sideline.

Having stipulated anguish as a man's basic condition, he said that she was rather Nordic, wasn't she? Then back to Pascal and Baudelaire. There was, she might as well know it now, nothing he disliked more than romanticism. As for living prudently, that was not living at all. He talked about freedom, like a Frenchman, about justice, order and anarchy, and, just occasionally, about Scotland, which he would, she suspected, like to see attached (in a highly liberal fashion) to France, if anywhere. Whatever he said, she let it be. He was an expert juggler. His tightrope was a high one, way above hers, all steel, professional steel, and he'd been on it a good many years now, too many to ever come down again for an hour or two, let alone a day. Unless . . . but this was to overestimate that power, the miraculous invention of women for men. Sometimes she thought he needed her – to sit on the steps, pick up the props, smile when only a smile would do. More often she did not. Whatever the terms that kept him up there twisting along, there was nothing easy about them. And she knew very well that the fall of a sparrow, however fond, would not be provided for. Meanwhile, if he claimed, for the moment, to be a follower of John Stuart Mill, then so, for the moment, did she.

It was late in November. He got busier, more evasive, said there were a lot of conferences going on. She offered half-jokingly to act as his secretary, but he was quite seriously afraid that would not be possible. He wanted to know just who she'd been speaking to, getting through to him on the phone, for it was always she who rang from the Leicester Square Lyons, always she who drove him home. Only the switchboard girls, she said. No one else? No, no one else. They drank in a colder, emptier pub, and even there, in the darkest corner with his back to the bar, he kept glancing round, hunching up, lowering his voice.

She parked the car in a different street and drove him back in a different way.

He was going to Scotland for a long weekend to see his son. Car? Yes, he'd got hold of a car thank you. There was clearly more to it than that. Paris was off, his presence there, in an advisory capacity, not required for the time being. That Mary said she didn't mind all that much was in his opinion a most Christian approach.

The Friday before he left for Scotland they were due to meet, soon after six, in the lounge this time, one of the upstairs lounges of the Charing Cross Hotel. It was a very large lounge, quite warm, designed presumably for private gatherings of a somewhat more businesslike nature than this one. He was nearly an hour late, carrying a new rubber ball, too big for its bag, and a new AA book of road maps. She told him then, for the first time, in a roundabout way, that she loved him . . . it

had been a very long week, would take a while for the froth to
settle, and wouldn't it be best to put the ball on an ashtray? It
might at least stay still there. He didn't seem to like the look of
the ball at all, anywhere. And it wouldn't quite fit into any
of the ashtrays. He reminded her then, very firmly, that the art
of living was largely a question of being a good loser. She said
you can't go on losing all the time surely, that there must be a
little more to it than that, and that anyhow she'd never been
much good at games – the whole wretched armoury flung up
against point-blank defeat.

He was gentler then, oddly attentive, and before getting out
of the car an hour or so later, at the jetty, he told her exactly
which day he'd be back and exactly what time would be best for
her to ring. It didn't seem quite so bad then, his going to
Scotland to see his son.

'Dear God,' he said, looking up at the sky, though there
weren't any stars out. And this time he watched while she
revved and stalled, backing up the lane.

He wasn't back the day he said . . . maybe tomorrow or the next
day. The switchboard girl, whom Mary was beginning to feel
she had sat next to for years at school, wanted to know if there
was anyone else she would like to speak to instead . . . The
third time she rang early, from the village post office in
Somerset. It was Thursday and he was back. She said she'd
have to be up in town after lunch anyway, to see the dentist.
He said he sometimes wondered whether she lived in Somerset
at all.

They met back in the wine house this time, and he was there
first waiting for her. He seemed more decisive than usual, said
straight away that he couldn't stay long. He'd had a good time
in Scotland, yes, climbed a mountain. No, not Arthur's Seat.

His son was very well, getting quite fond of Virgil. And then, just before they came to the second round, he wanted to know whether she could get away this coming weekend. She was almost sure she could. Saturday then, twelve o'clock, get off before the rush. They hadn't much time after all. Did he have to be back on the Monday as usual? Unfortunately it looked very much as if he did. They might go somewhere by the sea, he thought. Not Brighton? No, of course not. She could leave all the arrangements to him. Meanwhile how could he get in touch with her? She nearly said he could always ring, but, realising just in time what this would almost certainly mean, the way that instrument had squatted beside her in the past, she said she would let him know if anything went wrong. Otherwise Saturday, twelve o'clock or soon after. Here? Yes, here would do.

It was rather like being invited to join some brave and beautiful organisation, to lead a mission of the highest importance, as soon as you got your breath. And this after years on a rubbish dump, within sight of the latest headquarters, within shouting distance, if you could only shout, selling squash bottles with the labels picked off, at twopence each.

They got off before the rush. Here and there he pointed out national monuments which did not greatly appeal to him. Otherwise they said very little, making this time not for Slough and the West, but for Hatfield and the North. She said it was nice not to be driving him home, for once, to which he did not reply. Further on they stopped to eat at a roadhouse. He offered her a Pimms to start with, which didn't help very much, being rather too flippant a drink perhaps for such an occasion, though he didn't quite follow this. Getting back to the car he kissed her; that and the bottle of wine with the lunch made things much easier.

It was a long way to the coast, to the unspoilt village, the old coaching inn, with its tarred car park quite empty now, apart from a bright blue and yellow agricultural device and a milkman's electric scooter.

'Not much chance of our coming across any acquaintances this time of year,' he said. He had stayed here once before, years ago. There had been a fair then, in the car park he thought, though he couldn't be sure. A proper fair, smelling of engine oil, with swingboats and coconuts.

They left the car in a corner, all by itself, too tucked away to be anything but obviously not belonging to the place. For it wasn't Scotland, nor was it France, and it was all terribly tidy.

Their room was called Abraham Lincoln, in black Gothic script, just past the Bridal Chamber. It looked out on to a miniature Methodist mosque, an antique dealer specialising in ships' lanterns and a thatched and pargetted Barclays bank.

Mary changed for dinner. Her case – more the three-weeks than the two-day size – had been received and handled by Dermot with barely concealed disgust, as if such accessories were not merely extravagant but quite ridiculous in the circumstances. And so they were, the bottom layer consisting largely of what had not yet been unpacked from Sicily, because of the building. Still, having brought a dress along, she thought she might as well wear it. Much as a chronic invalid, alone late at night with another attack coming on, might rip out the curlers, grope for a hairbrush, not to be found wanting in the morning. Dermot shaved, though it was already a little late to do so, considering what he now referred to as her chin of glass. He had brought nothing with him, apart from a safety razor and several blades.

They dined in the alcove, second sitting, like a honeymoon couple. Not far off the wife of a certain ambassador was enter-taining various members of her family, resident presumably in the district. He knew her well. The children were already on to ice-creams, and when they next looked round, the party had moved on, jack-knives and dolls, reading glasses and all, which made things a little more comfortable.

'Wine in a bucket.' Mary laughed. 'The first sign of sin.'

'Not too bad, is it?' He refilled their glass.

'Not bad at all,' she said.

They did not have coffee in the non-resident lounge, nor liqueurs in the cocktail parlour, but one beer and one cider in the saloon bar. This was steadily filling up with rural pensioners, feeble greys and browns, and the odd not too disabled seaman, strict navy-blue, waiting for the summer. They were all smoking and drinking very very slowly, a few wheezing and snuffling over pegs and ancient cards, much like a birthday party in a geriatric ward. There were nothing but firebricks to sit on, so they left after the first round and went out to look at the sea.

'Should be a footpath somewhere near here,' he said. But they didn't look very far. It was cold and dark, and they hadn't much time.

They didn't look far in the morning either. The Methodist mosque had installed a carillon. Otherwise the sea hadn't much to contend with up there; they had, of course, both seen sea before, a good deal less tidy, and anyhow they didn't need sea just then. Or so it seemed, perhaps because it was too late now for them to try walking hand in hand by any water. Or possibly too soon. They got up for lunch, and after lunch they started back, by the coast road, though there wasn't much coast the way they were going, and the railway ran along it. It was all mapped out in miles to the inch. Monday morning, 10 a.m., he was due back on the office steps. Now and then they took a green up and down road, instead of a flat red one, but sooner or later the signs said London. Now and then she took a bend too fast on the wrong side. Neither much minded that.

It was getting on for five. Just over an hour and they'd be where he planned they should spend this night, be there in good time for dinner. Another old inn, on a river this time; the food there used to be good. He had not booked, but then this wasn't the flat racing season after all.

Mary hadn't spoken for some time. At the next lay-by she turned in, with a bit of a wave to no one behind her.

'Sorry,' she said, switching off, 'but my hands were starting to shake.'

He was looking straight ahead, and when he spoke it was quiet and slow, as if to himself.

'. . . quand il fallut s'asseoir à la croix dans deux routes
Et choisir le regret d'avecque le remords . . .'

She hardly heard him. She was looking for her cigarettes.

'. . . Et non point par vertu car nous n'en avons
      guère,
Et non point par devoir car nous ne l'aimons pas,
Mais momme un charpentier s'arme de son compas,
Par besoin de nous mettre au centre de misère.'*

'No,' she said, quite still now. 'No, not yet.'

He did not look round. 'You haven't any matches, have you?' she said, starting up again.

---

* '. . . when we had to sit down at the crossroads, to choose regrets rather than remorse . . .' ' . . . not at all because of virtue, for we can hardly lay claim to virtue, not at all because of duty, for we're not enamoured of duty, but like a carpenter taking up his compasses, through the need to place ourselves at the very centre of our wretchedness.'

When they reached the right inn, AA, RAC, soon after six, she went off to look for the river, while he saw to the booking. At least, he went in and she stayed out, following the only path, with its loops of fairy lanterns left over from the summer. Most bulbs were missing towards the end, and it ended in a rustic shelter stacked with kindling wood and chicken wire. There was a little more grass, if you wanted it, and then a fence. She could hear the river quite well now, but she couldn't get through to it; so she walked there where she was instead, beside the fence, turning always at the same spot, roots one end, tin cans the other. It seemed somehow that if she could only go on long enough, up and down beside that fence, something would snap and then it would all be quite different. She kept on walking, but all the same it got colder, and when she couldn't see the roots and tin cans any more she went in. He was sitting in the lounge.

'All right now?'

'Just cooling off,' she said.

'I thought you'd passed out. They said in the office that you'd gone upstairs to lie down.'

'Not me. Must have been someone else's girlfriend.'

'And here I was,' he grinned a little ruefully, 'getting slowly plastered.'

They went straight in to dinner. The food was still good and he talked about Fletcher, Andrew Fletcher, Laird of Saltoun, a great patriot. Not executed, no. Poisoned, quite accidentally it seemed, by drinking water from the Seine. No front-page story there. And Fletcher himself, what did he do? Well, he was not in his time much enamoured of that 'darling plea', as he called it, 'the dream of being one instead of two'. In fact he was at heart just a boy if you like, another of those well-meaning scholars in favour of virtuous city states. And his last words, yes the very last, were 'My poor country', in keeping mind you, quite in keeping with his chronic incapacity, when it came to studying anything from more than one point of view. But there it was. The generous and magnanimous always fail in life, Dermot said.

The dining room had been done up, hardly smelt of paint any more, but the residential section was still being redecorated. After some delay on the local lines, confirming percentages no doubt for handing on clients, they were booked into a much smaller hotel, just behind the market square in the nearest market town, the three bigger hotels there being already full for no particular reason.

Their room was high up at the back, very small, with an electric heater much like a mouth organ, the sort of wardrobe babies are left in, and a cracked pink rose on cream background jug, with matching wash-basin, on a black marble stand. The rest was all bed, covered in white cloth, the slightly suspect white of a male nurse's uniform. Later, a good deal later, something started to chink on and off outside the door, like an old woman counting her money, getting it wrong, starting over and over again. And there were cats down in the yard.

'What do you want?' she whispered through the night, her neck in his hand. 'What do you want?' Though she knew very well what it was now, for him anyway. He had made it quite clear. She also knew that there was nothing they could do about it, other than stay alive, that this was only the beginning and that there would never be anything else.

The market clock struck the hours, and the half-hours. The chinking went on. And the cats.

In the morning Mary had marmalade, seeing it was there on the tray, not standing for anything any more. He thought he had just enough money left to settle the bill. If not, he said they'd have to jump for it, by stages of course.

The car was slow in starting. He didn't think it was holding the road the way it should either. He said it might be a good idea to get the steering looked at some time. He'd had the same trouble himself before. And that was all, the whole way back to London. She drew up near Scotland Yard at ten minutes to ten.

'Drive carefully now,' he said, and was gone before she'd started to turn.

CHAPTER TWENTY-TWO

The only pelican was up by the railings, its pale feet planted on a wad of old newspaper. Its eyes were naked, watering slightly, its neck worn and matted, the great pouch withered away. Like an old man waiting for a free bench, it stood there beside the little basket, twitching and scratching, dozing off, studying crumbs. Perhaps it had some disease. The ducks seemed cheerful enough. Mary watched one chasing another in and out of the weeping ash roots, peck and scuttle and then the take-off, wing to wing, making for the ornamental rocks.

Fridays are frequent and reasons can usually be found for loitering in St James's Park. Having left the car in the only garage that claimed not only to understand the steering, but also to fix it free of charge, Mary had got the books that she couldn't get in Somerset, and the corkscrew she couldn't get there either. She had not so much as checked on the dentist's address this time, now had she any intention of going into a telephone booth for any other reason. It was twenty to one and the pelican had now started to shake all over. She turned, following the twig-brush men, wheeling their teak barrows off to lunch in one of the private pagodas. She did, of course, look up those steps, towards Clive of India and Whitehall, but she didn't mean to make use of them. It wasn't as if they were a short cut to anywhere she might be going.

Half-way up them she saw Dermot, edging his way between two of the cars parked to the left of Clive. He could hardly turn back at this stage. She smiled. He did not smile, but his face changed slightly.

'All right?' he said.

'Yes, fine thanks.' They stood aside to let the others pass.

'Up for the day?'

'Just getting the car serviced.'

'And the chin?'

'Healing up . . . I told Martin, had to really.'

'Oh?' His face changed a good deal more.

'Well, I'm a very elaborate liar, and there wasn't much scope for improvising this time. I mean you might borrow the wrong sort of face powder once, at a party, but you'd hardly be borrowing it again and again, especially if you're meant to be staying with a medical girlfriend.'

'And what did Martin have to say?'

'Oh, live and let live.' Though this was not what he'd said at all. In fact he'd started sleeping in his new oak-floored studio, with its wonderful view: part of the outhousing plan.

'Oh he did, did he? I see.'

From the tone of his voice, not to mention the look on his face, Mary was just beginning to realise that what Dermot saw more clearly than anything else was the imminent possibility of his career being wrecked. She was also just beginning to realise that frankness was its own reward.

'Shall we have a drink?' she said.

'I'm sorry.' He looked at his golden watch, his chronometer. 'I'm due at a departmental lunch, at the Travellers' Club, in five minutes' time. Perhaps you'd ring me though, later. Say about three?'

'All right,' she said. 'At the office?'

'Yes. I should be back there by then.' He went on down after that, and she went up, towards more books and coffee in the Charing Cross Road.

Soon after three she was back beside the pelican once more, moving this time in the direction of St James's Park underground station, in search of a telephone that worked, and a Smith's bookstall with a copy to spare of the weekly journal to which Dermot sometimes contributed. These contributions were quite unmistakable now that she knew him better – a learned blend of mischief and horror, great wit and subtlety, greater disgust, all set, suspended rather, in a matrix of molten iron – call it compassion, love of humanity. Molten but slightly suspect at times, seeing that compassion, outside its own instant of personal proof, is bound to be suspect, more suspect than most things, to those still trying to get by without concepts of any kind.

Past the pelican, round the bend, nearing the second THIS PARK IS BEAUTIFUL sign, she saw him coming up from the bridge behind a party of bull mastiffs, all leashed together, all carrying rubber rings in their mouths. There was only the one path just there, unless you took to the grass.

'Hallo,' she smiled uneasily, feeling the long arm of coincidence had somewhat overreached itself. 'Now I shan't have to telephone.'

He was carrying a copy of the journal, and he did not look at all pleased.

'Bit late for a drink now,' he said. 'Would you care for some coffee?'

She nodded, knowing he didn't drink coffee, wishing they hadn't met like this.

'This way, I think.' He turned towards the Guards barracks and the underground station. 'No car?' he said, taking her bag of books.

'No, not till later. They're seeing to the steering, putting in new shock absorbers too. Apparently you can't manage for long without a few shock absorbers.'

'Oh no, you need a few shock absorbers.'

'Up here?' she said, as they came to some walled steps. 'I never knew you could get through this way.' She went ahead up the wrinkled stone, lithe and springy, stepping high, with all the nonchalance of advanced anxiety. 'And now?' They were passing the Express Dairy. 'Not the Luncheon Basket?'

'No, not the Luncheon Basket.' They crossed the road. 'I think this will do.' He held back the door with its smoked orange glass advertising Churchman's cigarettes.

In spite of the entrance the place had not entirely escaped the continental approach. The coffee was made on steam. And beside the tiers of Pepsi-Cola and 7-Up, the glassed-in pies and coloured cakes, was a majolica basket full of green wax spaghetti and a Negro puppet with lips designed to receive donations for the Merchant Navy. They sat in the corner, behind a folding raffia screen and under a poster listing the more notable attractions of the Loire valley. Each table carried a sugar sifter, a brass cornucopia filled with heather and a Watney's ashtray. A few, including theirs, had small bottles of soya bean sauce. There was only one other customer, an Indian in a duffle coat with the hood still up; he was fingernailing things out of a copy of the *Horselover's Magazine*.

Having delivered two cappuccinos with cinnamon dust, the waitress returned to her conversation through the hatch.

'Sure, no kiddin'. Helluva baby mind he says. So I says.

Straight, mind you. I let him have it straight. Look here I says, if you're looking for a baby doll, you'd better look somewhere else.'

The Indian got up to put a coin in the jukebox. And Mary blew again at her coffee, denting the froth. There were several simple suggestions she wanted to make, like him letting her know in advance exactly where and when they might meet, once a week say, or once a month. Not just walking off the way he always did, leaving her there with the car. Like him sending her funny postcards perhaps, when he went away, fitting her into his life somewhere, loving her somehow.

'Anything in there this week?' she said, meaning the journal. He smoothed out a passage dealing with women and how they got in the way. She read it quickly, laughing once.

'Not bad,' she said, putting it down between the heather and the soya bean sauce. 'He seems to forget, though, that women are, after all, designed to please. They can't help it, though they do do their best to conceal it, of course, as far as they can. And naturally they spend a good deal of time looking for someone worth pleasing. Still, as a design – outside the nursery and the double bed, all the home trappings as he calls them – could anything be more perverse? Unless perhaps the gift of speech . . .' She looked at him. He was quite untouchable. She started twisting the sugar sifter, plugging, unplugging it with a match, turning it upside down. 'As if the crucial word could ever be more than a splutter.'

He nodded, as over a tune known far too well to be anything but irritating. He did not take her hand.

And a little later she said, 'I don't suppose they'd turn that thing off, do you?'

'I doubt if they'd understand,' he said. And the jukebox beat on.

'Look here . . .' she started, but he was already looking at his watch.

'Time I was getting back,' he said.

'Another mission?'

'I'm afraid so.' He got up, went to the counter. The waitress was now on the kitchen side of the hatch. He paid the bill through to her and then he came back. Mary lit a cigarette, not looking at him coming back, leaning over, picking up the journal. And then he turned. It was as if his face had suddenly been skinned.

'That's the lot,' he said, and walked out.

He did not trip, nor did he look back. The cigarette burned on. And when she went out of there, along the street, back down the steps the way they had come, she couldn't see him anywhere. At the litter basket, where the pelican had stood, she turned and went back to the café for her handbag and her books. The Indian had gone, but he had not taken them with him.

It was some way to the hospital where Theo worked in the afternoon. Mary turned in at the underground station and bought herself a ticket. From the connecting bridge both plat-forms looked quite empty. The rails, live and dead, shone on. At the first turn down the studded steps she slipped and twisted her ankle, just badly enough to attract the attention of the ticket collector. He helped her up with the books on to a bench beside the shuttered tobacco kiosk, outside the barrier.

'All right now miss?'

She nodded encouragingly.

'You'd sometimes think those steps were specially designed . . . Of course it's worse in the rain, far worse. Why they can't install an escalator here beats me. One of the busiest stations in London, this. You can't judge it now, at teatime, you know. Of course they're all much too busy upstairs decorating their offices. Danish lighting now, I ask you. I've seen those steps . . . Why, you couldn't clip a ticket for the ears sometimes. Now with an escalator . . .'

'Perhaps they'll install one soon,' she said.

'It'll have to be a good long one I'd say, the way things are going. Dunlopillo shelters, that's what we all want, isn't it?'

'I dare say we do.'

'Next circle train due in five minutes.'

'Thank you,' she said.

He went back to his post then and, some minutes later, she set out for the hospital on foot.

The streets were wide and empty, show streets mostly, dull red with concrete lamp-posts and disinfected tree stumps.

'Excuse me.' A grey rubber raincoat swished up alongside her. 'Is this right for the palace?'

'Yes.' She glanced down at the crêpe suede boots, the gabardine trousers with no turn-ups.

'You don't happen to have the time on you?'

'I don't happen to have anything at the moment,' she said, moving on.

'Just a nice little limp, eh?'

She went a bit faster.

'Easy now lady. Mind the girdle. You don't want to rush him, do you?'

She started across the street.

'OK, OK. He'll be there. Save a bit for me.' Another snigger, and the swishing veered off.

And when she next looked there was no one there, apart from a mounted policeman practising trotting.

Theo was not at the hospital. There was no clinic on Friday afternoons. She wasn't at home either. The girl who answered the phone seemed very disappointed in a Scandinavian kind of way. Mary wondered how long she'd been sitting there, that girl, by the phone; whether the baby ever got taken out as far as the park. Was there any message? No, no message.

The outpatients' department was just lighting up. It was warm there, colourful and complete – an elaborate neon network running on pain. Mary sat in the hall, waiting (she said) for a friend, watching the porters and trolleys, the meek bewildered family contingents, defining the nursing staff.

There was someone who came and went in green: green cap, green overalls and rubber boots. He seemed to be in charge, at least he was the only one who hesitated occasionally. The others moved from door to door, from screen to chart to steriliser, round and round unerringly, or were bundled sooner or later from one bench to the next. He reminded her somehow of Dermot, this one in green. Perhaps it was just the voice, a Scots voice too, saying 'no, not at the moment', or 'busy, yes, I'm afraid I am', that and the thick, peremptory build. It was certainly not the face. This face was puzzled and kind, cheerfully aware of its limitations. In fact it was all she had counted on till a few hours ago.

'Forgive me,' she said at last, going up to him. He wasn't in green any longer, just a short white coat, with a few bleached stains down the front, and a starched hole in one of the pockets, zigzagged in red thread. 'I know this may well sound absurd,' she went on, a little more loudly, 'but would it be possible, do you think, for me to wind bandages here for a while?'

His face stiffened, not kind or puzzled or cheerfully aware of anything any more.

'It needn't be bandages,' she said quickly. 'Paring corks, chopping up lint, pasting on labels, anything small in a row.'

'I'm sorry,' he looked at her coldly. 'We have a nursing staff, you know, to deal with all that.'

'Oh.' She started tracing cracks on the floor with her toe. He had changed his boots for plaited shoes with pinpoint decorations. 'So there isn't anything?'

'No, I'm afraid not. You're not a nurse by any chance?' She shook her head. 'There are of course a number of voluntary organisations. If you'd like to see the almoner, any morning ten to twelve, just along the corridor, first on the left.'

'Thank you,' she said. 'I'm sorry, I didn't realise . . .'

'That's quite all right.' He nodded at one of the porters. 'And now, if you'll excuse me?' He backed off briskly, looking much as before. And the trolleys rolled after him.

Mary went out into the street, which was, like all the other streets, getting ready for Christmas. Gold and china oxen kneeling there in the windows on velvet plush and fibreglass straw, Irish turkeys six shillings a pound, and another air crash on the newspaper placards, more threats to peace – as if nobody wanted planes to crash, nobody wanted war. But then there were plenty of coffee shops still open, selling cigarettes.

CHAPTER TWENTY-THREE

The tea things had been cleared away and Theo and Abigail were now sitting in the two armchairs, one on each side of the fire. On the table between them lay a miniature pirate's chest containing chocolate pastilles and wadding, a copy of the Upanishads (second series) and the December number of *Thought and Substance*, a magazine setting out to record the physical effects of mind over matter. The magazine cover bore witness this month in the shape of a pale, ectoplasmic cross on a streaky grey background – the impression produced on a nine by twelve inch photographic plate three hundred yards from a running tap, the water from this tap being blessed at the time by a bishop well known for his powers of concentration. There were these then, on the table, and winter branches all along the mantelpiece, some with berries, some without, a few painted white. Abigail's 'Beauty in the Bone' portrait was out on loan. In its place above the branches hung a framed tapestry illustrating simple sums and letters of the alphabet in uncial script – the product, one might be tempted to assume of a sheltered girlhood.

'Rather sweet, isn't it?' Abigail said, as if her nursery years, though somewhat remote, were still very dear to her. Theo agreed, aware that those nursery years, though they may well have included mixed weaving classes – girls to the bobbins, boys to the flax – could scarcely have catered for samplers. But then it was hard not to agree with Abigail these days. Every six months or so Theo came to tea, partly to reassure herself that the Oberall way of life still went on, and partly because she was interested in Abigail's feet. Not that there was anything very wrong with these feet – *hallus valgus*, true bunions, chopped off every day of the week. But they were ugly, the only ugly thing in Abigail's life, and Theo, though she had never actually seen them, had an idea they getting uglier. For some time now Abigail had worn slippers, glove-like leather slippers, both in and out of doors. As the years slyly creased and sallowed her, she bought more jars of night cream, more tubes of beauty paste; and if the lids of these jars were lost, the tubes split and peeling, eye-brushes caked, lipsticks not refilled, this was largely because she was thinking about her feet. She couldn't get them operated on, not yet she always said. They couldn't afford it. There was only one man in London she would dream of going to. And who would look after Nillie while she spent six months in bed? Like the baby, the beautiful baby girl for Nillie, it was all too difficult. But if Florentine mirrors, galactic skyscapes and the ways of Zen had apparently ousted the flouncing of cradles, hemming of bibs, they showed no signs of absorbing the feet. Abigail mentioned them less and less. And the odd fondling gestures she gave them were not very noticeable.

So far this afternoon Theo had mostly been checking up on the way of life. The Oberall fortunes had, it seemed, taken a slight turn for the better. For the past three months Nillie had been attached to the publicity department of a chocolate factory, concerned, along with its fellow home industries, in something different – new yet old – and what could be newer,

yet older, yet wiser than the continental taste? The transla-
tions had been suspended, the secretary dismissed. Abigail was
glad about the secretary – a silly little thing, she said, who
ruined the chairs with her steel-capped heels. She was not quite
so glad about the chocolate factory, though. Nillie was getting
terrible headaches, sitting in a basement all day long you see,
over a gas fire with the strip lights switched on. But then one
had to remember it was only a stop-gap, till something better
turned up. They had touched, Theo and Abigail over the tea,
upon other openings, irons in the fire. They had also touched
upon Abigail's father and his increasing addiction to champagne suppers of an artistic nature, suppers lavished, that is, on
the highways and hedges of Hampstead, Chelsea and South
Kensington. Admittedly the daily press hardly did him justice.
Those charabanc picnics for spastic orphans, festival stalls for
war widows, league of youth clubs, ten-day cargo trips on a
Rubel ticket for the leading pack of deaf and dumb Boy Scouts,
were only mentioned if somebody happened to slip a disc or get
flown home with food poisoning. Now he had a whole sonnet
sequence set for sheep bells, two likenesses – one in Indian ink
on a table napkin, the other glued to a garden table – also a set
of sacrificial stones bedded in his very own oyster shells, not to
mention numerous dedications still to come, all commemorat-
ing his fine integrity, guidance and sympathy, his services to
man. He called this keeping in touch with the younger generation, though his own family were inclined on the whole to
refer to it as poor father's last fling. Mother Rubel had recently
returned to her Church, whereas the sons and daughters continued to stand on their own feet. Or sit, seeing that several
played large musical instruments. For the Rubels were quite an
artistic family.

'I'm sorry I couldn't get to the wedding,' Theo said. 'Bernard wanted me up in Scotland canvassing for him. He didn't get that Chair after all, you know. They decided that what they really needed was an older man.' She smiled, thinking of Bernard and what he's said about the older man. 'I can't say I mind much. All granite and mist up there . . . and baking soda.' She started rubbing her thumbs over her fingers, steadily, patiently, nodding in the mean time to the humble back-breaking rhythm of ancient feminine tasks. 'Just right for mystics and supermen, all very noble and brave and drunk any time after 6 p.m., telling each other how very noble and brave and mystical they are, how knowledgeable too about sex and the state of the world, and what about X, will he get that job, do you think? Telling each other little legends the whole night through. The household gods would need to be pretty thickset to stand up to that sort of thing for long. Or else they'd turn into kelpies . . . water spirits,' she added, 'frequently taking the form of a horse.'

'I see.' Abigail was busy looking into the fire. 'So . . . what does that mean, exactly?'

Theo shrugged, an itchy sort of shrug. 'In this case it seems to mean America,' she said.

'Really?'

'As a matter of fact I'm quite looking forward to it . . . rearing kids on the campus,' she suggested.

'Are you, dear? I suppose the opportunities for medicine . . .?' Abigail finished less and less these days.

'Would be much the same,' Theo said. 'I'm coming to think that I'd rather sew encouraging mottoes on to T-shirts, even the same mottoes back and front, than run a whole suite of clinics.'

'Really?' Abigail was at her most mellow and resonant now. 'Of course your work here has not been exactly . . .'

'No,' Theo said. 'It has not. Birth control is all very well, but that clinic is more of a parcels office than anything else. One long Christmas rush. The whole place reeks of glue.'

Abigail was trying to pick coal out of the scuttle with a pair of tongs, old brass tongs.

'Bernard should do well in America,' Theo went on, a little more tentatively. 'I mean it's only the duds, saints and scholars who can carry on here. Don't you think so?'

Abigail clearly thought nothing of the sort. 'Raphael may be going to America soon,' she said.

'I was just going to ask you . . .' Theo stretched towards the little chest of chocolate pastilles. 'May I?'

'Of course, dear. Help yourself. We have several like that. Nillie is meant to be thinking up Christmas labels for them. But then, as he says, the whole conception is so very English, isn't it? You'll find some a little darker and thinner than others,' she hinted. 'Better to suck them, really.'

Theo nodded, reserving the rest of the darker, thinner doubloon for some future occasion. 'And how did the wedding go?' she said. 'I must admit it was about the last invitation I ever expected to get. They weren't childhood sweethearts, by any chance, were they? Raphael and . . . what was it?'

'Cornelia, Cornelia Anne. They met at a boat-race party.'

'Did they now? Not a boat race given by the Frosts, was it?'

Abigail started being busy again with the fire.

'What's she like?' Theo said, 'Cornelia Anne?'

'Very sweet really. A little overweight, poor girl, but then one must remember she is an only child. Adores Raphael, of course.'

'So it's quite a success then?'

'Well yes, I suppose it is. You know Nillie had always hoped that Raphael might re-establish certain links . . . But then the poor boy got so run down that there was simply no question of his finishing his studies in Germany, as we'd planned.'

Theo nodded not too sympathetically. 'All in all he seems to have made quite a remarkable recovery,' she said.

And Abigail agreed. 'The girl's family have a place in the Wye Valley,' she added casually.

'A fruit farm?'

'Well, I believe there are orchards on the estate. Perhaps you know it . . . Mafeking Priory?'

Theo did not.

'The old well is quite charming; the monks' penance, they call it. Something to do with the number of winds or holes in the bucket. I'm not sure which. Anyhow I really must make a little sketch of it next time we're down there.'

'And is the house quite comfortable?' Theo said.

'Well, my dear,' Abigail smiled her sad inscrutable smile, 'you know what those military families are. The guest wing is an old hop tower, with animal skins all round the walls. Poor Nillie came back absolutely convinced he had cancer of the throat. Even the London house is a bit of a barracks, one of those four-storey hospices, as Nillie calls them, just off Cadogan Square.'

'All out of soldiering?'

Abigail saw fit to admit a certain interest in soap. She was now fondling her feet.

Theo waited a bit. 'What did you wear at the wedding?' She said at last.

'Wear? What could anyone wear with slippers?' She laughed sharply. 'You know, Nillie just can't get over the child being called Sanders.'

'The child?'

'His grandson, the last of the line.' There was nothing mellow and resonant about Abigail now. 'Any child of ours would have been nothing,' she said, 'nothing at all. And now he has a grandson called Sanders.' She was still at the feet. 'They did that to soothe the old boy, of course, seeing there was hardly time to get their little church swept for the christening.'

'So there was a christening too?'

'Only a very small one in the end. Here in London. Just the family.'

'And Sanders senior?'

'No. He didn't come. Said he couldn't leave his cider press.' Abigail smiled. She was quieter now, started in on the scuttle and tongs again. 'They got some very nice silver one way and another. One of the loving cups is quite fascinating, almost Mithraic.'

'I suppose Sanders senior has connections in America?'

'Yes, I believe he has.'

At this point Nillie telephoned to say that he was entertaining a chocolate delegate from Leipzig and would not be back for dinner. Before sitting down again, Abigail got out one or two little things she thought Theo might be interested in. First there was the latest bulletin, issued by the owners of a certain Box, to which the Oberalls sent drops of blood on blotting paper, whenever they could afford to do so. This Box, now registered as a limited company, appeared from the photographs to consist of a suite of apartments lined with delicate dials, grouped presumably to transmit such waves as might be relevant. Recent developments included the full-time services of two skilled operators in white laboratory coats. Hairs, apparently could now be sent instead of blood. The rest of the issue was taken up with letters received from grateful owners of pedigree livestock, requesting prompt suspension of treatment, no more waves, that is, sent out their way at five guineas a time.

Theo exchanged this for an Ethiopian amulet, looking much like a coffee bean or rabbit turd. This little amulet, according to Abigail, served to impress one of the lower selves sufficiently to contact the High Self in times of trouble. It was all a question of energy and infinite layers of mind.

Once this had been handed back, stowed away in the antique cabinet, designed for the safe keeping of birds' eggs or coins or butterflies, they turned to the latest developments in psychotherapy. Here Theo had alas to admit that she had never so much as heard of ontoglossology. Abigail was not surprised, seeing that its principal exponent, a certain Dr Heinrich Ganzer, had only recently arrived in this country. This Ganzer was, in himself, a most exceptional man, a natural healer, you might say. He had spent many years in the East. Abigail was pretty sure that the best therapists were those in tune, as it were, with the Counterpart Body, that is to say the Vehicle of Prayer, in close touch for prolonged periods with the Oriental attitude to life. Anyhow, Ganzer was a most exceptional man. He had now established an institute providing public lectures and qualifying courses for would-be ontoglossologists. Nillie could not at the moment unfortunately afford the qualifying course, but they had both been attending the public lectures. All technical details were, of course, reserved for the qualifying course, seeing that Ganzer's whole approach depended, initially at any rate, on the element of surprise. Nevertheless, one way and another, Nillie now had a pretty good grasp of the subject, a pretty good idea of the technique involved. Given a trained mind, it didn't take long to get the gist of these things. There was no literature available as yet, apart from the official publication, which Abigail then produced.

The paper was think, the print uneven. There were one or two graphs; but as a whole the production could hardly compare with the *Box Bulletin*, or the December number of *Thought and Substance*. There were no eminent subscribers. But then this was, Theo gathered, only the first of the institute's publications. She also gathered that ontoglossology was a type of verbal shock therapy. And that its aim was to break down all associations in any way likely to interfere with the patient's freedom of action, on the principle that objects, once stripped of their haunting connections, may be handled without fear. At the end of a week's intensive treatment a simple working vocabulary was more or less guaranteed to replace a mess of linguistic taboos. This vocabulary would vary according to the patient's needs. Certain recalcitrant cases might require a further week's intensive treatment. Such cases were rare, occurring largely among those handicapped by prolonged sedentary habits. In any event all practitioners were at the disposal of their patients any time of the day or night during the first six months following the initial treatment, should any setbacks occur. Though their aim, it need hardly be repeated, was clear-cut self-reliance, rather than the confused dependence so frequently associated with the old analytical approach. Members of the public were warned that the forces released could be highly dangerous in unqualified hands. No accredited ontoglossologist could hold him or herself responsible for any lasting damage to the psyche resulting from unscrupulous practices associated with their name. A leaflet, in smaller, shakier print, stated – for the benefit of those who had difficulty in using the telephone – that the standard fee for a week's treatment was fifty guineas. A 25 per cent reduction would be considered should a further week prove necessary. Further consultations would be based on hourly terms.

'Well,' Theo said. 'It looks as if they're all set for a quick scoop.'

'What's that, dear?' Abigail was out in the hall just then, fitting a newly embroidered cover on to the telephone directory.

'I said it's all rather expensive, isn't it?'

'Not really.' She came in again with the cover that wouldn't quite fit. 'After all, just think what any ordinary analyst would charge for all those hours.' She started rummaging for coloured cotton in the birds' egg, coin, or butterfly cabinet. 'Did I ever tell you that the main reason why Nillie left Germany was because he couldn't pay his analyst's bill? That was years before I met him, mind you. The man was a charlatan, of course, a Czech. As Nillie says, what else can one expect from such hybrid *Untermenschen*.'

It was then that Theo remembered her Scandinavian mother's help, who was going to an Inter-Allied Ball that night. She stood up, slipping the half-eaten doubloon down the satin-striped side of the armchair.

'I was just wondering what you'd think of a few little experiments I've been making.' Abigail waved one slender artistic hand towards the door of her studio. 'Never mind, though. They're only a beginning. Just a little knack I've discovered. Abigail's very own contribution to this great big world.'

Theo did not insist. she said she'd very much rather not hurry over these little experiments. She only wished they had been mentioned before.

'You'll be back then, before going to America?'

'Of course. And you and Nillie must have dinner with us some time soon.' Theo had said this so often in the past that she could at times almost believe she meant it. But now, sure about the feet, she saw no reason why she and Abigail should ever meet again. Except that people mostly met again somehow, people who'd known one another well. 'New knocker?' she said at the front door.

'He's rather sweet, isn't he?' Abigail tweaked the forked brass beard. 'Just a little offering from Tibet. Here to watch over us . . . A present,' she added gravely, 'from a very dear friend.'

Theo smiled. 'It's nice to see everyone getting watched over,' she said, kissing Abigail goodbye. 'Give my love to Nillie. I'm sorry I missed him.'

And she went on down wondering on the nature of pathetic fallacies.

CHAPTER TWENTY-FOUR

Five minutes later Theo would have met Mary trying to work the lift, one of the cage on a rope sort, by means of which the more athletic residents on the fifth and sixth floors of the Oberall block kept themselves in training. But five minutes later Theo was standing outside the discreetly lit, not quite closed door of a nearby shop, wondering whether it could possibly deal in extra-large plastic baby pants.

Abigail, who had not seen Mary for over a year and was still waiting to be asked to Somerset, received her a little remotely. It was half-past seven and the Oberall larder did not allow for casual visitors.

'I'm sorry,' Mary said. 'I would have rung, but I seem to have lost the number.'

'We're in the book now,' Abigail said.

Mary nodded, as if this would hardly have made any difference. She said she would rather keep on her coat and produced a half-bottle of brandy. 'I'm afraid it's not very old.' She smiled placatingly. 'Do you think we might open it now?' She smiled a bit more, seeing that Abigail was looking less and less pleased to see her. 'I'm not feeling well,' she added. 'Not well at all.'

Less than an hour later she was lying tucked up on the chaise-longue in a pink quilted dressing gown, sipping a bowl of soup. The half-bottle of brandy was no longer in sight, and Abigail was telling her all about ontoglossology and its leading exponent, a natural healer you might say and a very dear friend of theirs.

He was, of course, extremely busy, but there was just a chance that he might have a week free soon, possibly even the coming one. You never knew. People did fall out occasionally. He liked to keep a certain amount of time for his own private research, but perhaps, in a special case like this . . . He was at his best with the highly intelligent. There were other practitioners too, but on the whole it might be wisest to wait for Ganzer. Anyhow, as soon as Nillie came back, she would get him to telephone. Ganzer might even come round later on. He didn't live very far off and he made a point of meeting prospective patients socially first, to get some idea of their normal environment, especially when this happened to be one he himself was accustomed to. Abigail was sure that he and Mary would get on splendidly. He was quite unassuming, so unassuming that one might at times be inclined to forget what a deeply religious person he was, almost a saint in his way. The treatment was pretty intensive. Mary did realise that, didn't she? While it was going on Abigail really thought it would hardly be safe for her to stay in London on her own. She'd been on her own far too long as it was. Could Martin come up? No, of course not. He could hardly be expected to. And the building was still going on, was it? How extraordinary. In that case Mary must stay here with them, just going out to see Ganzer in the mornings and afternoons. She could sleep in the studio, in fact there was no need really for her to go back to Somerset at all. She clearly wasn't fit to do so, not tonight

anyway; anyone could see that. And it wouldn't be putting
them out in the least; they'd love to have her. What were
friends for, if not to help out in times like these?

Mary was beginning to feel warmer now. She had only come
up not wanting to drink the brandy in a strange pub, or out in
the street, to chat a bit by a fire she knew. And then she was
going to call the garage to stop the car being packed away
behind a row of removal vans. She was trying hard not to think
of the drive back. It was all a question of planning, knocking up
steps and taking them steadily one by one. Another few hours
and she'd be asleep, and then it would be morning and so forth.
Meanwhile the afternoon coffee scene whirred on, round and
round like an old film strip, always jamming at the same spot.
Sometimes she tried dressing him up in a kilt, or that pin-stripe
suit he'd had, when they'd first met and she'd split the drink.
Sometimes she tried making him slip on a curl of butter or a
spoonful of jam. Sometimes playing the whole thing backwards
in slow motion, without that look on his face. But it didn't
help, any of it. The look on his face, that skinned look, was still
there, and so was the cigarette, and the raffia screen and the
two glass cups lined with froth and cinnamon dust.

What Mary had given Abigail, here on the chaise-longue,
was a fourpenny instalment of some amatory misadventure,
which had, in the telling, less and less connection with the
original. It was not until Abigail had started referring to the
characters concerned as 'he' and 'you' that she realised how
ludicrous it could all become, trying to tell anyone what
mattered most and why in serial form.

'You must remember,' she said, 'that there are alternative
versions. I sometimes think that the so-called art of living con-
sists largely in nourishing alternative versions.' She was
wondering then, as often before, just what alternative versions

Dermot had. 'Not that I've ever had any, crawling along from one pit to the next. But it stands to reason . . . everything stands to reason, doesn't it? Or falls by it. Like those milk bottles stacked up at the fun fair again and again, only waiting for the next knock-down. I'm on the side of the ball myself, the bright mad core. At least,' she smiled, 'I was. You might think I'd have a whole cupboardful of prizes by now. But no, not one clay poodle, not even a nickel cake fork to show for it. Underhand bowling, that's the trouble. The management only squirts out a few shots of candyfloss for that : . . Feathers,' she went.

Abigail, by this time, had either lost track of the argument, or was, more than ever, keeping herself to herself.

'Feathers,' Mary said. 'Fine feathers make fine birds at a distance, don't they?' But plucked . . . plucked, gutted and trussed. There's no concealing it.'

It was about then that Abigail had announced how terribly distressing it was to her that anyone she was so fond of should go on and on knocking their head against a stone wall. And Mary had said that if the wall were all stone she would have stopped knocking long ago. This, according to Abigail, was just what came of getting mixed up with words. A type of verbal block, which only ontoglossology could cure.

On and off, in spite of the exposition and the literature, Mary found herself almost prepared to believe in it. Words were the making, stretching and breaking, after all: the rollers on the great rack. Whether a system of grins and grunts, wriggles and twitches pinned out on a board, might have worked better was hardly the point. If there had been a point, the least speck of light about just then, she would not have been tucked up there in that pink quilted dressing gown, sipping soup. And to say no out loud, at the best of times, had always been a most intricate

manoeuvre, like sending a bagatelle ball clicking apologetically
from pin to pin right down the table, scoring alas nought. As
things were, by the time Nillie arrived she had more or less
offered to provide her own blankets. Whether it was his voice,
the dogmatic absurdity of everything he said, or more perhaps
the way he kept assessing his fingernails as if each were a rare
ancestral jewel, whatever it was, Mary found herself surrepti-
tiously collecting her belongings, trying hard to remember one
or two biblical admonishments concerning fools and their inner
parts and the needless crossing of their thresholds.

When it came to telephoning Ganzer, as it did, all too soon,
Mary pointed out how late it was, far too late to bother him
surely, especially now that she was feeling so much better, quite
different altogether, and anyhow she really felt it would be best
to talk the whole thing over with Martin first. She might just as
well have pointed out the number of twirls on the long brass
tongs. It was all fixed up by Nillie in the bedroom, an extension
installed, he explained cheerfully, entirely for the benefit of
Abigail's phantom lovers. Ganzer would be along for coffee in
the morning. It happened that this coming week was the only
one he could possibly manage before his Californian lecture
tour.

'Might it not be simpler to wait till he gets back?' Mary said.

They thought it would be most unwise.

'Well in that case . . .' She edged her legs towards the floor
out from under the pink quilted dressing gown. 'Do you think
we might have a little of that brandy?'

Abigail produced three fluted thimbles of Bristol glass from
the birds' egg, coin or butterfly cabinet, and the brandy from a
piece of furniture once designed to hold Wellington boots.

'Poison to me,' Nillie said, dismissing his share with a wistful
flutter of fingernails.

Mary took hers standing. 'If you don't mind,' she said, 'I think I'd better ring Martin. He'll be expecting me back by now.'

'Of course, dear.' Abigail showed her into the hall. 'Or would you rather use the other one?'

Mary said perhaps she'd use the other one; then she could tidy herself up a bit, while waiting to get through. This seemed reasonable enough. She sat for a while on the broad double bed, then got up and shut the door. She ran the garage. They would see what they could do, though she had left it rather late hadn't she, and all-day repair jobs remaining on the premises after 6 p.m. were liable for the all-night parking fee. She sat a few minutes longer, then got up, smoothed out the champagne spread and left five shillings in the gold-spotted ashtray shaped like a hand, palm up, amputated just above the wrist.

'Look,' she said, back in the sitting room, 'Martin would far rather I discussed the whole business with him before we went any further.'

'But Mary dear . . .' Abigail sounded like a famous head-mistress about to dismiss a favourite head-girl.

'It's all arranged now,' Nillie said, crossing and uncrossing his borzoi legs as if they were itching badly. 'Ganzer would never have accepted the case if he hadn't thought it was quite imper-ative that something should be done straight away. He wasn't so sure, mind you, that it might not be already too late, from what I told him.'

'I could always come back,' Mary said quickly, 'come back after the weekend. Wouldn't that do? You see –' she turned pleadingly from one to the other – 'it's just that Martin wants to know what's going on. I couldn't say much on the telephone. I mean it's not the sort of situation you can put across on a strict time basis.'

'Of course not, darling.' Abigail the famous headmistress

reinstated her charge with a sharp look at Nillie. 'You do whatever you think bet. I'm sure Ganzer would quite understand if
you were a day or two late. We could ring him now, if you like.'

'Oh no, please don't bother.' Mary was smiling once again.
'Perhaps the shortened course might be a little cheaper.'

'But surely,' Nillie glanced at her knowingly, 'under the
circumstances *cher Papa* would be only too willing to oblige.'

'I very much doubt if my father would be prepared to invest
in anything so recently established,' Mary said, not smiling any
more, 'anything in which supply so obviously exceeds demand.
After all there can't be very many people who'd give fifty
guineas to get rid of their vocabulary, or have it cut down
according to Ganzer and no more arguing about it. But there
you are,' she softened slightly. 'It's always the worst cases, the
crafty ones, who do their best to laugh the whole thing off,
isn't it? Like drunks at the careful stage.'

Nillie nodded gravely. '*Der letzte Trug*,' he said.

Mary poured herself out another mouthful of brandy.
'Forgive me. It's quite a long drive,' she said, wondering how she
could ever have thought of staying in that studio for a whole
week.

Abigail insisted on lending her an angora shawl, slightly less
pink than the dressing gown. 'Now darling you must be a good
sensible girl and wrap up warmly,' she said. 'Why Nillie, the
dear child has next to nothing on.' And the shawl was draped
firmly round Mary's shoulders, like a strait-jacket.

They checked on trains to Somerset and rang for a taxi to
Euston. Mary promised faithfully that on no account would she
dream of driving all that way back in the dark alone. She also
promised faithfully to ring them in the morning, or at any rate
on Sunday at the very latest.

*

And forty minutes after that she was doing sixty miles an hour on the Bath road, muttering 'poor mad creature' over and over again to herself, until she felt scornful enough to drive with reasonable care.

Nillie was dozing in his armchair, Abigail curled up below him, crotcheting the last of a set of table mats.

'It seemed the only chance,' she said, 'of your getting those details. Every day, lunch and dinner. You'd have had it all exactly then. And Ganzer need never have known. I suppose it's still just possible . . .'

Nillie shook his head sadly. 'As Tinkel says, the habitually self-destructive can only be salvaged by force. All the same you might have disconnected that telephone.'

'Poor Mary,' Abigail sighed, rethreading her needle. 'What about my shawl. Do you think I'll ever get it back?'

'*Ja, ja.*' He rubbed his nose reflectively. 'I should say you would get two shawls back in a few days, *mit Leib und Seele*. One for each.' He tweaked her breasts, one, two, the way he often did.

'Such messy lives some people lead,' she murmured, laying her head on his knees.

'A question of breeding, my dear,' he said.

CHAPTER TWENTY-FIVE

It was May yet again. Mary was up in her room in Somerset, writing to South America.

Dearest Daddy,

Thank you for your letters. I'm sorry economic conditions are not improving as much as you'd hoped, though it's nice to know private enterprise is being encouraged once again. Perhaps the southern bloc scheme will help, once it gets going properly, and there'll really be that one Latin America you've been waiting for. As you say, it wouldn't do to have all your assets in any one country these days, but all the same it sounds as if this would be a good time to consolidate things where you are. Europe is one large cafeteria now, except for a few little pastures like this. No *salón para familias*, no family gathering place.

I'm sorry you feel that way about the sheep. It wasn't Merino sheep, but Exmoor sheep – shaggy ones with horns – that Martin was thinking of. They do very well up here, being bred principally for crossing with softer, smoother varieties, ending up more as mutton than wool. These sheep like heather better than grass, and are not, as far as I know, prone to all the diseases you mention. Of course, to make it a really worthwhile proposition one would, as you say, need thousands of acres, but then Martin was merely hoping to make this place slightly more self-sufficient than it is at present. We are, as you know, considerably overdrawn on account of the building. I admit that such items as the outhouses, the ha-ha, the gravelling, the re-seeded park land and the hill fencing were undertaken without your approval, but Martin was determined to do the whole thing properly, as you yourself would have been, had you once paced the boundaries, as you surely will one of these days. There was no need, as it happens, to write to the bank about the title-deeds. It has not occurred to me to bond them. The fact remains that here we are, with this place, and no money to run it. Hence the sheep. If you take another quick look at Martin's letter, I think you'll see that there was nothing 'deliberately insulting' about it. He is, as you know, deeply attached to this way of life, and all it stands for. Naturally we do not wish to keep asking for more money – 'slowly killing you'. But as things stand, Martin is not prepared to pass the rest of his life as a full-time handyman. Nor is he prepared to stand by watching the weevils crawl in again. So there we are. He will probably go abroad for a while to get a fresh start on his sculpting. He could not possibly do it here, unless he had everything running properly. And I, needless to say, am not too keen to stay on by myself. Anyhow it looks very much as if I shall have to spend this summer in the hands of the doctors in London, getting my inside straightened out. Last month's little interlude was somewhat more drastic than the others. It was very nice of you to think of allowing Mamma to fly over, but I do see, of course, that her place is at your side just now. Next year perhaps she could come.

As to this blood pressure, as far as I can gather from the authorities here, it is not so much height as fluctuation that does the damage. The main thing, they say, is to avoid any sudden changes in your way of life. And aeroplanes. Even the pressurised ones are not, apparently, a good idea. So you'd better leave that spreading of assets, for a while anyway. I should not for a moment think of giving up those two little cups of coffee in the morning, or that half-glass of whisky in the evening. But you know best. There are, I am told, certain drugs designed to lower the blood pressure artificially, but these are still more or less in the experimental stage, requiring expert supervision. There are very few experts and very long queues, wherever the experts see fit to appear. At the Mayo clinic, for instance. But that's another streamlined cafeteria. On this side there's nothing streamlined about anything, just queues. Far the safest thing, from all accounts, is to go on quietly with your routine . . .

She stared out of the window, across the gravelled drive, the daffodil stalks. The docks were starting to sprout again, and the laurels. The rubble lining the yew walk had not yet dissolved. There were no yews yet, no urns either, no paved foundations, no pleasure ground. Only six rolls of five-strand sheep-wire, four lorryloads of weed-free manure, a few granite troughs towed up from a local farm. And, of course, the moors.

Dear Judith,

So that's where you've been. After that last postcard from Vienna, I thought of you hiking East, with a packful

of dictionaries, a judo manual, that old spirit stove perhaps, and a couple of drastic pills sewn into your island
socks. And here you are now, babbling of lakeshore drives
in Cadillacs; or was that just one trial spin and a stiff
stroll back? I do see that sitting over the gramophone in
a darkened library might be the soundest thing to do
most evenings in Winnipeg. Glad all the same the dollars
are coming in.

I gather from your occasional references to 'us' and
'ours' that Jaro is not too many lakes away. Also that
you're not thinking of clubbing together for a floating
home just yet. (*A nous la liberté.*) I'm sorry about the miscarriage. Don't let it get a habit, will you? *Et ego in
Arcadia*, but then in my case they seem to take the place
of heavy colds. Well well, all flesh is grass, but some grass
tastes better than others. All the same, I'm rather pleased
you've missed the Rilkean touch at last.

'*Erstaunte euch nicht auf attischen stelen die Vorsicht menschilicher Geste?! war nicht Liete und Abschied so leicht auf
die Schultern gelegt, als wär es aus anderm Stoffe gemacht als
bei uns? Gedenkt euch der Hände,* INDEED, *wie so drucklos
beruhon . . .*'*

I must admit that it is by no means these delicate gestures, this airy other stuff that I find my mind dwelling on
round about 6 p.m.

Getting back to those evenings in Winnipeg, instead of
going south in the fall with that wonder-pack of dollars, to
listen to longer records in larger libraries, would you not

---

* 'Did not the delicacy of human gestures astonish your Attic souls?! Were not
love and parting so lightly borne, as if they were made of a different substance
from what we know? Think of the hands, how they touch so softly . . .'

consider sharing a flat in London with me? Martin is setting out on his travels again, the high ground of Somerset
having proved not exactly more bracing than searching
(as the guidebooks say), but a good deal more feudal than
feminine. I would have suggested Paris, if it weren't that
we'd be a little more affluent in London. I mean I could
provide the flat, if you'd like to live in it. If the setting
doesn't tempt you, there are other cities we might try,
though it's not as if anyone speaks English in London
nowadays, except in a few station waiting-rooms and at all
Greenline bus stops. I gather the original inhabitants still
make use of the town for purposes of trade, but are not in
any way obtrusive . . .

Oh God, she thought, staring out of the window again. The
shared salads, the little boxes of cheese . . . two pairs of stockings
on the radiator, two hands on the telephone.

Darling,
    There was surely no need to sweep off spraying gravel
all over the grass like that. From here it still looks very
much as if we'd been holding a tractor rally. (Did you
leave the car at the station? I haven't been down yet to
see.) I'm sorry I got so worked up, but women all do that
now and then. Sorry too about that letter from South
America, but I did warn you, didn't I, that farming was a
particularly sore topic. Perhaps I should have told you
about Uncle Karl, who had an affair with a gaucho girl,
got mixed up with the *peons*, which was at the time far
worse than getting mixed up with the *descamisados* or
sumergidos or any other noticeably underprivileged section of society. Anyhow for twenty years he was kept out

of the foothills of the Andes, the barren windswept Patagonian coast. And there he farmed, was set up by Papa that is, with pigs and chickens, cows, crops, quick-growing timber, rare bulbs, even little llamas, I think, which some people eat, or perhaps they just used the droppings for fuel. Anyhow, at the age of seventy-five, he was given his last chance. Five hundred pounds and not one penny/*peso* more. Six months later he shot himself in a little hotel down by the waterfront in B.A., the Boca, having settled the account with his last fiver and *pesos* to spare for the staff. The farm has now been sold, apart from the mineral rights. Both daughters married into the landed gentry, *estancieroi* class. Still, as far as I know, this Uncle Karl never went in for sheep. So if you really want them, I dare say it might be arranged, without 'bonding' anything. I shan't do that ever. It's just signing on to big business, getting tied up with the whole system, so please don't insist. I have written back to try and calm things down a bit, partly so as you could have the sheep, if you really etc., and partly because I am still mildly interested in not getting cut off at the moment. We could admittedly sell up here and split the proceeds, if anyone wants to take over the place, which I rather doubt. There would probably be an international lawsuit pending pretty soon after that, Gallen versus Freemantle, which would all be a little embarrassing. Personally, if the house weren't insured – big business again – I should be very much tempted to burn it down, especially on an evening like this, but I do see that any such grand manoeuvre might well be dismissed as the product of an unsound mind. You know you got yourself quite the wrong sort of wife. She should have been very sweet and simple and sweetly and simply rich. But really, honey, you were expecting rather a lot – beautiful books, pictures, furniture, food. And now sheep on the hill, shepherd boys in the loft, and enough spare cash to leave all this ticking over while you pace the docks of the Middle East looking for fresh inspiration. Well now, you have the house. To get the family you'd probably need another wife. You might still manage the sheep. You might even sit in the car outside the local cinema night after night, while a succession of shepherd boys cuddled their girlfriends, and the sheep knelt down and died. The more that died of course, the less you'd get abroad. And as for abroad, I admit there are women who live on weeping and polishing, but they have on the whole been much assisted by wonderful letters from L'Afrique du Nord. So you'd have to write wonderful letters too, and even then I doubt if you'd find those old slippers restitched and warming for you by the fire. Not up on these moors.

As for the sculpting, you can't really blame me for your getting carried away like that designing the ideal setting for your work. You see now that keeping the setting in good repair could well be another full-time job. And anyhow you're not going to get quite the audience you want off the pages of Country Life. I'm afraid artists are still expected to live pretty low, at the start anyway. Not much backing for the Compleat Man yet, though maybe that will come with more and more leisure hours all round. I know it's all very well for me to draw such fine distinctions. I've never been really poor and so on. But then we all have our own style of sinning, and this is not mine. Which does not mean I'm quite ready yet for the Carmelite grille or that beat off Curzon Street. Not

quite ready either to cut loose completely from South
America, what with the overdraft and nowhere particular to go.

So there now. What do you say? There are boats for
Finland most days surely, and you left your raincoat
behind. Rollo was to come this weekend. Could you not
get back to show him round? Then we could talk the
whole thing over, without so much gravel flying about.

I'm sending this to the Travellers' Club, in case you call
in there for a few letters of introduction . . .

The dog had been barking in the courtyard on and off most
apologetically for some hours now. It was a black and white dog,
rather like Jake, only smaller, more shrinking and it had no
name. It slept in one of the lofts and was going to be trained for
the sheep. Martin didn't believe in making a fuss over dogs, or
letting Mary do so. She went down to it, brought it in, for
which it was very grateful, almost happy, though it wasn't a
happy dog. On the kitchen table, very long, natural oak, specially designed, lay a leaf torn from last year's car insurance
calendar, bearing a pencilled message to the effect that the
woman who came up from the village in the mornings would
not be coming any more. She found the place too lonely, her
husband was sick again and needed looking after, and could her
wages please be left at the post office. Here followed a small
sum, including farm eggs and butter, with deductions for telephone calls made on the premises. Alongside this message was
a pannier or chip basket containing leeks and soil and a section
of birch bark inscribed in purple ink:

Just a little flutter-by.
The tulips are nearly touching this year,

the mill-stones mounted at last,
making a new girl of
       Your Own Moor Hen.
Could I have the basket back please?

The Moor Hen came from over the hill, had a Bentley, a husband who lived on a yacht and children at boarding-school.

Mary took the dog, and the wine left over from earlier on, back upstairs, wondering whether loneliness might not be made a capital offence. Then the real addicts would have to keep out and about. Anyone found living alone would be kept under close surveillance. There would soon be underground movements of course, Singular Brigades, all only too willing to die at any time for their cause, their right in this case to be lonely. Indeed there already were. What else did anyone want, after all, but some jolly good reason for dying? Belonging to a brigade. That was the thing. Camaraderie. Funny how serious thought always seemed to boil down to something quite obvious. Perhaps if you stuck it long enough . . .

She took the pocket diary away from the dog. It was an old one of Martin's, a present from his nanny. They came every year. This one was in brown Morocco, with a golden ace of diamonds on the cover. She started thumbing through the damp pages, not bitten across the print so far . . .

Information given in this diary is correct at the time of going to press.
Purification of B.V.M./Candlemas(Scottish Quarter Day)/ new moon/Ramadan ends/longest day
drinks top floor No. 6.
Duke of Edinburgh born
dentist dentist dentist

Transfiguration/grouse shooting begins/autumnal equinox
Manoli Angelakis Canada House WHI 9741 – immigration 61
Green Street W
23rd After Trinity (last)/annual motor licences renewable
Art of Crete 10gns. ?Publisher . . .

Mary gave the diary back and watched the dog, busy again.
When dogs weren't busy they barked, or slept. The wine didn't
taste of anything, but she went on drinking it, smoking, staring.
And the moors stared back. It was taking a very long time to get
dark . . .

Dear Dermot . . .

She had quite a collection of 'Dear Dermots' by now. A few
had even been posted earlier in the year, to be forwarded to
whatever country he might be spending those few months abroad
in. They had all been heavily disguised to get past the secretary,
if he had a secretary, a great friend of his wife's perhaps. She
didn't know. One had contained a newspaper clipping of a
Whitefaced Scoops Owl, one of the few surviving members of
its species, facing the camera for the very first time, only a few
weeks before its death, her death rather (she was called
Martha), in a Saskatchewan zoo. Clipped to this was a typed
note suggesting that Mr McNeill might be kind enough to consider this bird in his New Year issue of *Ways and Means*. Others
had been a little more practical, like the one on *Empress of
France* notepaper.

Dear Mr McNeill,
    For reasons which will doubtless become clear to you, I
am not at the moment at liberty to reveal the name of the

organisation I have the honour to represent. Suffice it to
say that if not quite the biggest in its line, it can certainly
claim to have achieved the most far-reaching effects to
date. I believe you are an authority on Scottish
Parliamentary History. Well now, what d'you say boy, if
you'll pardon the patter, to lending a hand with *The Long
Break, Life and Times of A. Fletcher Esq.*, a late of Saltoum.
No pipe and skirt stuff. The boss wants it played straight
this time, speeches and all, on the old principle that men
like Fletcher just don't happen any more. OK? That's the
boy. This Saturday then, 6 p.m. Savoy lounge. Beaver hat
and two-way specs, that's me. Round table conference
upstairs later.

Yours cordially,
Sol Steinberg
(travelling secretary)

She had run through her three sheets of *Empress of France*
notepaper, practising the signature. There was also a card, a
thick crenellated card, with *One Month Old Today* engraved in
gold and a space below for the appropriate photograph. On the
back of this she had written in best marking ink *With the
Compliments of the Management*. But there was no photograph.
Only that nightgowned dervish adrift on a dinghy, drawn late
one night in the nursing home, and still no doubt tucked away
in a pocket edition of *War and Peace*. One stick-like arm had
just lost touch with a bottle labelled . . .

For private reasons I must have the truth, remember . . .
Expect to be here another ten days at least.

Somehow, the next morning, this *War and Peace* taped up in a fruiterers' bag, with 'Review Copy Only' hand-printed in shaky capitals on the smoothest corner, had looked a little too un-official to give to the first or to the second newspaper boy to post. She had not tried getting in touch with him since then. For since then, with the last-minute assistance of Theo packing up for America, she had got the truth, a few facts that is, the sort of facts you usually get from friends about friends. That the McNeill marriage was far from ideal did not surprise her. As to what was wrong with it, there opinions differed considerably. But that Dermot's home life, in the accepted meals, bath and bed sense, had been almost nonexistent for several years was a little disconcerting considering all that driving him back to Putney she'd done on Fridays soon after eight. Just what she'd driven him back to was not very clear. Nor could it be clear, nothing like clear, if he wanted to keep his job. Obviously he did very much want to keep his job. There were the children to be supported. And even if he wasn't quite where he wanted to be, he'd been a long time getting there, and would be very much longer getting anywhere else. Anyhow Dermot was hardly the man to put his feelings first. He was, they said, in the long run, essentially this, essentially that . . . opinions again, prismatic effects, matching and clashing, some penetrating, some as grotesque as a school report. And if they sat there, these friends, murmuring gravely – too brilliant, ambitious, tor-mented, bound to crack up before very long – and if Mary could hardly sit on there with them murmuring gravely like that, what else could she say to herself and to them but, 'Weren't we all bound to crack up somehow or other before very long?'

The great fact remained that there was someone else, another sweet intelligent girl, unmarried, who worked in the Protocol Department, had known him for years, came indeed from his part of the country, was deeply religious (not in any odd way if you know what I mean), very fond of France, and had, presumably, been on leave late November last. Or climbing that mountain with him maybe, the one that hadn't been Arthur's Seat.

It was quite dark now. The dog was still chewing. One of the four mousetraps had snapped.

Dear Dermot,

Forgive me for not writing before, but there's been a lot going on lately. You know how hard it can be at times to pick up the threads you want. One way and another the most unexpected people seem to find these moors growing on them. I should have thought, the way the world is just now, that most of them could hardly be spared to lie here day after day shredding the heather, flourishing storm-lighters, assessing the wing span of owls. But there it is. Who's to remind them half-way through some favourite parody of theirs, that they mustn't forget their toothbrush or their special shaving cream this time? I am only beginning now, you see, to get some idea of what can be meant by a long weekend.

As for this evening, you really should have been here. *Le bon Dieu*, and some other old friends you probably know, dropped in for a drink. Towards the end I couldn't help thinking they'd come for good. But then the wine ran out, and they wouldn't touch whisky, oddly enough. Something to do with driving at night I suppose.

The other day in London I was having a quick coffee at one of those Hamburger Halls, when a woman came in. I don't suppose I'd have noticed her if she hadn't been standing quite still by herself, not near anything. She was of a respectable age, you might say, and elegant in the

sketchy way of those who can no longer afford nor quite
forget how to dress well. Whether it was the little spotted
veil, the long gloves, bracelets, high-buttoned dress, or
more perhaps the way she carried them off, but anyhow I
thought of her as French. You know the taint and tang of
it. She was, as I said, standing still. She didn't join either
queue. And then she started walking slowly down the
space between the counter and the window stools. Now
and then she paused, nodding to one side or the other,
that half-greeting half-blessing sort of nod you give, coming on old friends enjoying themselves in their own way.
I couldn't see her eyes properly, because of the veil, but
she was smiling all the time. It was as if this hall were her
own room, her regular salon. She wasn't shy in the least,
being alone out there on the marble floor with everyone
looking on. She had, presumably, loved and lost, must, as
they say, have been very beautiful once. And now they
were all here – lovers, friends, family – her life guests.
And she could pass between them, not cursing or weeping, but quietly welcoming, dismissing, moving on,
nodding like that. I would have followed her out the other
door, but before I could catch the right waitress to pay, she
was back again, where I'd first seen her, doing the same
thing all over again. As she came nearer her lips were
murmuring, the nods seemed sharper this time, almost
abrupt, and the smile had quite gone. I paid my bill. And
when I next turned round she was smiling again, unbut-
toning her dress. Most people weren't looking at her any
more, but then a man near me – just a man in the latest
tie – let out a whistle, the first whistle most boys learn.
Would you have hit him too I wonder, more effectively
perhaps? (I only broke his cup.) Or would you have gone

long before, or turned away, or made a note on something else? You don't drink coffee though, do you?

THIS CORRESPONDENCE IS NOW CLOSED.

Mary took up a small blue pocket book of squared paper, bought in Paris three years back, before setting out for Sicily. It was labelled DEER. She turned the page, printed the day and date at the top and then ticked off the central square very neatly. The second mousetrap snapped.

CHAPTER TWENTY-SIX

Rollo and Mary were having coffee on the veranda in Somerset.

'Nice view,' he said.

'Yes isn't it.' She was looking down *The Times* personal column. 'Quite misty for May. It could be anywhere really on a day like this.'

'Not quite as chilly as I thought. We might even have a shot at this later.' He slid the camera strap off his shoulder, licked two fingers and started rubbing at a scratch on the shining leather case. 'Of course you'd need to be pretty mad to live up here like this for long.'

'Yes,' she said. 'You would. That looks very smart. Is it new?'

'Oh no . . . Western Zone I'd say. Fully guaranteed though.' He held up the case, tilting and weighing it, as though it had diddled him somehow. 'I've often wondered what happened to old P.K.Z. Probably now equipped himself with the latest model, just getting the wife and kiddies lined up on deck for that first glimpse of the Corinth canal. The latest model sells at ninety-five guineas, or thereabouts. Very little difference between them, mind you.' He had the camera out of its case now, started testing various levers. 'They took fifty-two pounds

ten off me for this,' he added a while later. And then one of the
levers stuck. He cursed, apologised for his language, admitting
a little later, with marked reluctance, that this wasn't the only
film he had. There should be another two rolls like it somewhere in his luggage.

'Would you like me to make sure?' she said, starting helpfully
towards the luggage lying in the hall.

He disengaged one hand to indicate that he'd very much
rather she left his luggage alone. He cursed again.

Mary, still standing, broke off the straightest bit of what had
once been a geranium. There were several of these, planted by
the previous owner's wife in the more ornamental sections of an
old gas plant and ranged at various vantage points round the
house. Somehow, in spite of the building, most of them had
stayed on where they'd always been.

'He doesn't bring them back like Jake,' she said, throwing the
hollow stem several yards short of the dog.

'Well, that's something, isn't it? . . . Christ, back to front
again, what a bloody farce.' He touched the spool gingerly. 'I
hear the old boy's died,' he went on, squinting down various
slits. 'Kidneys, wasn't it? Some doggy disease like that.'

'Oh? I didn't know.' Mary sat down again. 'So you've seen
Pete then?'

'Yes, only three months ago. They'd come up from Cardiff for
the day. An outing, I take it, for that car of his.'

'What car?'

'Don't ask me, dear. Made out of ten vacuum cleaners I
should say, from the look of the bonnet. All pipes and straps.
Very fast apparently.'

'I suppose he's much the same, Pete?'

'Yes, much the same. Just built himself a tape recorder. One
thing I did notice though, there was a lot more talk about

money than there used to be. How to come by the cheapest and best on the market, lamp bulbs for instance. And currants. He'd got currants just where he wanted them. Still, with a new nipper to feed, I suppose you'd need to watch that sort of thing.'

Mary nodded. She knew about the nipper. 'I didn't tell you, did I?' she said, kicking at a knot of greenery established between the great flags, got years back from somebody else's kitchen to make this veranda. 'Well,' she said. 'Not so long ago, or since we last met, I came across all, a good deal more anyway than I'd ever bargained for. He had, as you might expect, a lot on his mind. And he said' – here she tossed the greenery, roots and the rest, far out over the gravel – 'he said . . . poor little rich girl, let's go away for the weekend.'

'And did you go?'

'Of course . . . More coffee?'

'Not just now, dear.'

'In the multitude of dreams and many words there are also diverse vanities,' she said. 'I wanted the child. Don't know why really, except perhaps on the off-chance of having the same head of hair within reach. Though it's not as if I'm in any way likely to forget what he looked like. Anyhow,' she studied her cup to see if there was anything left worth drinking in it, 'once again we have the same old story, set in a private nursing home.'

Rollo stirred slightly. 'For one who claims to lead such a secluded life, you seem to cover a lot of ground.'

'Do you really think so?' She smiled at him trustingly, as if to assure herself he meant no harm. 'In a way I'd always thought that sort of thing only happened to Gretchens. And milkmaids, of course, jogging in the new-mown hay, you know. Sing fal the dal-diddle all day. But there we are. C'est une femme qu'il faut absolument tromper, car elle n'est pas de la classe de celles qu'on *quitte.*[*] That's what comes of being carefully brought up, far from those stark realities called only human after all.'

'What about Martin?' Rollo said, offhand as ever, only a little more so. 'How did he take all this?'

'Martin? Not well, not well at all. He knew, of course. I wasn't planning any lifelong deception. Why should I? All the same he wasn't too sympathetic. It seems –' she smiled – 'It seems to me that home might be quite a happy place if all the 2 a.m. talk could be carried out, when the talk was true. Some of it, anyway, and not too many complaints about the consequences. If you are to go in for family life, allowances should surely be made for one or two fruits of passion along with the apples and pears. But what do you get? Lovers, yes, any time, any place, just as long as you give me a few details. While it's going on if you can, but if you can't . . . No of course not darling, I quite understand. You tell me about it when it's all over . . . But children. Oh no. They draw the line at that. Not that Martin, say, would have had to support his children, or anyone else's. But still, as a matter of principle . . . Principles. Men. If they do draw the line at any-thing, you can be pretty sure they've crossed it already, and just don't care to be followed. Still,' she was smiling once again, 'perhaps I'm a little biased.'

'You're getting quite a tongue,' he said.

'Would you rather I wept on your shoulder? I could, you know, quite easily. But on the whole it's only the ladies with very small wrists who get comforted.'

'I must say, if you were *my* wife now . . .'

'Yes dear. You'd keep me in order. But then you don't want a wife, do you? I still like to think that in the right hands I

---

[*] She's a woman one simply must be unfaithful to, since she's in a different class from the sort of woman one leaves.

should have made the most exemplary companion.'

Rollo looked a little dubious.

'We all start off with some set of rules,' she said.

'Inhibitions for the most part,' he muttered, feeling through his pockets for something.

'All right. Inhibitions then, though they sound a bit clinical. Anyhow, one by one they get broken and have to be replaced. Mine were in Celtic lettering early on: pastel knots, more or less innocent beasts, translated some time later into French . . . A B C,' she added quietly, *et puis glissade*.' Whereupon she added other words, both English and French, under her breath, removed them, added them again. Some way through these experiments a tattered shadow croaked across the coffee cups, making for the wood. 'Ravens back, I see.' She laughed a bit, not looking up. 'There are also honey buzzards and peregrine falcons. And deer, of course, red deer. So far I've managed not to see the deer. It's a sort of game that keeps me going up here. Like not treading on the lines, except that it lasts much longer. You can't help hearing them in the autumn, though. It's the hinds I think, looking for the stags. What you might call a very deep-rooted cry. Do you know it?'

Rollo nodded. 'Not the sort of sound I'd care to hear often,' he said, staring at the small curved face of a small curved instru-ment in a plush-lined leather case, matching the other, but with no initials on it. He tapped the glass suspiciously, but the needle stayed where it was. 'Do you see that chap, what's his name, still?'

'No,' she said, 'I do not. Somehow the suggestion that we should always remain good friends just didn't arise. Perhaps I should have mentioned that he happened to earn his living as a diplomat.'

'One of those fine-strung personal relationships, no doubt.'

He frowned a little primly. 'I must say I've never seen the point of them myself.'

'Haven't you?' She looked at him curiously. 'It must be nice to be so self-absorbed. I find that my most single-minded approaches are apt to crumble pretty rapidly in the face of a clearly superior power. I suppose that comes of not having quite enough private hallucinations to be getting on with, not being able to take them all that seriously for very long. Except of course this last winter.' She looked up at him. 'Am I boring you?'

He shook his head. 'Of course not dear. You chat away.'

'This last winter now, you might have seen me any day in a long plaid shawl and carpet slippers selling sprays from an old tin pram at the foot of a certain flight of steps just of Whitehall. Or any night in strapless velvet up Cheyne Walk seducing First Secretaries one by one. If I get any more attacks like that, may I let you know? Perhaps you'd bring your camera along . . . Everybody smiling? That's the ticket. Just a bit closer. Right. Hold it now . . . And then,' she laughed, 'watch out for that camera.'

'Not a small man, I gather.' Rollo bent and stretched each arm in turn, fingering the principal muscles, as though they usually belonged to someone else. 'Violence has never appealed to me,' he said.

Mary turned away, suddenly hating him. 'In this case violence would be rather out of place.' She leant down, stroking the dog's head, picking knots out of its ears. 'I suppose if anyone has been very unhappy for a very long time, there's not much you can do but give them a drink when they ask for it.'

'If I were you I'd stay well away from the Diplomatic Service in future,' he said.

'It wasn't very practical, was it?'

She gave up the ears. 'I think I'd better go down to the village for that tea.' She was standing now, all bright and brisk.

'We'll need it tomorrow anyway. I'm afraid that without Martin here, and the daily help gone back to her husband, supplies are running rather low.'

'By the way – ' He looked up from *The Times* sporting news – 'what exactly do you do with yourself here all day?'

'The idea of work was impressed on me very early on,' she said, hunting through her bag for the car key. 'Though just what form it ought to take has never been very clear. Meanwhile you might say I attend to my studies,' she smiled at him, 'like a good girl.'

'I see.' He smiled back. 'Anderson was asking. I said I thought you read a lot, but he seemed to have other ideas.'

'You'd better tell Anderson I run a brothel up here.' She was quite fierce now. 'For stag hunters only.' And finding herself all tears she sat down again and asked for a handkerchief. 'You see,' she went on, mopping up, 'I didn't tell you that Martin's not just away. He's gone . . . to Finland.'

'Finland?'

'Yes.' She gave back the handkerchief. 'British Council. The only vacancy they could spare. It was my fault really. I'd had enough, only perhaps it wasn't quite the time to say so.' She sniffed once more. 'I don't know quite why it is, but some people have a hypnotic effect on me. I do what they want done, say what they'd like to hear, even talk the way they do, about things that don't much matter to me one way or the other. It's a kind of protective colouring, a patchwork quilt tacked here and there, never quite settled on, never sewn up. Bit by bit, the pieces fade, split apart. They may last minutes, sometimes years, but then, all of a sudden they've no connection, none whatsoever. Look at this now.' She waved back at the shining pillars, the oval windows, the anti-downdraught chimneypots, and then to the laurel roots, the five-strand sheep wire, the moors.

'Nothing to do with me. Nothing at all. This last week, here on my own, waiting for you to come . . .'

'What'll you do with the place, then? Sell it?' He spoke as if the selling of houses required some special equipment he would far rather not possess.

'It's what you might call tied up,' she said, studying the palm of her hand, not so much to see what this palm might hold, as to remind herself that things were what they had been and what they would have to be, including the old burst beer bottle cut. 'There's only one thing to be done,' she said, 'and that is to get into the car, of which I now have the key, to get into this car and drive off, take a job. People do do that sort of thing, don't they?' She looked at him hopefully. 'I mean it can be done.' She looked at him even more hopefully, as if he had only to uncap his pen and scribble something in the right space and then it would all be fixed up.

'I must say I don't know where I'd be without my job,' he said. 'Oddly enough I find myself earning a certain amount of respect these days.' He dusted one creaseless pale green trouser knee to confirm that this was so.

'You've not gone and published the diaries, have you?'

'Good Lord no.' He yawned and stretched like a cat, limb by limb. 'Just see to that lot some day.' He yawned again, as if the whole problem could hardly be expected to interest him. 'Just a few choice tips,' he said, out of this last yawn, 'well seasoned, wisely placed. It's all a knack, you know, this getting through life. I dare say you'll get your own slant on it.'

She said nothing, gripping and ungripping the arms of that sitting-room chair brought out on to that veranda.

'Then there's the school,' he went on. 'They've robbed enough parents' pockets at last to put up a new music wing, with its very own concert hall. And they want my advice, my advice mind you, my considered opinion.' He smiled narrowly. 'As if I had nothing better to do with my time than assess the elevation of their bevelled platform from the front row of their stalls. If the whole troupe of little miss madrigals were to slip through those maple planks into boiling cauldrons within the first five minutes of the opening matinée, I, for one, should be more than thankful . . . I've got over all that now, you know,' he added, a little despondently.

'You can get over a little too much,' she said, leaning towards him, trying to make him hear. 'I know it's hardly your affair, but I really don't see at the moment how I'm going to get out of here. I've been trapped in places before, but this is the worst, quite the worst.'

'Is it?' he said absently. 'I should have thought it was pretty well appointed myself.'

'I don't see how I'm going to get out,' she said again, very slowly very clearly, as if to a child who should have been talking long ago.

'You're not broke, are you?' He looked at her guardedly.

'Money?' She bowed her head. 'There's always money in the post.'

'I don't know, dear.' He touched her arm tentatively. 'You've always been a bit of an enigma to me.'

She smiled, seeing that for life to go on just then, only a smile would do. 'Look here,' she said, 'do you think I'm employable? . . . Good-looking girl, bone structure etc., seeks new setting, fairly central. Follows some languages better than others. Fair acquaintance with sin. Good with small bush babies and cactus plants, not avocado pears. Own car. No means of driving it at present. Would travel far for a living wage in the right company . . . You can't think of anything, can you?'

He shook his head. 'Sounds a little far-fetched to me.'

'I know, I know. No chance of jumping the queue, is there? The trouble is I'm a very slow learner. Too young and fair, and far too proud to settle for less.' She laughed, going back to the handbag again, this time for a small black book of pocket matches, on which was inscribed in joined-up gold: *Chaque Échec est un Pas vers le Succès*. 'Present from Paris,' she said, twisting off the one match left and striking it with such a dash that it crumpled up without lighting at all.

And then the telephone rang.

'That was Martin,' she said, coming out again some ten minutes later. 'Back late tonight. He seems to have changed his mind about Finland.'

Rollo was winding off lilac-backed film, as though it were bandage that had stuck, his own bandage, stuck to himself. 'So you're starting a new life together,' he suggested, very priestlike.

'Well, hardly that' – though, as it happened, those were the very words she'd heard. 'People do change,' she said firmly. 'Lots of them, all the time. I don't mean the cunning ones nailed to their own devices, but the others. The ones who still somehow see fit to speak their mind, one word at a time, and mean it. They might change a bit, mightn't they?' She was looking at him hopefully again. 'Take shorter steps? Pick up their own clothes? Play the gramophone quietly? Use postcards, say, instead of trunk calls? Of course,' she sat back quietly considering, 'it's mostly the wording that changes, isn't it? I believe in this now, not that any more. The little ways are the last to go. As long as Martin, for instance, is married to me he'll always be wanting the best writing paper, engraved with the best address. And that means more and more begging letters to South America, with all the old phrases used up long ago. He's a pretty pathetic monster, my father, from a distance anyway. Till it comes to money, and then. Dear God. Money and taste.

That's the good life nowadays, isn't that so? The discreet hand-made harmonious best?'

'Don't ask me.' His voice was dry and deliberate. 'I live in a world of fantasy. And I might as well tell you now I'd go a very long way not to see it disturbed.'

'But with no fantasies?' she murmured, turning from him, not to the dog, not to anything, because of his face just then, and others like it.

'Anyhow,' she went on lightly, as lightly as she could, 'it looks as if I'll be able to get off these moors after all. That's the main thing. And then . . . well then I suppose I'll have to see about making another of those clean breaks.'

Rollo frowned uneasily.

'That's all right.' She patted his shoulder. 'I wasn't thinking of asking you to take me to Brighton or anything like that, knowing how you feel about the law.'

The frown cleared slightly.

'I suppose there are people who do these things,' she went on a little doubtfully. 'Without slitting your throat?'

'What about that Whitehall chap?'

'Oh no,' she said, 'that wouldn't do at all. Render unto Caesar the hotel register, the twin beds facing the sea.'

'Well dear, I dare say you know best.' Rollo stood up, examining his sleeve for paint. 'Won't be so easy though this time, will it?'

'No,' she said. 'Not easy at all. Six days ago I didn't think I could do it. But six days up here with a dog . . .'

Rollo was getting his little leather cases together, snapping them shut. 'Midges rising,' he said warningly. 'I think, if you don't mind, I'd better check on those films, just in case the dove should descend at this late hour,' he tried out one or two grins, 'along with the dancing girls . . . Damn nuisance about that tripod though, with the light like this.' He shambled off towards the hall door, scowling irritably.

'It must be still in the car,' she called after him. 'I'll have another look.'

Once away from the house there was no strolling. You could either go up or down. Mary went up, nowhere near the car, round behind the outhouses, where the old paint tins, torn pockets of plaster, cracked slates still lay, and on then into the wood, for the first time that year, taking the path she had always taken, and the dog with her. The leaves were very small and pale, paper thin, not hiding anything. One or two primroses had been out. Half-way up the dog chased off after something she couldn't see, and when she came down again Rollo had disappeared. She went on slowly down the gravelled drive, scuffing here and there at the weeds. Then back over the gate that stuck, across the re-seeded parkland, with its best mixed grass already too high for sheep. On the last slope she saw him, higher up near the split elm, the one that someone had said was dangerous and ought to come down. In the still grey light with his back to her, he looked too short, like a new armless scarecrow slipped down its pole.

'So you found it all right,' she said, drawing up behind him, surprised to see the tripod set up there in front of him.

One hand crept out, tapping air, hushing her. He nodded ahead. She came a bit closer, examining the view. And then, below the house, along by the sunken fence – dug, staked and partly wired – she saw the deer. Just one, a hind, with its eyes full on them.

'But surely,' she whispered, breathing again, glancing at Rollo. But Rollo was busy counting to himself. She crept aside, tiptoeing clumsily from tuft to tuft towards the elm, hiding there, edging on, away from Rollo, nearer the deer. Suddenly

she stopped, quite still, part of the picture. Then she turned ar
ran.

It was almost dark when he found her, face down in the woo
with her fists full of last year's mould.

'Not dead,' she said, trying to laugh.

He knelt beside her, stroking her head. 'I'm, sorry, honey
really I am.' And he went on kneeling there, picking out th
twigs. 'You see, from where I was it looked all right.'

'Yes,' she said. 'I know it did. Never mind. You go in now
Please. I'll be along.'

'Need a curry-comb for this.' He settled himself as best he
could between the rocks and the roots, still stroking her head.

'What did you do with it,' she said at last, not wanting to know.
But his hand had already stopped stroking, lay stiff and dumb. She
turned towards him, almost sitting now. 'With the tripod?'

'Mostly . . . yes.'

'And the fawn? There should have been a fawn somewhere.'

'No, there was no fawn.'

They sat on there, side by side, still and separate as the trees,
but blurred, almost gone.

'It wasn't just the deer, wrapped up in the wire like that,' she
said, 'but the whole thing, my slant if you like, ripped wide
open again and again. And it doesn't fit into the photographs.
You do see that, don't you? . . . I was keeping deer because
they're simple . . . and gentle, most gentle. And gentleness is all
we have. Isn't it . . . isn't it?' Yet she knew very well it was not,
knew the race now to the swift, the battle to the strong, and
death deciding nothing.

And soon after, he kissed her, and she him, seeing they were
old friends – though hardly looking for the same thing.

'Owls about,' she said, lost long ago in another night.